Amanda M. Dou

The Old Woman Who Lived in A Shoe

Amanda M. Douglas

The Old Woman Who Lived in A Shoe

1st Edition | ISBN: 978-3-75233-798-3

Place of Publication: Frankfurt am Main, Germany

Year of Publication: 2020

Outlook Verlag GmbH, Germany.

Reproduction of the original.

THE
OLD WOMAN WHO LIVED IN A SHOE
BY
AMANDA M. DOUGLAS

CHAPTER I.

JOE'S GRAND DISCOVERY.

Hal sat trotting Dot on his knee,—poor little weazen-faced Dot, who was just getting over the dregs of the measles, and cross accordingly. By way of accompaniment he sang all the Mother Goose melodies that he could remember. At last he came to,—

> "There was an old woman who lived in a shoe:
>
> She had so many children she didn't know what to do;
>
> To some she gave broth without any bread,"—

and Harry stopped to catch his breath, for the trotting was of the vigorous order.

> "And a thrashing all round, and sent them to bed!"

finished Joe, thrusting his shaggy head in at the window after the fashion of a great Newfoundland dog.

Dot answered with a piteous cry,—a sort of prolonged wail, heart-rending indeed.

"Serve you right," said Joe, going through an imaginary performance with remarkably forcible gestures.

"For shame, Joe! You were little once yourself, and I dare say cried when you were sick. I always thought it very cruel, that, after being deprived of their supper, they should be"—

"Thrashed! Give us good strong Saxon for once, Flossy!"

Flossy was of the ambitious, correct, and sentimental order. She had lovely light curls, and soft white hands when she did not have to work too hard, which she never did of her own free will. She thought it dreadful to be so poor, and aspired to a rather aristocratic ladyhood.

"I am sorry you were not among them," she replied indignantly. "You're a hard-hearted, cruel boy!"

"When the thrashings went round? You're a c-r-u-e-l girl!" with a prodigious length of accent. "Why, I get plenty of 'em at school."

"'Trot, trot, trot. There was an old woman'—what are you laughing at, Joe?" and Hal turned red in the face.

"I've just made a brilliant discovery. O my poor buttons! remember Flossy's hard labor and many troubles, and do not *bust*! Why, we're the very children!"

At this, Joe gave a sudden lurch: you saw his head, and then you saw his heels, and the patch on the knee of his trousers, ripped partly off by an unlucky nail, flapped in the breeze; and he was seated on the window-sill right side up with care, drumming both bare heels into the broken wall. He gave a prolonged whistle of satisfaction, made big eyes at Dot, and then said again,—

"Yes, we are the *very* children!"

"What children? Joe, you are the noisiest boy in Christendom!"

"Flossy, the old woman who lived in a shoe is Granny, and no mistake! I can prove it logically. Look at this old tumble-down rookery: it is just the shape of a huge shoe, sloping gradually to the toe, which is the shed-end here. It's brown and rusty and cracked and patched: it wants heeling and toeing, and to be half-soled, greased to keep the water out, and blacked to make it shine. It was a famous seven-leaguer in its day; but, when it had lost its virtue, the giant who used to wear it kicked it off by the roadside, little dreaming that it would be transformed into a cabin for the aforesaid old woman. And here we all are sure enough! Sometimes we get broth, and sometimes we don't."

Dot looked up in amazement at this harangue, and thrust her thumbs in her mouth. Hal laughed out-right,—a soft little sound like the rippling of falling water.

"Yes, a grand discovery! Ladies and gentlemen of the nineteenth century, I rise to get up, to speak what I am about to say; and I hope you will treasure the words of priceless wisdom that fall from my lips. I'm not backward about coming forward"—

Joe was balancing himself very nicely, and making tremendous flourishes, when two brown, dimpled hands scrubbed up the shock of curly hair, and the sudden onslaught destroyed his equilibrium, as Flossy would have said, and down he went on the floor in crab fashion, looking as if he were all arms and legs.

"Charlie, you midget! just wait till I catch you. I haven't the broth, but the other thing will do as well."

But Charlie was on the outside; and her little brown, bare feet were as fleet as a deer's. Joe saw her skimming over the meadow; but the afternoon was very warm, and a dozen yards satisfied him for a race, so he turned about.

"Joe, you might take Dot a little while, I think," said Hal beseechingly, as Joe braced himself against the door-post. "I've held her all the afternoon."

"She won't come—will you, Dot?"

But Dot signified her gratification by stretching out her hands. Joe was a good-natured fellow; and, though he might have refused Hal easily, he couldn't resist Dot's tender appeal, so he took her on his shoulder and began trotting off to Danbury Cross. Dot laughed out of her sleepy eyes, highly delighted at this change in the programme.

"Oh, dear!" and Hal rubbed his tired arms. "I shouldn't think grandmother would know what to do, sure enough! What a host of us there are,—six children!"

"I'm sure I do my best," said Flossy with a pathetic little sniff. "But it's very hard to be an orphan and poor."

"And when there are six of us, and we are all orphans, and all poor, it must be six times as hard," put in Joe with a sly twinkle.

Then he changed Dot from her triumphal position on his shoulder to a kind of cradle in his arms. Her eyelids drooped, and she began to croon a very sleepy tune.

Hal looked out of the window, over to the woods, where the westward sun was making a wonderful land of gold and crimson. Sometimes he had beautiful dreams of that softened splendor, but now they were mercenary. If one could only coin it all into money! There was poor grandmother slaving away, over at Mrs. Kinsey's,—she should come home, and be a princess, to say the very least.

"I guess I'll clear up a bit!" said Hal, coming down from the clouds, and glancing round at the disorderly room. "Granny will be most tired to death when her day's work is done. Flossy, if you wouldn't mind going in the other room."

Flossy gathered up her skirts and her crocheting, and did not take the invitation at all amiss.

Then Hal found the stubby broom, and swept the floor; dusted the mantle, after removing an armful of "trash;" went at the wooden chairs, that had once been painted a gorgeous yellow with green bars; and cleared a motley accumulation of every thing off of the table, hanging up two or three articles, and tucking the rest into a catch-all closet. A quaint old pitcher, that had lost both spout and handle, was emptied of some faded flowers, and a fresh lot cut,—nothing very choice; but the honeysuckle scented the room, and the coxcombs gave their crimson glow to the top of the pyramid.

"Why, Mrs. Betty," said Joe, "you've made quite a palace out of your end of the shoe, and this miserable little Dot has gone to sleep at last. Shall I put her in the cradle, or drop her down the well?"

Hal smiled a little, and opened the door. It was the best room, quite large, uncarpeted, but clean; and though the bed was covered with a homemade spread, it was as white as it could be. The cradle was not quite as snowy; for the soiled hands that tumbled Dot in and out left some traces.

To get her safely down was a masterpiece of strategy. Joe bumped her head; and Hal took her in his arms, hushing her in a low, motherly fashion, and pressing his brown cheek to hers, which looked the color of milk that had been skimmed, and then split in two, and skimmed again. She made a dive in Hal's hair with her little bird's claw of a hand, but presently dropped asleep again.

"I guess she'll take a good long nap," whispered Hal, quite relieved.

"I'm sure she ought," sighed Florence.

Hal went back to his housekeeping. He was as handy as a girl, any day. He pulled some radishes, and put them in a bowl of cold water, and chopped some lettuce and onions together, the children were all so fond of it. Then he gleaned the raspberries, and filled the saucer with currants that were not salable.

Joe, in the meanwhile, had gone after Mrs. Green's cows. She gave them a quart of milk daily for driving the cows to and from the pasture, and doing odd chores.

"If you see the children, send them home," had been Hal's parting injunction. "Grandmother will soon be here."

She came before Joe returned. The oddest looking little old woman that you ever saw. Florence, at fourteen, was half a head taller. Thin and wrinkled and sunburned; her flaxen hair turning to silver, and yet obstinately full of little curls; her blue eyes pale and washed out, and hosts of "crows'-feet" at the corners; and her voice cracked and tremulous.

Poor Grandmother Kenneth! She had worked hard enough in her day, and was still forced to keep it up, now that it was growing twilight with her. But I don't believe there was another as merry a houseful of children in all Madison.

Joe's discovery was not far out of the way. The old woman, whose biography and family troubles were so graphically given by Mother Goose, died long before our childhood; but I think Granny Kenneth must have looked like her, though I fancy she was better natured. As for the children, many and many a time she had not known what to do with them,—when they were hungry, when they were bad, when their clothes were worn out and she had nothing to make new ones with, when they had no shoes; and yet she loved the whole six, and toiled for them without a word of complaint.

Her only son, Joe, had left them to her,—a troublesome legacy indeed; but at that time they had a mother and a very small sum of money. Mrs. Joe was a pretty, helpless, inefficient body, who continually fretted because Joe did not get rich. When the poor fellow lay on his death-bed, his disease aggravated by working when he was not able, he twined his arms around his mother's neck, and cried with a great gasp,—

"You'll be kind to them, mother, and look after them a little. God will help you, I know. I should like to live for their sakes."

A month or two after this, Dot was born. Now that her dear Joe was dead, there was no comfort in the world; so the frail, pretty little thing grieved herself away, and went to sleep beside him in the churchyard.

The neighbors made a great outcry when Grandmother Kenneth took the children to her own little cottage.

"What could she do with them? Why, they will all starve in a bunch," said one.

"Florence and Joe might be bound out," proposed another.

A third was for sending them to the almshouse, or putting them in some orphan asylum; but five years had come and gone, and they had not starved yet, though once or twice granny's heart had quaked for fear.

Every one thought it would be such a blessing if Dot would only die. She had been a sight of trouble during the five years of her life. First, she had the whooping cough, which lasted three times as long as with any ordinary child. Then she fell out of the window, and broke her collar-bone; and when she was just over that, it was the water-pox. The others had the mumps, and Dot's share was the worst of all. Kit had the measles in the lightest possible form, and actually had to be tied in bed to make him stay there; while it nearly killed poor Dot, who had been suffering from March to midsummer, and was still poor as a crow, and cross as a whole string of comparisons.

6

But Granny was patient with it all. The very sweetest old woman in the world, and the children loved her in their fashion; but they seldom realized all that she was doing for them. And though some of her neighbors appreciated the toil and sacrifice, the greater part of them thought it very foolish for her to be slaving herself to death for a host of beggarly grandchildren.

"Well, Hal!" she exclaimed in her rather shrill but cheery voice, "how's the day gone?"

"Pretty well: but you're tired to death. I suppose Mrs. Kinsey's company came, and there was a grand feast?"

"Grand! I guess it was. Such loads of pies and puddings and kettles of berries and tubs of cream"—

Granny paused, out of breath from not having put in any commas.

"Ice-cream, you mean? Freezers, they call 'em."

"You do know every thing, Hal!" And granny laughed. "I can't get all the new-fangled names and notions in my head. There was Grandmother Kinsey, neat as a new pin, and children and grandchildren, and aunts and cousins. But it was nice, Hal."

The boy smiled, thinking of them all.

"Half of the goodies'll spile, I know. Mrs. Kinsey packed me a great basket full; and, Hal, here's two dollars. I'm clean tuckered out."

"Then you just sit still, and let me 'tend to you. Dot's asleep; and if I haven't worried with her this afternoon! That child ought to grow up a wonder, she's been so much trouble to us all. Joe's gone after the cows, and Florence is busy as a bee. Oh, what a splendid basket full! Why, we shall feast like kings!"

With that Hal began to unpack,—a plate full of cut cake, biscuits by the dozen, cold chicken, delicious slices of ham, and various other delicacies.

"We'll only have a few to-night," said Hal economically. "'Tisn't every day that we have such a windfall. I'll put these out of the children's sight; for there they come."

The "children" were Charlie and Kit, with barely a year between; Kit being seven, and Charlie—her real name was Charlotte, but she was such a tomboy that they gave her the nickname—was about eight. Hal was ten, and Joe twelve.

"Children," said Hal, "don't come in till you've washed yourselves. Be quiet, for Dot is asleep."

Thus admonished, Charlie did nothing worse than pour a basin of water over Kit, who sputtered and scolded and kicked until Hal rushed out to settle them.

"If you're not quiet, you shall not have a mouthful of supper; and we've lots of goodies."

Kit began to wash the variegated streaks from his face. Charlie soused her head in a pail of water, and shook it like a dog, then ran her fingers through her hair. It was not as light or silken as that of Florence, and was cropped close to her head. Kit's was almost as black as a coal; and one refractory lock stood up. Joe called it his "scalp-lock waving in the breeze."

"Now, Charlie, pump another pail of water. There comes Joe, and we'll have supper."

Charlie eyed Joe distrustfully, and hurried into the house. Hal hung up Granny's sun-bonnet, and placed the chairs around.

"Come, Florence," he said, opening the door softly.

"My eyes!" ejaculated Joe in amaze. "Grandmother, you're a trump."

"Joe!" exclaimed Hal reproachfully.

Joe made amends by kissing Granny in the most rapturous fashion. Then he escorted her to the table in great state.

"Have you been good children to-day?" she asked, as they assembled round the table.

"I've run a splinter in my toe; and, oh! my trousers are torn!" announced Kit dolefully.

"If you ever had a whole pair of trousers at one time the world would come to an end," declared Joe sententiously.

"Would it?" And Kit puzzled his small brain over the connection.

"And Charlie preserves a discreet silence. Charlie, my dear, I advise you to keep out of the way of the ragmen, or you will find yourself on the road to the nearest paper-mill."

Florence couldn't help laughing at the suggestion.

"Children!" said their grandmother.

Full of fun and frolic as they were, the little heads bowed reverently as Granny asked her simple blessing. She would as soon have gone without eating as to omit that.

"I really don't want any thing," she declared. "I've been tasting all day,— a bit here and a bit there, and such loads of things!"

"Tell us all about it," begged Joe. "And who was there,—the grand Panjandrum with a button on the top. Children's children unto the third and fourth generation."

"O Joe! if you only wouldn't," began Granny imploringly.

"No, I won't, Granny;" and Joe made a face as long as your arm, or a piece of string.

"Of course I didn't see 'em all, nor half; but men and women and children and babies! And Grandmother Kinsey's ninety-five years old!"

"I hope I'll live to be that old, and have lots of people to give me a golden wedding," said Charlie, with her mouth so full that the words were pretty badly squeezed.

"This isn't a golden wedding," said Florence with an air of dignity: "it's a birthday party."

"Ho!" and Joe laughed. "You'll be,—

'Ugly, ill-natured, and wrinkled and thin,

Worn by your troubles to bone and to skin.'"

"She's never been much else," rejoined Flossy, looking admiringly at her own white arm.

"I'm not as old as you!" And Charlie flared up to scarlet heat.

"Oh! you needn't get so vexed. I was only thinking of the skin and bone," said Florence in a more conciliatory manner.

"Well, I don't want to be a 'Mother Bunch.'"

"No fear of you, Charlie. You look like the people who live on some shore,—I've forgotten the name of the place,—and, eat so many fish that the bones work through."

Charlie felt of her elbows. They were pretty sharp, to be sure. She was very tall of her age, and ran so much that it was quite impossible to keep any flesh on her bones.

"Hush, children!" said grandmother. "I was going to tell you about the party. Hal, give me a little of your salad, first."

The Kinseys had invited all their relations to a grand family gathering.

Granny told over the pleasant and comical incidents that had come under her notice,—the mishaps in cooking, the babies that had fallen down stairs, and various entertaining matters.

By that time supper was ended. Florence set out to take some lace that she had been making to a neighbor; Hal washed the dishes, and Charlie wiped them; Joe fed the chickens, and then perched himself astride the gate-post, whistling all the tunes he could remember; Kit and Charlie went to bed presently; and Hal and his grandmother had a good talk until Dot woke up, strange to say quite good-natured.

"Granny," said Hal, preparing a bowl of bread and milk for his little sister, "some day we'll all be grown, and you won't have to work so hard."

"Six men and women! How odd it will be!" returned Granny with a smile shining over her tired face.

"Yes. We'll keep you like a lady. You shall have a pretty house to live in, and Dot shall wait upon you. Won't you, Dot?"

Dot shook her head sagely at Granny.

And in the gathering twilight Hal smiled, remembering Joe's conceit. Granny looked happy in spite of her weariness. She, foolish body, was thinking how nice it was to have them all, even to poor little Dot.

CHAPTER II.

PLANNING IN THE TWILIGHT.

It was a rainy August day, and the children were having a glorious time up in the old garret. Over the house-part there were two rooms; but this above the kitchen was kept for rubbish. A big wheel, on which Granny used to spin in her younger days, now answered for almost any purpose, from a coach and four, to a menagerie: they could make it into an elephant, a camel, or a hyena, by a skilful arrangement of drapery.

There were several other pieces of dilapidated furniture, old hats, old boots, a barrel or two of papers; in fact, a lot of useless traps and a few trophies that Joe had brought home; to say nothing of Charlie's endless heaps of trash, for she had a wonderful faculty of accumulation; herbs of every kind, bundles of calamus, stacks of "cat-tails," the fuzz of which flew in every direction with the least whiff of wind.

The "children" had been raising bedlam generally. Joe was dressed in an old scuttle-shaped Leghorn bonnet and a gay plaid cloak, a strait kind of skirt plaited on a yoke. Granny had offered it to Florence for a dress, but it had been loftily declined. Kit was attired as an Indian, his "scalp-lock" bound up with rooster feathers; and he strutted up and down, jabbering a most uncouth dialect, though of what tribe it would be difficult to say. Charlie appeared in a new costume about every half-hour, and improvised caves in every corner; though it must be confessed Joe rather extinguished her with his style. He could draw in his lips until he looked as if he hadn't a tooth in his head, and talk like nearly every old lady in town.

Such whoops and yells and shouts as had rung through the old garret would have astonished delicate nerves. In one of the bedrooms Granny was weaving rag-carpet on a rickety loom, for she did a little of every thing to lengthen out her scanty income; but the noise of that was as a whiff of wind in comparison.

At last they had tried nearly every kind of transformation, and were beginning to grow tired. It was still very cloudy, and quite twilight in their den, when Florence came up stairs, and found them huddled around the window listening to a wonderful story that Joe made up as he went along. Such fortunes and adventures could only belong to the Munchausen period.

"Dear!" exclaimed Florence, "I thought the chief of the Mohawks had declared war upon the Narragansetts, and everybody had been scalped, you subsided so suddenly. You've made racket enough to take off the roof of the house!"

"It's on yet," was Joe's solemn assurance.

"O Joe!" begged Charlie: "tell us another story,—something about a sailor who was wrecked, and lived in a cave, and found bags and bags of money!"

"That's the kind, Charlie. Flo, come on and take a seat."

"Where's Dot?"

"Here in my arms," replied Hal; "as good as a kitten; aren't you, Dot?"

Dot answered with a contented grunt.

"Oh, let's all tell what we'd like to do!" said Charlie, veering round on a new tack. "Flo'll want to be Cinderella at the king's ball."

Florence tumbled over the pile of legs, and found a seat beside Hal.

"Well, I'll lead off," began Joe with a flourish. "First, I'm going to be a sailor. I mean to ship with a captain bound for China; and hurra! we'll go out with a flowing sea or some other tip-top thing! Well, I guess we'll go to China,—this is all suppos'n, you know; and while I'm there I'll get such lots of things!—crape-shawls and silks for you, Flossy; and cedarwood chests to keep out moths, and fans and beautiful boxes, and a chest of tea, for Granny. On the way home we shall be wrecked. You'll hear the news, and think that I'm dead, sure enough."

"But how will Flo get her shawls?" asked Charlie.

"Oh, you'll hear presently! That's way in the end. I shall be wrecked on an island where there's a fierce native chief; and first he and his men think they'll kill me." Joe always delighted in harrowing up the feelings of his audience. "So I offer him the elegant shawls and some money"—

"But I thought you lost them all in the wreck!" interposed quick-brained Charlie.

"Oh, no! There's always something floats ashore, you must remember. Well, he concluded not to kill me, though they have a great festival dance in honor of their idols; and I only escape by promising to be his obedient slave. I find some others who have been cast on that desolate shore, and been treated in the same manner. The chief beats us, and makes us work, and treats us dreadfully. Then we mutiny, and have a great battle, for a good many of the natives join us. In the scrimmage the old fellow is killed; and there's a tremendous rejoicing, I can tell you, for they all hate him. We divide his treasure, and it's immense, and go to live in his palace. Well, no boat ever comes along; so we build one for ourselves, and row to the nearest port and tell them the chief is dead. They are very glad, for he was a cruel old fellow. Then we buy a ship, and go back for the rest of our treasures. We take a great many of the beautiful things out of the palace, and then we start for home, double-quick. It's been a good many years; and, when I come back, Granny is old, and walking with a cane, Florence married to a rich gentleman, and Dot here grown into a handsome girl. But won't I build a stunning house! There'll be a scattering out of this old shoe, I tell you."

"Oh, won't it be splendid!" exclaimed Charlie, with a long-drawn breath. "It's just like a story."

"Now, Hal, it's your turn."

Hal sighed softly, and squeezed Dot a little.

"I shall not go off and be a sailor"—

"Or a jolly young oysterman," said Joe, by way of assistance.

"No. What I'd like most of all"—and Hal made a long pause.

"Even if it's murder, we'll forgive you and love you," went on tormenting Joe.

"O Joe, don't!" besought Florence. "I want to hear what Hal will choose, for I know just what I'd like to have happen to me."

"So do I," announced Charlie confidently.

"I don't know that I can have it," said Hal slowly; "for it costs a good deal, though I might make a small beginning. It's raising lovely fruit and flowers, and having a great hot-house, with roses and lilies and dear white blossoms in the middle of the winter. I should love them so much! They always seem like little children to me, with God for their father, and we who take care of them for a stepmother; though stepmothers are not always good, and the poor wicked ones would be those who did not love flowers. Why, it would be like fairy-land,—a great long hot-house, with glass overhead, and all the air sweet with roses and heliotrope and mignonette. And it would be so soft and still in there, and so very, very beautiful! It seems to me as if heaven must be full of flowers."

"Could you sell 'em if you were poor?" asked Charlie, in a low voice.

"Not the flowers in heaven! Charlie, you're a heathen."

"I didn't mean that! Don't you suppose I know about heaven!" retorted Charlie warmly.

"Yes," admitted Joe with a laugh: "he could sell them, and make lots of money. And there are ever so many things: why, Mr. Green paid six cents apiece for some choice tomato-plants."

"When I'm a man, I think I'll do that. I mean to try next summer in my garden."

"May I tell now?" asked Charlie, who was near exploding with her secret.

"Yes. Great things," said Joe.

"I'm going to run away!" And Charlie gave her head an exultant toss, that, owing to the darkness, was lost to her audience.

Joe laughed to his utmost capacity, which was not small. The old garret fairly rang again.

Florence uttered a horrified exclamation; and Kit said,—

"I'll go with you!"

"Girls don't run away," remarked Hal gravely.

"But I mean to, and it'll be royal fun," was the confident reply.

"Where will you go? and will you beg from door to door?" asked Joe quizzically.

"No: I'm going out in the woods," was the undaunted rejoinder. "I mean to find a nice cave; and I'll bring in a lot of good dry leaves and some straw, and make a bed. Then I'll gather berries; and I know how to catch fish, and I can make a fire and fry them. I'll have a gay time going off to the river and rambling round, and there'll be no lessons to plague a body to death. It will be just splendid."

"Suppose a bear comes along and eats you up?" suggested Joe.

"As if there were any bears around here!" Charlie returned with immense disdain.

"Well, a snake, or a wild-cat!"

"I'm not afraid of snakes."

"But you'd want a little bread."

"Oh! I'd manage about that. I do mean to run away some time, just for fun."

"You'll be glad to run back again!"

"You see, now!" was the decisive reply.

"Florentina, it is your turn now. We have had age before beauty."

Florence tossed her soft curls, and went through with a few pretty airs.

"I shouldn't run away," she said slowly; "but I'd like to *go*, for all that. Sometimes, as I sit by the window sewing, and see an elegant carriage pass by, I think, what if there should be an old gentleman in it, who had lost his wife and all his children, and that one of his little girls looked like—like me? And if he should stop and ask me for a drink, I'd go to the well and draw a fresh, cool bucketful"—

"From the north side—that's the coldest," interrupted Joe.

"Hush, Joe! No one laughed at you!"

"Laugh! Why, I am sober as an owl."

"Then I'd give him a drink. I wish we could have some goblets: tumblers look so dreadfully old-fashioned. I mean to buy *one*, at least, some time. He would ask me about myself; and I'd tell him that we were all orphans, and had been very unfortunate, and that our grandmother was old"—

>   "'Four score and ten of us, poor old maids,—
>
>   Four score and ten of us,
>
>   Without a penny in our *puss*,
>
>   Poor old maids,'"

sang Joe pathetically, cutting short the *purse* on account of the rhyme.

"O Joe, you are too bad! I won't tell any more."

"Yes, do!" entreated Hal. "And so he liked you on account of the resemblance, and wanted to adopt you."

"Exactly! Hal, how could you guess it?" returned Florence, much mollified. "And so he would take me to a beautiful house, where there were plenty of servants, and get me lovely clothes to wear; and there would be lots of china and silver and elegant furniture and a piano. I'd go to school, and study music and drawing, and never have to sew or do any kind of work. Then I'd send you nice presents home; and, when you were fixed up a little, you should come and see me. And maybe, Hal, as you grew older, he would help you about getting a hot-house. I think when I became a woman, I would take Dot to educate."

"I've heard of fairy godmothers before, but this seems to be a godfather. Here's luck to your old covey, Florrie, drunk in imaginary champagne."

"Joe, I wish you wouldn't use slang phrases, nor be so disrespectful."

"I'm afraid I'll have to keep clear of the palace."

"Oh, if it only could be!" sighed Hal. "I think Flo was meant for a lady."

Florence smiled inwardly at hearing this. It was her opinion also.

"Here, Kit, are you asleep?" And Joe pulled him out of the pile by one leg. "Wake up, and give us your heart's desire."

Kit indulged in a vigorous kick, which Joe dodged.

"It'll be splendid," began Kit, "especially the piano. I've had my hands over my eyes, making stars; and I was thinking"—

"That's just what we want, Chief of the Mohawk Valley. Don't keep us in suspense."

"I'm going to save up my money, like some one Hal was reading about the other day, and buy a fiddle."

A shout of laughter greeted this announcement, it sounded so comical.

Kit rubbed his eyes in amazement, and failed to see any thing amusing. Then he said indignantly,—

"You needn't make such a row!"

"But what will you do with a fiddle? You might tie a string to Charlie, and take her along for a monkey; or you might both go round singing in a squeaky voice,—

'Two orphan boys of Switzerland.'"

"You're real mean, Joe," said Kit, with his voice full of tears.

"Kit, I'll give you the violin myself when I get rich," Florence exclaimed in a comforting tone, her soft hand smoothing down the refractory scalp-lock; "but I would say violin, it sounds so much nicer. And then you'll play."

"Play!" enunciated Kit in a tone that I cannot describe, as if that were a weak word for the anticipated performance. "I'd make her talk! They'd sit there and listen,—a whole houseful of people it would be, you know; and when I first came out with my fiddle,—violin. I mean,—they would look at me as if they thought I couldn't do much. I'd begin with a slow sound, like the wind wailing on a winter night,—I guess I'd have it a storm, and a little lost child, for you can make almost any thing with a violin; and the cries should grow fainter and fainter, for she would be chilled and worn out; and presently it should drop down into the snow, and there'd be the softest, strangest music you ever heard. The crowd would listen and listen, and hold their breath; and when the storm cleared away, and the angels came down for the child, it would be so, so sad"—and there was an ominous falter in Kit's voice, "they couldn't help crying. There'd be an angel's song up in heaven; and in the sweetest part of it all, I'd go quietly away, for I wouldn't want any applause."

"But you'd have it," said Hal softly, reaching out for the small fingers that were to evoke such wonderful melody. "It almost makes me cry myself to think of it! and the poor little girl lost in the snow, not bigger than Dot here!"

"Children!" called Granny from the foot of the stairs, "ain't you going to come down and have any supper? I've made a great pot full of mush."

There was a general scrambling. Hal carried Dot in his arms, for she was fast asleep. Two or three times in the short journey he stopped to kiss the soft face, thinking of Kit's vision.

"Oh, we've been having such a splendid time!" announced Charlie. "All of us telling what we'd like to do; and, Granny, Joe's going to build you an *elegant* house!" with a great emphasis on the word, as Charlie was not much given to style, greatly to the sorrow and chagrin of Florence.

Granny gave a cheerful but cracked treble laugh, and asked,—

"What'll he build it of, my dear,—corn-cobs?"

"Oh, a *real* house! He's going to make lots of money, Joe is, and get shipwrecked."

Granny shook her head, which made the little white curls bob around oddly enough.

"How you do mix up things, Charlie," said Joe, giving her a poke with his elbow. "You're a perfect harum-scarum! I don't wonder you want to live in the woods. Go look at your head: it stands out nine ways for Sunday!"

Charlie ran her fingers through her hair, her usual manner of arranging it.

"Granny, here's this little lamb fast asleep. She's grown to be one of the best babies in the world;" and Hal kissed her again.

He had such a tender, girlish heart, that any thing weak or helpless always appealed to him. Their sleek, shining Tabby had been a poor, forlorn, broken-legged kitten when he found her; and there was no end to the birds and chickens that he nursed through accidents.

But for a fortnight Dot had been improving, it must be confessed, being exempt from disease and broken bones.

"Poor childie! Just lay her in the bed, Hal."

There was a huge steaming dish of mush in the middle of the table; and the hungry children went at it in a vigorous manner. Some had milk, and some had molasses; and they improvised a dessert by using a little butter, sugar, and nutmeg. They spiced their meal by recounting their imaginary adventures; but Granny was observed to wipe away a few tears over the shipwreck.

"It was all make believe," said Joe sturdily. "Lots of people go to sea, and don't get wrecked."

"But I don't want you to go," Granny returned in a broken tone of voice.

"Pooh!" exclaimed Joe, with immense disdain. "Don't people meet with accidents on the land? Wasn't Steve Holder killed in the mill. And if I was on the cars in a smash-up, I couldn't swim out of that!"

Joe took a long breath, fancying that he had established his point beyond a cavil.

"But sailors never make fortunes," went on Granny hesitatingly.

"Captains do, though; and it's a jolly life. Besides, we couldn't all stay in this little shanty, unless we made nests in the chimney like the swallows; and I don't know which would tumble down first,—we or the chimney."

Charlie laughed at the idea.

"I shall stay with you always, Granny," said Hal tenderly. "And Dot, you know, will be growing into a big girl and be company for us. We'll get along nicely, never fear."

Some tears dropped unwittingly into Granny's plate, and she didn't want any more supper. It was foolish, of course. She ought to be thankful to have them all out of the way and doing for themselves. Here she was, over fifty, and had worked hard from girlhood. Some day she would be worn out.

But, in spite of all their poverty and hardship, she had been very happy with them; and theirs were by no means a forlorn-looking set of faces. Each one had a little beauty of its own; and, though they were far from being pattern children, she loved them dearly in spite of their faults and roughnesses. And in their way they loved her, though sometimes they were great torments.

And so at bed-time they all crowded round to kiss the wrinkled face, unconsciously softened by the thought of the parting that was to come somewhere along their lives. But no one guessed how Granny held little Dot in her arms that night, and prayed in her quaint, fervent fashion that she might live to see them all grown up and happy, good and prosperous men and women, and none of them straying far from the old home-nest.

I think God listened with watchful love. No one else would have made crooked paths so straight.

CHAPTER III.

A CHANCE FOR FLOSSY.

The vacation had come to an end, and next week the children were to go to school again. Florence counted up her small hoard; for though she did not like to sweep, or wash dishes, she was industrious in other ways. She crocheted edgings and tidies, made lamp-mats, toilet-sets, and collars, and had earned sixteen dollars. Granny would not have touched a penny of it for the world.

So Florence bought herself two pretty delaine dresses for winter wear, and begged Granny to let Miss Brown cut and fit them. Florence had a pretty, slender figure; and she was rather vain of it. Her two dresses had cost seven dollars, a pair of tolerably nice boots three and a half, a plaid shawl four, and then she had indulged in the great luxury of a pair of kid gloves.

It had come about in this wise. Mrs. Day had purchased them in New York, but they proved too small for her daughter Julia. She was owing Florence a dollar; so she said,—

"Now, if you have a mind to take these gloves, Florence, I'd let you have them for seventy-five cents. I bought them very cheap: they ask a dollar and a quarter in some stores;" and she held them up in their most tempting light.

Florence looked at them longingly.

"They are lovely kid, and such a beautiful color! Green is all the fashion, and you have a new green dress."

There was a pair of nice woollen gloves at the store for fifty cents; and although they were rather clumsy, still Florence felt they would be warmer and more useful.

"I don't know as I can spare you the dollar now," continued Mrs. Day, giving the dainty little gloves a most aggravating stretch.

"I'd like to have them," said Florence hesitatingly.

"I suppose your grandmother won't mind? Your money is your own."

Now, Mrs. Day knew that it was wrong to tempt Florence; but the gloves were useless to her, and she felt anxious to dispose of them.

"Grandmother said I might spend all my money for clothes," was the rather proud reply.

"Kid gloves always look so genteel, and are so durable. You have such a pretty hand too."

"I guess I will take them," Florence said faintly.

So Mrs. Day gave her the gloves and twenty-five cents. Florence carried them home in secret triumph, and put them in *her* drawer in Granny's big bureau. She had not told about them yet; and sometimes they were a heavier burden than you would imagine so small a pair of gloves could possibly be.

Joe had earned a little odd change from the farmers round, and bought himself a pair of new trousers and a new pair of boots; while Hal had been maid-of-all-work in doors, and head gardener out of doors.

"Just look at these potatoes!" he said in triumph to Granny. "There's a splendid binful, and it'll last all winter. And there'll be cabbage and pumpkins and marrow-squash and Lima beans, and lots of corn for the chickens. The garden has been a success this summer."

"And you've worked early and late," returned Granny in tender triumph. "There isn't such another boy in the State, I'll be bound!" And she gave him the fondest of smiles.

"But the best of all is Dot. She's actually getting fat, Granny; and she has a dimple in her cheek. Why, she'll be almost as pretty as Flossy!"

Granny gave the little one a kiss.

"She's as good as a kitten when she is well," was the rejoinder, in a loving tone.

Kit and Charlie still romped like wild deers. They had made a cave in the wood, and spent whole days there; but Charlie burned her fingers roasting a bird, and went back to potatoes and corn, that could be put in the ashes without so much risk.

The old plaid cloak had been made over for a school-dress, and Charlie thought it quite grand. Kit and Hal had to do the best they could about clothes.

"Never mind me, Granny," Hal said cheerfully; though he couldn't help thinking of his patched Sunday jacket, which was growing short in the sleeves for him.

So on Saturday the children scrubbed and scoured and swept, and made the place quite shine again. Hal arranged the flowers, and then they all drew a restful breath before the supper preparations began.

"There's Mrs. Van Wyck coming!" and Charlie flew up the lane, dashing headlong into the house, to the imminent peril of her best dress, which she had been allowed to put on for an hour or two.

"Mrs. Van Wyck!"

Granny brushed back her bobbing flaxen curls, washed Dot's face over again with the nearest white cloth, which happened to be Flossy's best handkerchief that she had been doing up for Sunday.

"Oh!" the young lady cried in dismay, and then turned to make her prettiest courtesy. Mrs. Van Wyck was very well off indeed, and lived in quite a pretentious cottage,—villa she called it; but, as she had a habit of confusing her V's and W's, Joe re-christened it the Van Wyck Willow.

"Good-afternoon, Mrs. Kenneth. How d'y do, Florence?"

Florence brought out a chair, and, with the most polite air possible, invited her to be seated.

Mrs. Van Wyck eyed her sharply.

"'Pears to me you look quite fine," she said.

Florence wore a white dress that was pretty well outgrown, and had been made from one of her mother's in the beginning. It had a good many little darns here and there, and she was wearing it for the last time. She had tied a blue ribbon in her curls, and pinned a tiny bouquet on her bosom. She looked very much dressed, but that was pretty Flossy's misfortune.

Mrs. Van Wyck gathered up her silk gown,—a great staring brocade in blue and gold, that might have been her grandmother's, it looked so ancient in style.

"I've come over on some business," she began, with an important air and a mysterious shake of the head.

Granny sat down, and took Dot upon her lap. Kit and Charlie peered out of their hiding-places, and Joe perched himself upon the window-sill.

"How do you ever manage with all this tribe?" And Mrs. Van Wyck gave each of them a scowl.

"There's a houseful," returned Granny, "but we *do* get along."

"Tough scratching, I should say."

"And poor pickings the chickens might add, if they had *such* an old hen," commented Joe *soto voce*. "There'd be something worse than clucking."

Hal couldn't help laughing. Mrs. Van Wyck was so ruffled and frilled, so full of ends of ribbon about the head and neck, that she did look like a setting hen disturbed in the midst of her devotions.

"Them children haven't a bit of manners," declared Mrs. Van Wyck, in sublime disregard of syntax. "Trot off, all of you but Florence: I have something to say to your grandmother."

Joe made a somerset out of the window, and placed himself in a good listening position; Hal went out and sat on the doorstep; and Charlie crawled under the table.

"I don't see how you manage to get along with such a houseful. I always did wonder at your taking 'em."

"Oh! we do pretty well," returned Granny cheerily.

"They're growing big enough to help themselves a little. Why don't you bind Joe out to some of the farmers. Such a great fellow ought to be doing something besides racing round and getting into mischief."

Joe made a series of such polite evolutions, that Hal ran to the gate to have a good laugh without being heard.

"He's going to school," said Granny innocently. "They all begin on Monday."

"Going to school?" And Mrs. Van Wyck elevated her voice as if she thought them all deaf. "Why, *I* never went to school a day after I was twelve year old, and my father was a well-to-do farmer. There's no sense in children having so much book-larnin'. It makes 'em proud and stuck up, and good for nothing.

"Oh! where's that dog? Put him out! Put him out! I can't bear dogs. And the poorer people are, the more dogs they'll keep."

Joe, the incorrigible, was quite a ventriloquist for his years and size. He had just made a tremendous ki-yi, after the fashion of the most snarling terrier dog, and a kind of scrabbling as if the animal might be under Mrs. Van Wyck's feet.

"Oh, my! Take the nasty brute away. Maybe he's full of fleas or has the mange"—

"It is only Joe," explained Florence, as soon as she could put in a word.

"I'd Joe him, if I had him here! You're a ruining of these children as I've always said; and you may thank your stars if Joe escapes the gallows. I've positively come on an errand of mercy."

"Not for Joe," declared the owner of the name with a sagacious shake of the head, while Mrs. Van Wyck paused for breath.

"Yes. Not one of them'll be worth a penny if they go on this way. Now, here's Florence, growing up in idleness"—

"She keeps pretty busy," said Granny stoutly.

"Busy! Why, you've nothing for her to do. When I was a little girl, my mother made me sit beside her, and sew patchwork; and before I was twelve year old I had finished four quilts. And she taught me the hymn,—

> 'Satan finds some mischief still
>
> For idle hands to do.'"

"They always learn a verse for Sunday," said Granny deprecatingly.

"But you let 'em run wild. I've seen it all along. I was a talkin' to Miss Porter about it; and says I, 'Now, I'll do one good deed;' and the Lord knows it's needed."

Everybody listened. Joe from the outside made a pretence of picking his ears open with the handle of a broken saucepan.

"Florence is getting to be a big girl, and it's high time she learned something. As I was a sayin' to Miss Porter, 'I want just such a girl; and it will be the making of Florence Kenneth to fall into good hands.'"

"But you don't mean"—and Granny paused, aghast.

"I mean to make the child useful in her day and generation. It'll be a good place for her."

Mrs. Van Wyck nodded her head until the bows and streamers flew in every direction.

Granny opened her eyes wide in surprise.

"What do you want of her, Mrs. Van Wyck?"

Charlie peeped out from between the legs of the table to hear, her mouth wide open lest she should lose a word.

"Want of her?" screamed the visitor. "Why, to work, of course! I don't keep idle people about me, I can tell you. I want a girl to make beds, and sweep, and dust, and wash dishes, and scour knives, and scrub, and run errands, and do little chores around. It'll be the making of her; and I'm willing to do the fair thing."

Granny was struck dumb with amazement. Florence could hardly credit her ears. Hal sprang up indignantly, and Joe doubled his fists as if he were about to demolish the old house along with Mrs. Van Wyck.

"Yes. I've considered the subject well. I always sleep on a thing before I tell a single soul. And, if Florence is a good smart girl, I'll give her seventy-five cents a week and her board. For six dollars a month I could get a grown girl, who could do all my work."

Granny looked at Florence in helpless consternation; and Florence looked at Granny with overwhelming disdain.

"Well! why don't you answer?" said the visitor. She had supposed they would jump at the offer.

"I don't expect to go out doing housework, Mrs. Van Wyck," said Florence loftily.

"Hoity-toity! how grand we are! I've never been above doing my own housework; and I could buy and sell the whole bunch of you, a dozen times over."

"Florence wouldn't like it, I'm afraid," said Granny mildly.

"A fine way to bring up children, truly! You may see the day when you'll be thankful to have a home as good as my kitchen."

There was a bright red spot in Florence's cheeks.

"Mrs. Van Wyck," Florence began in a quiet, ladylike manner, although she felt inclined to be angry, "grandmother is right: I should not like it. I have no taste for housework; and I can earn more than you offer to give by doing embroidering and crocheting. Through the six weeks of vacation I earned sixteen dollars."

"Fancy work! What is the world coming to? Children brought up to despise good, honest employment."

"No, I don't despise it," amended Florence; "but I do not like it, and I think it a hard way of earning a little money. If I can do better, of course I have the right."

Granny was amazed at the spirit Florence displayed.

"You'll all be paupers on the town yet, mark my words. Flaunting round in white dresses and ribbons, and"—

She glanced around for some further vanity to include in her inventory.

"I am sure we are obliged to you," said Granny mildly. "But Florence"—

"Yes, Florence is too good to work. There's no sense in such high-flown names. I'd have called her plain Peggy. She must curl her hair, and dress herself—oh my lady, if I had you, you'd see!"

And Mrs. Van Wyck arose in great wrath, her streamers flying wildly.

"You'll remember this when you come to beggary,—refusing a good home and plenty. Your grandmother is a foolish old woman; and you're a lazy, shiftless, impudent set! I wash my hands of the whole lot."

"I'm sorry," began Granny.

"There's no use talking. I wouldn't have the girl on any account. I can get her betters any day. You'll come to no good end, I can tell you!"

With that, Mrs. Van Wyck flounced out; but at the first turn tumbled over Kit, who had rolled himself in a ball on the doorstep.

Down she went, and Joe set up a shout. Hal couldn't help laughing, and Charlie ran to pull out Kit.

"You good-for-nothing, beggarly wretches!"

While she was sputtering and scrambling about, Joe began a hideous caterwauling.

"Drat that cat! Pity I hadn't broken his neck! And my second-best bonnet!"

Kit hid himself in his grandmother's gown, sorely frightened, and a little bruised.

"It's the last time I'll ever step inside of this place. Such an awful set of children I never did see!"

To use Joe's expressive phraseology, she "slathered" right and left, her shrill voice adding to the confusion.

Granny watched the retreating figure with the utmost bewilderment.

"The mean old thing!" began Florence, half crying. "Why, I couldn't stand her temper and her scolding, and to be a common kitchen-girl!"

"She meant well, dear. In my day girls thought it no disgrace to live out."

"Wasn't it gay and festive, Granny? I believe I've burst every button, laughing; and you'll have to put a mustard plaster on my side to draw out the soreness. And oh, Kit, what a horrible yell you gave! How could you be the ruin of that second best bonnet?"

"'Twasn't me," said Kit, rubbing his eyes. "But she most squeezed the breath out of me."

"Flossy, here is your fortune, and your coach-and-four. My dear child, I hope you will not be too much elated, for you must remember"—

"'Satan finds some mischief still,' &c."

Joe whisked around, holding Dot's apron at full length in imitation of a streamer.

"I wonder if she really thought I would go. Scouring and scrubbing, and washing dishes. I'd do with one meal a day first."

"She is a coarse, ill-bred woman," said Hal; "not a bit like Mrs. Kinsey."

"We will not be separated just yet," exclaimed Granny, with a sigh for the time that must come.

"And I don't mean to live out," was the emphatic rejoinder of Florence.

"My dear, you mustn't be too proud," cautioned Granny.

"It isn't altogether pride. Why should I wash dishes when I can do something better?"

"That's the grit, Flossy. I'll bet on you!"

"O Joe! don't. I wish you would learn to be refined. Now, you see all Mrs. Van Wyck's money cannot make her a lady."

Joe put on a solemn face; but the next moment declared that he must keep a sharp look out, or some old sea-captain would snap him up, and set him to scrubbing decks, and holystoning the cable.

And yet they felt quite grave when the fun was over. Their merry vacation had ended, and there was no telling what a year might bring forth.

"I think I should like most of all to be a school-teacher," Florence declared.

"You'll have to wait till you're forty. Who do you s'pose is going to mind a little gal?"

"Not you; for you never mind anybody," was the severe reply.

Florence felt quite grand on the following day, attired in her new green delaine, and her "lovely" gloves. Granny was so busy with the others that she never noticed them; and Florence quieted her conscience by thinking that the money was her own, and she could do what she liked with it. She kept self generally in view, it must be admitted.

Mrs. Van Wyck's overture was destined to make quite a stir. She repeated it to her neighbors in such glowing terms that it really looked like an offer to adopt Florence; and she declaimed bitterly against the pride and the ingratitude of the whole Kenneth family.

Florence held her head loftily, and took great pains to contradict the story; and Joe became the stoutest of champions, though he teased her at home.

"But it's too bad to have her tell everybody such falsehoods; and, after all, three dollars a month would be very low wages. Why, Mary Connor gets a dollar a week for tending Mrs. Hall's baby; and she never scrubs or scours a thing!"

Truth to tell, Florence felt a good deal insulted.

But the whole five went to school pretty regularly. Hal was very studious, and Florence also, in spite of her small vanities; but Joe was incorrigible everywhere.

Florence gained courage one day to ask Mr. Fielder about the prospect of becoming a teacher. She was ambitious, and desired some kind of a position that would be ladylike.

"It's pretty hard work at first," he answered with a smile.

"But how long would I have to study?"

"Let me see—you are fourteen now: in three years you might be able to take a situation. Public schools in the city are always better for girls, for they can begin earlier in the primary department. A country school, you see, may have some troublesome urchins in it."

Florence sighed. Three years would be a long while to wait.

"I will give you all the assistance in my power," Mr. Fielder said kindly. "And I may be able to hear of something that will be to your advantage."

Florence thanked him, but somehow the prospect did not look brilliant.

Then she thought of dressmaking. Miss Brown had a pretty cottage, furnished very nicely indeed; and it was her boast that she did it all with her own hands. She kept a servant, and dressed quite elegantly; and all the ladies round went to her in their carriages. Then she had such beautiful pieces for cushions and wonderful bedquilts,—"Though I never take but the least snip of a dress," she would say with a virtuous sniff. "I have heard of people who kept a yard or two, but to my mind it's downright stealing."

There was a drawback to this picture of serene contentment. Miss Brown was an old maid, and Florence hoped devoutly that would never be her fate. And then Miss Skinner, who went out by the day, was single also. Was it the natural result of the employment?

CHAPTER IV.

THE IDENTICAL SHOE.

They did pretty well through the fall. Joe came across odd jobs, gathered stores of hickory-nuts and chestnuts; and now and then of an evening they had what he called a rousing good boil; and certainly chestnuts never tasted better. They sat round the fire, and told riddles or stories, and laughed as only healthy, happy children can. What if they were poor, and had to live in a little tumble-down shanty!

Sometimes Joe would surprise them with a somerset in the middle of the floor, or a good stand on his head in one corner.

"Joe," Granny would say solemnly, "I once knowed a man who fell that way on his head off a load of hay, and broke his back."

"Granny dear, 'knowed' is bad grammar. When you go to see Florence in her palace, you must say knew, to rhyme with blew. But your old man's back must have grown cranky with rheumatism, while mine is limber as an eel."

"He wasn't old, Joe. And in my day they never learned grammar."

"Oh, tell us about the good old times!" and Hal's head was laid in Granny's lap.

The children were never tired of hearing these tales. Days when Granny was young were like enchantment. She remembered some real witch stories, that she was sure were true; and weddings, quiltings, husking-bees, and apple-parings were full of interest. How they went out sleigh-riding, and had a dance; and how once Granny and her lover, sitting on the back seat, were jolted out, seat and all, while the horses went skimming along at a pace equal to Tam O'Shanter's. And how they had to go to a neighboring cottage, and stay ever so long before they were missed.

"There'll never be such times again," Joe would declare solemnly.

Florence would breath a little sigh, and wonder if she could ever attain to beaux and merriment, and if any one would ever quarrel about dancing with her. How happy Granny must have been!

Dot had a dreadful cold, and Granny an attack of rheumatism; but they both recovered before Christmas. Every one counted so much on this holiday. All were making mysterious preparations. Joe and Hal and Florence had their heads together; and then it was Granny and Florence, or Granny and Hal.

"I don't dare to stir out," said Joe lugubriously, "lest you may say something that I shall not hear."

Hal killed three fine young geese. Two were disposed of for a dollar apiece, and the third he brought to the kitchen in triumph.

"There's our Christmas dinner, and a beauty too!" he announced.

Hal had sold turkeys and chickens enough to buy himself a good warm winter coat.

Granny had a little extra luck. In fact, it was rather a prosperous winter with them; and there was nothing like starvation, in spite of Mrs. Van Wyck's prediction.

They all coaxed Granny to make doughnuts. Joe dropped them in the kettle, and Hal took them out with the skimmer. How good they did smell!

Kit and Charlie tumbled about on the floor, and were under everybody's feet; while Dot sat in her high chair, looking wondrous wise.

"How'll we get the stockings filled?" propounded Joe, when the supper-table had been cleared away.

They all glanced at each other in consternation.

"But where'll you hang 'em?" asked Kit after a moment or two of profound study.

"Some on the andirons, some on the door-knob, some on the kettle-spout, and the rest up chimney."

"I say, can't we have two?" was Charlie's anxious question.

"Lucky if you get one full. What a host of youngsters! O Granny! did you know that last summer I discovered that you were the old woman who lived in a shoe?"

"O Joe! don't;" and Hal raised his soft eyes reproachfully.

Granny laughed, not understanding Hal's anxiety.

"Because I had so many children?"

"Exactly; but I think you are better tempered than your namesake."

Granny's eyes twinkled at this compliment.

"It was an awful hot day, and Dot was cross enough to kill a cat with nine lives."

"But she's a little darling now," said Hal, kissing her. "I think the sandman has been around;" and he smiled into the little face with its soft drooping eyes.

"Yes, she ought to be in bed, and Kit and Charlie. Come, children."

"I want to see what's going to be put in my stocking," whined Charlie in a very sleepy tone.

"No, you can't. March off, you small snipes, or you will find a whip there to-morrow morning."

That was Joe's peremptory order.

They had a doughnut apiece, and then went reluctantly. Charlie was very sure that she was wider awake than ever before in her life, and could not get asleep if she tried all night. Kit didn't believe that morning would ever come. Hal put on Dot's nightgown, and heard her say, "Now I lay me down to sleep;" while Joe picked up the cat, and irreverently whispered,—

> "Now I lay me down to sleep,
>
> All curled up in a little heap.
>
>
> If I should wake before 'tis day,
>
> What do you s'pose the doctor'd say?"

"O Joe!" remonstrated Granny.

"That's Tabby's prayers. Tabby is a high principled, moral, and intellectual cat. Now go to sleep, and dream of a mouse."

Tabby winked her eyes solemnly, as if she understood every word; and it's my firm belief that she did.

Then Granny, Florence, Joe, and Hal sat in profound thought until the old high clock in the corner struck nine.

"Well," said Joe, "what are we waiting for?"

Hal laughed and answered,—

"For some one to go to bed."

"What is to be done about it?"

Florence looked wise, and said presently,—

"We'll all have to go in the other room except the one who is to put something in the stockings."

"That's it. Who will begin?"

"Not I," rejoined Joe. "I don't want to be poked down into the toe."

"And I can't have my gifts crushed," declared Florence.

"Hal, you begin."

Hal was very cheerful and obliging. Granny lighted another candle, and the three retired. He disposed of his gifts, and then called Joe.

Joe made a great scrambling around. One would think he had Santa Claus himself, and was squeezing him into the small stocking, sleigh, ponies, and all.

"Now, Granny, it's your turn."

Granny fumbled about a long while, until the children grew impatient. Afterward Florence found herself sorely straitened for room; but she had a bright brain, and what she could not put inside she did up in papers and pinned to the outside, giving the stockings a rather grotesque appearance, it must be confessed. There they hung in a row, swelled to dropsical proportions, and looking not unlike stumpy little Dutchmen who had been beheaded at the knees.

"Now, Granny, you must go to bed," said Joe with an air of importance. "And you must promise to lie there until you are called to-morrow morning, —honor bright!"

Granny smiled, and bobbed her flaxen curls.

"Now," exclaimed Florence, bolting the middle door so they would be sure of no interruption.

Joe went out to the wood-shed, and dragged in a huge shoe. The toe was painted red, and around the top a strip of bright yellow, ending with an immense buckle cut out of wood.

"Oh, isn't it splendid!" exclaimed Florence, holding her breath.

"That was Hal's idea, and it's too funny for any thing. Granny could crawl into it head first. If we haven't worked and conjured to keep Kit and Charlie out of the secret, then no one ever had a bit of trouble in this world."

Joe laughed until he held his sides. It was a sort of safety escape-valve with him.

"H-u-s-h!" whispered Hal. "Now, Flossy."

Florence brought a large bundle out of the closet. There were some suppressed titters, and "O's," and "Isn't it jolly?"

"Now you must tie your garters round the bedpost, put the toe of your shoes toward the door, and go to bed backward. That'll make every thing come out just right," declared Joe.

"Oh, dear! I wish it was morning!" said Hal. "I want to see the fun."

"So don't this child. I must put in some tall snoring between this and daylight."

They said good-night softly to each other, and went off to bed. Joe was so full of mischief, that he kept digging his elbows into Hal's ribs, and rolling himself in the bedclothes, until it was a relief to have him commence the promised snoring.

With the first gray streak of dawn there was a stir.

"Merry Christmas!" sang out Joe with a shout that might have been heard a mile. "Hal and Kit"—

"Can't you let a body sleep in peace?" asked Kit in an injured tone, the sound coming from vasty deeps of bedclothes.

Joe declared they always had to fish him out of bed, and that buckwheat cakes was the best bait that could be used.

"Why, it's Christmas. Hurrah! We're going to have a jolly time. What do you suppose is in your stocking?"

That roused Kit. He came out of bed on his head, and commenced putting his foot through his jacket sleeve.

"I can't find my stockings! Who's got 'em?"

"The fellow who gets up first always takes the best clothes," said Joe solemnly.

With that he made a dive into his. It was the funniest thing in the world to see Joe dress. His clothes always seemed joined together in some curious fashion; for he flung his arms and legs into them at one bound.

"Oh, dear! Don't look in my stocking, Joe. You might wait. I know you've hidden away my shoe on purpose."

With this Kit sat in the middle of the floor like a heap of rains, and began to cry.

Hal came to the rescue, and helped his little brother dress. But Joe was down long before them. He gave a whoop at the door.

"Merry Christmas!" exclaimed Florence with a laugh, glad to think she had distanced him.

"Merry Christmas! The top o' the mornin' to you, Granny! Long life and plenty of 'praties and pint.' Santa Claus has been here. My eyes!"

Hal and Kit came tumbling along; but the younger stood at the door in amaze, his mouth wide open.

"Hush for your life!"

But Kit had to make a tour regardless of his own stocking, while Joe brandished the tongs above his head as if to enforce silence.

Hal began to kindle the fire. Charlie crept out in her nightgown, with an old shawl about her, and stood transfixed with astonishment.

"Oh, my! Isn't that jolly? Doesn't Granny know a bit?"

"Not a word."

"Mrs. McFinnegan," said Joe through the chink of the door, "I have to announce that the highly esteemed and venerable Mr. Santa Claus, a great traveller and a remarkably generous man, has made a call upon you during the night. As he feared to disturb your slumbers, he left a ball of cord, a paper of pins, and a good warm night-cap."

Florence was laughing so that she could hardly use buttons or hooks. Dot gave a neglected whine from the cradle.

"Is Granny ready?" Hal asked as she came out.

"She's just putting on her cap."

Hal went in for a Christmas kiss. Granny held him to her heart in a fond embrace, and wished the best of every thing over him.

"Merry Christmas to you all!" she said as Hal escorted her out to the middle of the room.

Joe went over on his head, and then perched himself on the back of a chair. The rest all looked at Granny.

"Is this really for me?" she asked in surprise, though the great placard stared her in the face.

The children set up a shout. Kit and Charlie paused, open-mouthed, in the act of demolishing something.

"Why, I never"—

"Tumble it out," said Joe.

"This great shoe full"—

Florence handed the first package to Granny. She opened it in amaze, as if she really could not decide whether it belonged to her or not.

There was a paper pinned on it, "A Merry Christmas from Mrs. Kinsey."

A nice dark calico dress-pattern, at which Granny was so overcome that she dropped into the nearest chair.

Next a pair of gloves from Joe; a pretty, warm hood from Mrs. Howard, the clergyman's wife; a bowl of elegant cranberry sauce from another neighbor; a crocheted collar from Florence, and then with a big tug—

"Oh!" exclaimed Granny, "is it a comfortable, or what?"

A good thick plaid shawl. Just bright enough to be handsome and not too gay, and as soft as the back of a lamb.

"Where did it come from?"

Granny's voice trembled in her excitement.

"From all of us," said Florence. "I mean, Joe and Hal and me. We've been saving our money this ever so long, and Mrs. Kinsey bought it for us. O Granny!"—

But Granny had her arms around them, and was crying over heads golden and brown and black; and Hal, little chicken-heart, was sobbing and smiling together. Joe picked a big tear or two out of his eye, and began with some nonsense.

"And to keep it a secret all this time! and to make this great shoe! There never was such a Christmas before. Oh, children, I'm happier than a queen!"

"What makes you cry then, Granny?" asked Charlie. "But oh! wasn't it funny? And if it only had runners it would make a sleigh. Look at the red toe."

They kissed dozens of times, and inspected each other's gifts. Florence had made each of the boys two dainty little neckties, having begged the silk from Miss Brown. Charlie and Kit had a pair of new mittens, Joe and Hal a new shirt with a real plaited bosom, and a host of small articles devised by love, with a scarce purse. But I doubt if there was a happier household in richer homes.

It was a long while before they had tried every thing,

tasted of all their "goodies," and expressed sufficient delight and surprise. Dot was taken up and dressed, and Kit found that she fitted into the shoe exact. Her tiny stocking was not empty. They all laughed and talked; and it was nine o'clock before their simple breakfast was ready.

Joe had to take a turn out to see some of the boys; Florence made the beds, and put the room in order; and Hal kept a roaring fire to warm it up, so that they might have a parlor. Kit and Charlie were deeply interested in the shoe; and Granny had to break out every now and then in surprise and thankfulness.

"A shawl and hood and gloves and a dress! Why, I never had so many things at once, I believe; and how hard you must all have worked! I don't see how you could save so much money!"

"It's better than living with Mrs. Van Wyck," returned Florence with pardonable pride. "Embroidering is real pretty work, and it pays well. Mrs. Howard has asked me to do some for a friend of hers."

"You're a wonder, Florence, to be sure. I can't see how you do 'em all so nice. But my fingers are old and clumsy."

"They know how to make pies and doughnuts," said Kit, as if that was the main thing, after all.

They went to work at the dinner. It was to be a grand feast. Joe kept the fire brisk; while Hal waited upon Granny, and remembered the ingredients that went to make "tip-top" dressing.

"It is a pity you were not a Frenchman," said Florence. "You would make such a handy cook."

Hal laughed, his cheeks as red as roses.

"I couldn't keep house without him," appended Granny.

There was a savory smell of roasting goose, the flavor of thyme and onions, which the children loved dearly. Charlie and Kit went out to have a good run, and came back hungry as bears, they declared. Joe went off to see some of the boys, and compare gifts. Though more than one new sled or nice warm overcoat gave his heart a little twinge, he was too gay and happy to feel sad very long; and, when he had a royal ride down hill on the bright sleds that flashed along like reindeers, he returned very well content.

Florence sighed a little as she arranged the table. Three kinds of dishes, and some of them showing their age considerably. If they were all white it wouldn't be so bad. She did so love beauty!

But when the goose, browned in the most delicious manner, graced the middle dish, the golden squash and snowy mound of potatoes, and the deep wine color of the cranberries lent their contrast, it was quite a picture, after all. And when the host of eager faces had clustered round it, one would hardly have noticed any lack. They were all in the gayest possible mood.

Hal did the carving. The goose was young and tender, and he disappeared with marvellous celerity.

Wings, drumsticks, great juicy slices with crisp skin, dressing in abundance; and how they did eat! For a second helping they had to demolish the rack; and Charlie wasn't sure but picking bones was the most fun of all.

"Hal, you had better go into the poultry business," said Joe, stopping in the midst of a spoonful of cranberry.

"I've been thinking of it," was the reply.

"I should think he was in it," said Charlie slyly.

Joe laughed.

"Good for you, Charlie. They must feed you on knives at your house, you're so sharp. But I have heard of people being too smart to live long, so take warning."

Charlie gave her head a toss.

"Why wouldn't it be good?" pursued Joe. "People do make money by it;

and I suppose, before very long, we must begin to think about money."

"Don't to-day" said Granny.

"No, we will not worry ourselves," rejoined Hal.

One after another drew long breaths, as if their appetites were diminishing. Dot sat back in her high chair, her hands and face showing signs of the vigorous contest, but wonderfully content.

"Now the pie!" exclaimed Joe.

Florence gathered up the bones and the plates, giving Tabby, who sat in the corner washing her face, a nice feast. Then came on the Christmas pie, which was pronounced as great a success as the goose.

"Oh, dear!" sighed Joe. "One unfortunate thing about eating is, that it takes away your appetite."

"It is high time!" added Florence.

They wouldn't allow Granny to wash a dish, but made her sit in state while they brought about order and cleanliness once more. A laughable time they had; for Joe wiped some dishes, and Charlie scoured one knife.

Afterward they had a game at blind-man's-buff. Such scampering and such screams would have half frightened any passer-by. They coaxed Granny to get up and join; and at last, to please Hal, she consented.

If Joe fancied he could catch her easily, he was much mistaken. She had played blind-man's-buff too many times in her young days. Such turning and doubling and slipping away was fine to see; and Charlie laughed so, that Joe, much chagrined, took her prisoner instead.

"Granny, you beat every thing!" he said. "Now, Charlie."

Charlie made a dive at the cupboard, and then started for the window, spinning round in such a fashion that they all had to run; but even she was not fleet enough.

After that, Kit and Florence essayed; and Joe, manœuvring in their behalf, fell into the trap himself, at which they all set up a shout.

"I'm bound to have Granny this time," he declared.

Sure enough, though he confessed afterwards that he peeped a little; but Granny was tired with so much running: and, as the short afternoon drew to a close, they gathered round the fire, and cracked nuts, washing them down with apples, as they had no cider.

"It's been a splendid Christmas!" said Charlie, with such a yawn that she nearly made the top of her head an island.

"I wonder if we'll all be here next year?" said Joe, rather more solemnly than his wont.

"I hope so," responded Granny, glancing over the clustering faces. Dot sat on Hal's knee, looking bright as a new penny. She, too, had enjoyed herself amazingly.

But presently the spirit of fun seemed to die out, and they began to sing some hymns and carols. The tears came into Granny's eyes, as the sweet, untrained voices blended so musically. Ah, if they could always stay children! Foolish wish; and yet Granny would have toiled for them to her latest breath.

"Here's long life and happiness!" exclaimed Joe, with a flourish of the old cocoanut dipper. "A merry Christmas next year, and may we all be there to see!"

Ah, Joe, it will be many a Christmas before you are all there again.

CHAPTER V.

GOOD LUCK FOR JOE.

"Hooray!" said Joe, swinging the molasses jug over his head as if it had been a feather, or the stars and stripes on Fourth of July morning.

"O Joe!"

"Flossy, my darling, you are a poet sure; only poetry, like an alligator, must have feet, or it will lose its reputation. Here's your 'lasses, Granny; and what do you think? Something has actually happened to me! Oh, my! do guess quick!"

"You've been taken with the 'lirium"—and there Charlie paused, having been wrecked on a big word.

"Delirium tremen*jous*. Remember to say it right hereafter, Charlie."

Charlie looked very uncertain.

"Maybe it's the small-pox," said Kit, glancing up in amazement.

"Good for you!" and Joe applauded with two rather blue thumb-nails. "But it's a fact. Guess, Granny. I'm on the high road to fortune. Hooray!"

With that, Joe executed his usual double-shuffle, and a revolution on his axis hardly laid down in the planetary system. He would have said that it was because he was not a heavenly body.

"O Joe, if you were like any other boy!"

"Jim Fisher, for instance,—red-headed, squint-eyed, and freckled."

"He can't help it," said Hal mildly. "He is real nice too."

"You're not going"—began Granny with a gasp.

"Yes, I'm going"—was the solemn rejoinder.

"Not to sea!" and there came a quick blur in Hal's eyes.

"Oh, bother, no! You're all splendid at guessing, and ought to have a prize leather medal. It's in Mr. Terry's store; and I shall have a dollar and a half a week! Good by, Mr. Fielder. Adieu, beloved grammar; and farewell, most fragrant extract of cube-root, as well as birch-oil. O Granny! I'm happy as a big sunflower. On the high road to fame and fortune,—think of it!"

"Is it really true?" asked Florence.

"Then, I won't need to go for any thing," appended Charlie.

"No; but you'll have to draw water, and split kindlings, and hunt up Mrs. Green's cows."

"In Mr. Terry's store! What wonderful luck, Joe!"

Granny's delight was overwhelming. All along she had experienced a sad misgiving, lest Joe should take a fancy to the sea in real earnest.

"Yes. It's just splendid. Steve Anthony's going to the city to learn a trade. He had a letter from his uncle to-day, saying that he might start right away. I thought a minute: then said I, 'Steve, who's coming here?' 'I don't know,' said he. 'Mr. Terry'll have to look round.' 'I'm your boy,' said I, 'and no mistake.' And with that I rushed in to Mr. Terry, and asked him. He gave me some columns of figures to add up, and questioned me a little, and finally told me that I might come on Monday, and we'd try for a week."

"There's Joe's fortune," said Hal, "and a good one too. You will not need to go to sea."

There was an odd and knowing twinkle in Joe's merry hazel eye, which showed to an observing person that he was not quite sound on the question.

"Tate Dotty;" and two little hands were outstretched.

"O Dot! you're a fraud, and more trouble to me than all my money."

With that, Joe sat her up on his shoulder, and she laughed gleefully.

Granny lighted a candle, and began to prepare for supper. While Charlie set the table, Granny brought out the griddle, and commenced frying some Indian cakes in a most tempting manner. Joe dropped on an old stool, and delighted Dot with a vigorous ride to Banbury Cross.

Kit stood beside him, inhaling the fragrance of the cakes, and wondering at the dexterity with which Granny turned them on a slender knife.

"I don't see how you do it. Suppose you should let 'em fall?"

"Ho!" said Charlie, with a sniff of disdain. "Women always know how."

"But they can't come up to the miners," suggested Joe. "They keep house for themselves; and their flapjacks are turned,—as big as Granny's griddle here."

"One cake?"

"Yes. That's where the art comes in."

"They must take a shovel," said Charlie.

"No, nor a knife, nor any thing."

With that Joe shook his head mysteriously.

"With their fingers," announced Kit triumphantly.

"My mother used to bake them in a frying-pan," said Granny. "Then she'd twirl it round and round, and suddenly throw the cake over."

"There!"

Kit gave a nod as much as to say, "Beat that if you can."

"That isn't a circumstance," was Joe's solemn comment.

"But how then?" asked Charlie, who was wound up to a pitch of curiosity.

"Why, *they* bake them in a pan too, and twirl it round and round, and then throw it up and run out of doors. The cake goes up chimney, and comes down on the raw side, all right, you see, and drops into the pan before you can count six black beans."

"Oh, I don't believe it!" declared Charlie. "Do you, Granny?"

"They'd have to be pretty quick," was the response.

"You see, a woman never could do it, Charlie," Joe continued in a tormenting manner.

"But, Charlie, a miner's cabin is not very high; and the chimney is just a great hole in the roof," explained Hal.

"'Tory, 'tory," said Dot, who was not interested in the culinary art.

"O Dotty! you'll have a piece worn off the end of my tongue, some day. It's high time you were storing your mind with useful facts; so, if you please, we will have a little English history."

"What nonsense, Joe! As if she could understand;" and Florence looked up from her pretty worsted crocheting.

"To be sure she can. Dot comes of a smart family. Now, Midget;" and with that he perched her up on his knee.

Charlie and Kit began to listen.

"'When good King Arthur ruled the land,

He was a goodly king:

He stole three pecks of barley-meal

To make a bag pudding.'"

"I don't believe it," burst out Charlie. "I was reading about King Arthur"—

"And he was a splendid cook. Hear his experience,—

'A bag pudding the king did make,

And stuffed it well with plums;

And in it put great lumps of fat,

As big as my two thumbs.'"

Dot thought the laugh came in here, and threw back her head, showing her little white teeth.

"It really wasn't King Arthur," persisted Charlie.

"It is a fact handed down to posterity. No wonder England became great under so wise and economical a rule; for listen—

'The king and queen did eat thereof,

And noblemen beside;

And what they could not eat that night,

The queen next morning fried,'—

as we do sometimes. Isn't it wonderful?"

"Hunnerful," ejaculated Dot, wide-eyed.

"I hope you'll take a lesson, and"—

"Come to supper," said Granny.

Irrepressible Charlie giggled at the ending.

They did not need a second invitation, but clustered around eagerly.

"I'm afraid there won't be any left to fry up in the morning," said Joe solemnly.

After the youngsters were off to bed that evening, Joe began to talk about his good fortune again.

"And a dollar and a half a week, regularly, is a good deal," he said. "Why, I can get a spick and span new suit of clothes for twelve dollars,—two months, that would be; and made at a tailor's too."

"The two months?" asked Florence.

"Oh! you know what I mean."

"You will get into worse habits than ever," she said with a wise elder-sister air.

"I don't ever expect to be a grand gentleman."

"But you *might* be a little careful."

"Flo acts as if she thought we were to have a great fortune left us by and by, and wouldn't be polished enough to live in state."

"The only fortune we shall ever have will come from five-finger land," laughed Hal good-naturedly.

"And I'm going to make a beginning. I do think it was a streak of luck. I am old enough to do something for myself."

"I wish I could find such a chance," said Hal, with a soft sigh.

"Your turn will come presently," Granny answered, smiling tenderly.

Joe went on with his air-castles. The sum of money looked so large in his eyes. He bought out half of Mr. Terry's store, and they were to live like princes,—all on a dollar and a half a week.

Granny smiled, and felt proud enough of him. If he would only keep to business, and not go off to sea.

So on Friday Joe piled up his books, and turned a somerset over them, and took a farewell race with the boys. They were all sorry enough to lose him. Mr. Fielder wished him good luck.

"You will find that work is not play," he said by way of caution.

Early Monday morning Joe presented himself bright as a new button. He had insisted upon wearing his best suit,—didn't he mean to have another soon? for the school clothes were all patches. He had given his hair a Sunday combing, which meant that he used a comb instead of his fingers. Mr. Terry was much pleased with his promptness.

A regular country store, with groceries on one side and dry goods on the other, a little sashed cubby for a post-office, and a corner for garden and farm implements. There was no liquor kept on the premises; for the mild ginger and root beer sold in summer could hardly be placed in that category.

Joe was pretty quick, and by noon had mastered many of the intricacies. Old Mr. Terry was in the store part of the time,—"father" as everybody called him. He was growing rather childish and careless, so his son instructed Joe to keep a little watch over him. Then he showed him how to harness the horse, and drove off with some bulky groceries that he was to take home.

"All things work together for good, sonny," said Father Terry with a sleepy nod, as he sat down by the stove.

"What things?"

"All things," with a sagacious shake of the head.

This was Father Terry's favorite quotation, and he used it in season and out of season.

The door opened, and Mrs. Van Wyck entered. She gave Joe a sharp look.

"So *you're* here?" with a kind of indignant sniff.

"Yes. What will you have?"

There was a twinkle in Joe's eye, and an odd little pucker to his lips, as if he were remembering something.

"You needn't be so impudent."

"I?" and Joe flushed in surprise.

"Yes. You're a saucy lot, the whole of you."

With that Mrs. Van Wyck began to saunter round.

"What's the price of these cranberries?"

"Eighteen cents," in his most respectful tone.

"They're dear, dreadful dear. Over to Windsor you can get as many as you can carry for a shillin' a quart."

Joe was silent.

"Say sixteen."

"I couldn't," replied Joe. "If Mr. Terry were here"—

"There's Father Terry." She raised her voice a little. "Father Terry, come and look at these cranberries. They're a poor lot, and you'll do well to get a shillin' a quart."

Joe ran his fingers through them. Plump and crimson, very nice he thought for so late in the season.

"I don't s'pose I'd get more'n two good quarts out of three. They'll spile on your hands. Come now, be reasonable."

Father Terry looked undecided. Joe watched him, thinking in his heart that he ought not fall a penny.

"Say a shillin'."

The old man shook his head.

"Well, fifteen cents. I want three quarts, and I won't give a penny more."

The old gentleman studied Joe's face, which was full of perplexity.

"Well," he said with some reluctance.

Joe measured them. Mrs. Van Wyck gave each quart a "settle" by shaking it pretty hard, and Joe had to put in another large handful.

"Now I want some cheese."

The pound weighed two ounces over.

"You can throw that in. Mr. Terry always does."

"How much?"

"Twenty-three cents."

"No: you can't fool me, youngster. I never pay more than twenty cents."

"I'm sure Mr. Terry told me that it was twenty-three."

Father was appealed to again, and of course went over to the domineering enemy.

Then two pounds of butter passed through the same process of cheapening. Joe began to lose his temper. Afterward a broom, some tape and cotton, and finally a calico dress.

"Now, here's three dozen eggs for part pay. They're twenty-four cents a dozen."

"Why, that's what we sell them for," said astonished Joe, mentally calculating profit and loss.

"Oh! they've gone up. Hetty Collins was paid twenty-five over to Windsor. I'd gone there myself if I'd had a little more time."

"I wish you had," ejaculated Joe inwardly.

She haggled until she got her price, and the settlement was made.

"She's a regular old screwer," said Joe rather crossly. "I don't believe it was right to let her have those things in that fashion."

"All things work together for good."

"For *her* good, it seems."

Father Terry went back to his post by the stove. Joe breathed a little thanksgiving that Flossy was not Mrs. Van Wyck's maid-of-all-work.

Joe's next customer was Dave Downs, as the boys called him. He shuffled up to the counter.

"Got any *reel* good cheese?"

"Yes," said Joe briskly.

"Let's see."

Joe raised the cover. Dave took up the knife, and helped himself to a bountiful slice.

"Got any crackers?"

"Yes," wondering what Dave meant.

"Nice and fresh?"

"I guess so."

"I'll take three or four."

"That will be a penny's worth."

When Dave had the crackers in his hand he said, raising his shaggy brows in a careless manner,—

"Oh! you needn't be so perticelar."

Then he took a seat beside Father Terry, and munched crackers and cheese. "Cool enough," thought Joe.

Old Mrs. Skittles came next. She was very deaf, and talked in a high, shrill key, as if she thought all the world in the same affliction.

She looked at every thing, priced it, beat down a cent or two, and then concluded she'd rather wait until Mr. Terry came in. At last she purchased a penny's worth of snuff, and begged Joe to give her good measure.

After that two customers and the mail. Father Terry bestirred himself, and waited upon a little girl with a jug.

Joe was rather glad to see Mr. Terry enter, for he had an uncomfortable sense of responsibility.

"Trade been pretty good, Joe?" with a smile.

"I've put it all down on the slate, as you told me."

"Hillo! What's this!"

A slow stream of something dark was running over the floor back of the lower counter.

"Oh, molasses!" and with a spring Joe shut off the current, but there was an ominous pool.

"I did not get that: it was"—and Joe turned crimson.

"Father. We never let him go for molasses, vinegar, oil, or burning fluid. He is sure to deluge us. Run round in the kitchen, and get a pail and a mop."

"It's my opinion that this doesn't work together for good," said Joe to himself as he was cleaning up the mess.

"So you had Mrs. Skittles?" exclaimed Mr. Terry with a laugh. "And Mrs. Van Wyck. Why, Joe!"

"She beat down awfully!" said Joe; "and she wanted every thing thrown in. Mr. Terry"—

"She called on father, I'll be bound. But she has taken off all the profits; and then to make you pay twenty-four cents for the eggs."

"I'd just like to have had my own way. If you'll give me leave"—

"You will have to look out a little for father. He's getting old, you know; and these sharp customers are rather too much for him."

"I'll never fall a penny again;" and Joe shook his head defiantly.

"You will learn by degrees. But it is never necessary to indulge such people. There's the dinner-bell."

Dave Downs had finished his crackers and cheese, and now settled himself to a comfortable nap. Joe busied himself by clearing up a little, giving out mail, and once weighing some flour. Then he discovered that he had scattered it over his trousers, and that with the molasses dabs it made a not very delightful mixture. So he took a seat on a barrel-head and began to scrub it off; but he found it something like Aunt Jemima's plaster.

"Run in and get some dinner, Joe," said Mr. Terry after his return to the store.

"But I was going home," replied Joe bashfully.

"Oh! never mind. We will throw in the dinner."

So Joe ran around, but hesitated at the door of Mrs. Terry's clean kitchen. She was motherly and cordial, however, and gave him a bright smile.

"I told Mr. Terry that you might as well come in here for your dinner. It is quite a long run home."

"You are very kind," stammered Joe, feeling that he must say something, in spite of his usual readiness of speech deserting him.

"You ought to have an apron, Joe, or a pair of overalls," she said kindly. "You will find grocery business rather dirty work sometimes."

"And my best clothes!" thought Joe with a sigh.

But the coffee was so delightful, and the cold roast beef tender as a chicken. And Joe began to think it was possible for a few things to work together for good, if they were only the right kind of things.

Altogether he went home at night in very good spirits.

"But my trousers will have to go in the wash-tub, Granny," he exclaimed. "I believe I wasn't cut out for a gentleman, after all."

"O Joe, what a sight! How could you?"

"It was all easy enough. If you'd had molasses to scrub up, and flour to get before it was dry, you would have found the sticking process not at all difficult. And oh! Mrs. Van Wyck came in."

Florence flushed a little at this.

"Yes, wait till I show you." With that, Joe sprang up, and wrapped Granny's old shawl about him, and began in his most comical fashion. In a moment or two the children were in roars of laughter.

"I don't know as it is quite right, Joe dear," interposed Granny mildly, "to make fun of any one."

"My conscience don't trouble me a bit;" for now he was in a high glee. "I owe her a grudge for making me pay twenty-four cents for eggs. And, Granny, when you come to the store, don't beat me down a penny on any thing; nor ask me to throw in a spool of cotton nor a piece of tape, nor squeeze down the measure. I wonder how people can be so mean!"

"Rich people too," added Florence in an injured tone of voice, still thinking of Mrs. Van Wyck's overture.

"There's lots of funny folks in the world," said Joe with a grave air. "But I like Mr. Terry, and I mean to do my very best."

"That's right;" and Granny smiled tenderly over the boy's resolve.

"And I'll put on my old clothes to-morrow. Who knows but I may fall into the mackerel-barrel before to-morrow night?"

Kit laughed at this. "They'll have to fish you out with a harpoon, then."

"Oh! I might swim ashore."

The next day Joe improved rapidly. To be sure, he met with a mishap or two; but Mr. Terry excused him, and only charged him to be more careful in future. And Father Terry administered his unfailing consolation on every occasion.

But on Saturday night Joe came home in triumph.

"There's the beginning of my fortune," he said, displaying his dollar and a half all in hard cash. For that was a long while ago, when the eagle, emblem of freedom, used to perch on silver half-dollars.

CHAPTER VI.

FORTUNES AND MISFORTUNES.

"I think I'll go into business," said Hal one evening, as he and Granny and Florence sat together.

They missed Joe so much! He seldom came home until eight o'clock; and there was no one to stir up the children, and keep the house in a racket.

"What?" asked Granny.

"I am trying to decide. I wonder how chickens would do?"

"It takes a good deal to feed 'em," said Granny.

"But they could run about, you know. And buckwheat is such a splendid thing for them. Then we can raise ever so much corn."

"But where would you get your buckwheat?" asked Florence.

"I was thinking. Mr. Peters never does any thing with his lot down here, and the old apple-trees in it are not worth much. If he'd let me have it ploughed up! And then we'd plant all of our ground in corn, except the little garden that we want."

"What a master hand you are to plan, Hal!"

Granny's face was one immense beam of admiration.

"I want to do something. It's too hard, Granny, that you should have to go out washing, and all that."

Hal's soft brown eyes were full of tender pity.

"Oh! I don't mind. I'm good for a many day's work yet, Hal."

"I hope some of us will get rich at last."

Florence sighed softly.

"I thought you were going to have a green-house," she said.

"I'm afraid I can't manage the green-house now, though I mean to try some day. And I noticed old Speckly clucking this morning."

"But we haven't any eggs," said Granny.

"I could get some."

"How many chickens would you raise?" asked Florence.

"Well, if we should set the five hens,—out of say sixty-four eggs we ought to raise fifty chickens; oughtn't we, Granny?"

"With good luck; but so many things happen to 'em."

"And if I could clear thirty dollars. Then there's quite a good deal of work to do in the summer."

"I shall soon be a fine lady, and ride in my carriage," Granny commented with a cheerful chirrup of a laugh.

"Mrs. Kinsey's chickens are splendid," said Florence.

"Yes. Shall I get some eggs, and set Speckly?"

"It's rather airly to begin."

"But I'll make a nice coop. And eggs are not twenty-four cents a dozen."

Hal finished off with a quiet smile at the thought of Mrs. Van Wyck.

So he went to Mrs. Kinsey's the next morning, and asked her for a dozen of eggs, promising to come over the first Saturday there was any thing to do, and work it out.

"I'll give you the eggs," she said; "but we will be glad to have you some Saturday, all the same."

So old Speckly was allowed to indulge her motherly inclinations to her great satisfaction. Hal watched her with the utmost solicitude. In the course of time a tiny bill pecked against white prison walls; and one morning Hal found the cunningest ball of soft, yellow down, trying to balance itself on two slender legs, but finding that the point of gravity as often centred in its head. But the little fellow winked oddly, as much as to say, "I know what I'm about. I'll soon find whether it is the fashion to stand on your head or your feet in this queer world."

One by one the rest came out. Hal had a nice coop prepared, and set Mrs. Speckly up at housekeeping. Dot caught one little "birdie," as she called it, and, in running to show Granny, fell down. And although Dot wasn't very heavy, it was an avalanche on poor "birdie." He gave two or three slow kicks with his yellow legs, and then was stiff for all time.

"Hal's boofer birdie," said Dot. "See, Danny!"

"O Dot! what have you done?"

"Him 'oont 'alk;" and Dot stood him down on the doorstep, only to see him tumble over.

"Oh, you've killed Hal's birdie! What will he say?"

"I 'ell down. Why 'oont him run, Danny?"

What could Granny do? Scolding Dot was out of the question. And just then Hal came flying up the road.

Granny had seen the fall, and explained the matter.

"But she mustn't catch them! You're a naughty little Dot!"

Dot began to cry.

"Poor little girl!" said Hal, taking her in his arms. "It is wrong to catch them. See, now, the little fellow is dead, and can never run about any more. Isn't Dot sorry? She won't ever touch Hal's birdies again, will she?"

So Dot promised, and Hal kissed her. But she carried the dead birdie about, petting it with softest touches, and insisting upon taking it to bed with her.

One more of the brood met with a mishap, but the other ten throve and grew rapidly. By the time the next hen wanted to set, Hal had a dozen eggs saved.

He asked Farmer Peters about the lot. It was just below their house, between that and the creek, a strip of an acre and a half perhaps. The old trees were not worth much, to be sure; and Mr. Peters never troubled himself to cultivate the plot, as it was accounted very poor.

"Yes, you may have it in welcome; but you won't git enough off of it to pay for the ploughin'?"

"I'm going to raise chickens; and I thought it would be nice to sow buckwheat, and let them run in it."

"Turnin' farmer, hey? 'Pears to me you're makin' an airly beginnin'."

Hal smiled pleasantly.

"You'll find chickens an awful sight o' bother."

"I thought I'd try them."

"Goin' to garden any?"

"A little."

"Hens and gardens are about like fox an' geese. One's death on the other. But you kin have the lot."

So Hal asked Abel Kinsey to come over and plough. In return he helped plant potatoes and drop corn for two Saturdays. By this time there was a third hen setting.

House-cleaning had come on, and Granny was pretty busy. But she and Hal were up early in the morning garden-making. The plot belonging to the cottage was about two acres. Hal removed his chicken-coops to the lot, and covered his young vegetables with brush to protect them from incursions,— pease, beans, lettuce, beets, and sweet-corn; and the rest was given over to the chickens.

"I am going to keep an account of all that is spent for them," he said; "and we will see if we can make it pay."

When Joe had saved three dollars, he teased Granny to let him order his clothes.

"I don't like running in debt, Joe," she said with a grave shake of the head.

"But this is very sure. Mr. Terry likes me, and I shall go on staying. There will be four dollars and a half to pay down by the time they are done, and in five weeks I can earn the rest."

"How nice it seems!" said Hal. "You and Flo earn a deal of money."

Flo gave a small sniff. She wanted some new clothes also. And Kit and Charlie were going to shreds and patches. Charlie, indeed, was shooting up like Jack's bean-stalk, Joe declared, being nearly as tall as Hal. She was wild as a colt, climbed trees, jumped fences, and wouldn't be dared by any of the boys.

"I'm sure I don't know what you'll come to," Granny would say with a sigh.

Joe carried his point, and ordered his clothes; for he insisted that he could not think of going to Sunday school until he had them. It was quite an era in his life to have real store clothes. He felt very grand one day when he went to Mr. Briggs the tailor, and selected the cloth. There were several different patterns and colors; but he had made up his mind that it should be gray, just like Archie Palmer's.

He was so dreadfully afraid of being disappointed, that he dropped in on Friday to see if they were progressing. There was the jacket in the highest state of perfection.

"But the pants?" he questioned.

"Never you mind. Them pants'll be done as sure as my name's Peter Briggs."

"All right," said Joe; and he ran on his way whistling.

"Kit," he announced that evening, "I've just found out a good business for you."

"What?" and Kit roused himself.

"You shall be a tailor. I was thinking to-day how you would look on the board, with your scalp-lock nodding to every stitch."

"I won't," said Kit stoutly; and he gave a kick towards Joe's leg.

"It's a good business. You will always have plenty of cabbage."

"You better stop!" declared Kit.

"It will be handy to have him in the house, Granny. He can do the ironing by odd spells. And on the subject of mending old clothes he will be lovely."

With that Kit made another dive.

Granny gave a sudden spring, and rescued the earthen jar that held the cakes she had just mixed and set upon the stove-hearth.

"O Kit! Those precious pancakes! We are not anxious to have them flavored with extract of old shoes."

"Nor to go wandering over the floor."

Kit looked sober and but half-awake.

"Never mind," said Granny cheerily. "You mustn't tease him so much, Joe."

"Why, I was only setting before him the peculiar advantages of this romantic and delightful employment;" and with that, Joe executed a superior double-shuffle quickstep, accompanied by slapping a tune on his knee.

"You'd do for a minstrel," said Kit.

Joe cleared his voice with a flourish, and sang out,—

"I'd be a tailor,
　　Jolly and free,
With plenty of cabbage,
　　And a goose on my knee.
Monday would be blue,
　　Tuesday would be shady,
Wednesday I'd set out
　　To find a pretty lady."

"Much work you would do in that case," commented Florence.

"It's time to go to bed, children," said Granny.

"Yes," Joe went on gravely. "For a rising young man, who must take time by the fore-lock, or scalp-lock, and who longs to distinguish himself by some great and wonderful discovery, there's nothing like,—

'Early to bed, and early to rise,
　　To make a man healthy, wealthy, and wise.'"

With that Joe was up stairs with a bound.

"Joe!" Charlie called in great earnest.

"Well?"

"You better take a mouthful of Granny's rising before you go."

"Good for you, Charlie; but smart children always die young. Granny, won't you put a stone on Charlie's head for fear?"

Hal said his good-night in a tenderer manner.

They were all wonderfully interested in Joe's clothes; and, though it was always later on Saturday night when he reached home, they begged to sit up, but Kit took a nap by the chimney-corner with Tabby. Granny sat nodding when they heard the gay whistle without.

"Hurrah! The country's safe!" exclaimed Joe. "Get out your spectacles, all hands."

"You act as if you never had any thing before, Joe," said Florence, with an

57

air of extreme dignity.

"But these are real 'boughten' clothes," said Joe, "and gilt buttons down the jacket. I shall feel like a soldier-boy. Just look now."

The bundle came open with a flourish of the jack-knife. All the heads crowded round, though the one candle gave a rather dim light.

Such exclamations as sounded through the little room, from every voice, and in almost every key.

"But where are the trousers?" asked Hal.

"The trousers?—why"—

Granny held up the beautiful jacket. There was nothing else in the paper.

"Why—he's made a mistake. He never put them in, I am sure."

"You couldn't have lost 'em?" asked Granny mildly.

"Lost them—and the bundle tied with this strong twine! Now, that's mean! I'll have to run right back."

Off went Joe like a flash. He hardly drew a breath until his hand was on Mr. Brigg's door-knob.

"Well, what now, Joe?" asked the astonished Mr. Briggs.

"You didn't put in the trousers!"

"Didn't? Dan done 'em up. Dan!"

Dan emerged from a pile of rags under the counter, where he was taking a snooze.

"You didn't put in Joe's trousers."

"Yes I did."

"No you didn't," said Joe, with more promptness than politeness.

Dan began to search. A sleepy-looking, red-headed boy, to whom Saturday night was an abomination, because his father was always in the drag, and cross.

"I'm sure I put 'em in. Every thing's gone, and they ain't here."

"Look sharp, you young rascal!"

"He has lost 'em out."

"Lost your grandmother!" said Joe contemptuously; "or the liberty pole out on the square! Why, the bundle was not untied until after I was in the house."

"Dan, if you don't find them trousers, I'll larrup you!"

Poor Dan. Fairly wide awake now, he went tumbling over every thing piled on the counter, searched the shelves, and every available nook.

"Somebody's stole 'em."

Dan made this announcement with a very blank face.

"I know better!" said his father.

"You are sure you made them, Mr. Briggs," asked Joe.

"Sure!" in a tone that almost annihilated both boys.

"If you don't find 'em!" shaking his fist at Dan.

Dan began to blubber.

Joe couldn't help laughing. "Let me help you look," he said.

Down went a box of odd buttons, scattering far and wide.

"You Dan!" shouted his father, with some buttons in his mouth, that rendered his voice rather thick. "Just wait till I get at you. I have only six buttons to sew on."

"They're not here, Mr. Briggs," exclaimed Joe.

"Well, I declare! If that ain't the strangest thing! Dan, you've taken them trousers to the wrong place!"

A new and overwhelming light burst in upon Dan's benighted brain.

"That's it," said Joe. "Now, where have you taken them?"

"I swow!" ejaculated the youth, rubbing his eyes.

"None o' your swearin' in this place!" interrupted his father sternly. "I'm a strictly moral man, and don't allow such talk in my family."

"Tain't swearin'," mumbled Dan.

Mr. Briggs jumped briskly down from the board, with a pair of pantaloons in one hand, and a needle and thread in the other. Dan dodged round behind Joe.

"You took 'em over to Squire Powell's, I'll be bound!"

Another light was thrown in upon Dan's mental vision.

"There! I'll bet I did."

"Of course you did, you numskull! Start this minute and see how quick you can be gone."

"I will go with him," said Joe.

So the two boys started; and a run of ten minutes—a rather reluctant performance on Dan's part, it must be confessed—brought them to Squire Powell's. There was no light in the kitchen; but Joe beat a double tattoo on the door in the most scientific manner.

"Who's there?" asked a voice from the second story window.

"Dan Briggs!" shouted Joe.

"Guess not," said the squire. The sound was so unlike Dan's sleepy, mumbling tone.

"There was a mistake made in some clothes," began Joe, nothing daunted.

"Oh, that's it! I will be down in a minute."

Pretty soon the kitchen-door was unlocked, and the boys stepped inside.

"I didn't know but you sent these over for one of my girls," said the squire laughingly. "They were a *leetle* too small for me. So they belong to you, Joe?"

"Yes, sir," said Joe emphatically, laying hold of his precioustrousers.

"Look sharper next time, Dan," was the squire's good advice.

"I wish you'd go home with me, Joe," said Dan, after they had taken a few steps. "Father'll larrup me, sure!"

"Maybe that will brighten your wits," was Joe's consoling answer.

"But, Joe—I'm sure I didn't mean to—and"—

"I'm off like a shot," appended Joe, suiting the action to the word; and poor Dan was left alone in the middle of the road.

"Why, what *has* happened, Joe?" said Granny as he bounced in the kitchen-door.

"Such a time as I've had to find 'them trousers,' as Mr. Briggs calls them! Dan had packed them off to Squire Powell's!"

"That Dan Briggs is too stupid for any thing," commented Florence.

"There's time to try them on yet," Joe exclaimed. "Just you wait a bit."

Joe made a rush into the other room.

"Don't wake up Dot," said Hal.

"Oh! I'll go as softly as a blind mouse."

"There, Granny, what do you think of that?"

"You want a collar and a necktie, and your hair brushed a little," said Florence with critical eyes.

"But aren't they stunners!"

Granny looked at him, turned him round and looked again, and her wrinkled face was all one bright smile. For he was so tall and manly in this long jacket, with its narrow standing collar, and the trousers that fitted to a charm.

"Oh," said Hal with a long breath, "it's splendid!"

"You bet! When I get 'em paid for, Hal, I'll help you out."

Florence sighed.

"O Flo! I can't help being slangy. It comes natural to boys. And then hearing them all talk in the store."

"Wa-a!" said a small voice. "Wa-a-a Danny!"

"There!" exclaimed Hal; and he ran in to comfort Dot.

But Dot insisted upon being taken up, and brought out to candle-light. The buttons on Joe's jacket pleased her fancy at once, and soothed her sorrow.

"I must say, Dot, you are a young woman of some taste," laughed Joe.

"Granny," said Kit, after sitting in deep thought, and taking a good chew out of his thumb, "when Joe wears 'em out, can you cut 'em over for me?"

"O Kit! Prudent and economical youth! To you shall be willed the last remaining shreds of my darling gray trousers, jacket, buttons and all."

They had a grand time admiring Joe. Charlie felt so sorry that she wasn't a boy; and Flo declared that "he looked as nice as anybody, if only he wouldn't"—

"No, I won't," said Joe solemnly.

Granny felt proud enough of him the next day when he went to church. Florence was quite satisfied to walk beside him.

"I wish there was something nice for you, Hal," said Granny in a tone of tender regret.

"My turn will come by and by," was the cheerful answer.

For Hal took the odds and ends of every thing, and was content.

"They're a nice lot of children, if I do say it myself," was Granny's comment to Dot. "And I'm glad I never let any of them go to the poor-house or be bound out, or any thing. We'll all get along somehow."

Dot shook her head sagely, as if that was her opinion also.

The story of Joe's Saturday night adventure leaked out; and poor Dan Briggs was tormented a good deal, the boys giving him the nickname of Trousers, much to his discomfort.

Joe discovered, like a good many other people, that whereas getting in debt was very easy, getting out of debt was very hard. He went along bravely for several weeks, and then he began to find so many wants. A new straw hat he *must* have, for the weather was coming warm, and they had such beauties at the store for a dollar; and then his boots grew too rusty, so a pair of shoes were substituted. He bought Dot a pretty Shaker, which she insisted upon calling her "Sunny cool Shaker." She was growing very cunning indeed, though her tongue was exceedingly crooked. Hal laughed over her droll baby words; and Kit's endeavor to make her say tea-kettle was always crowned with shouts of laughter.

Joe succeeded pretty well at the store, but occasionally all things did not work together for good. His margin of fun was so wide that it sometimes brought him into trouble. One day he inadvertently sold old Mrs. Cummings some ground pepper, instead of allspice. That afternoon the old lady flew back in a rage.

"I'll never buy a cent's wuth of this good-for nothin', car'less boy!" she ejaculated. "He does nothin' but jig around the store, and sing songs. An' now he's gone and spiled my whole batch of pies."

"Spoiled your pies?" said Mr. Terry in astonishment.

"Yes, spiled 'em! Four as good pies as anybody in Madison makes. Green apple too!"

"Why, I never saw your pies!" declared Joe.

"I'd like to make you eat 'em all,—to the last smitch!" and she shook her fist.

"But what did he do?" questioned Mr. Terry.

"That's what I'm tryin' to tell you. I run in this mornin' and bought two ounces of allspice; for I hadn't a speck in the house. Seth's so fond of it in apple-pies. Well, I was hurryin' round; an' I lost my smell years ago, when I had the influenzy, so I put in the allspice; an' sez I at dinner, 'Seth, here's the fust green-apple pies. I don't believe a soul in Madison has made 'em yet!

They're nice an' hot.' With that he tasted. 'Hot!' sez he, 'hot! I guess they air, and the've somethin' more'n fire in 'em too!' 'What's in 'em?' sez I; and sez he, 'Jest you taste!' an' so I did, an' it nigh about burnt my tongue off. 'Why,' sez I, 'it's pepper;' an' Seth sez, 'Well, if you ain't smart!' That made me kinder huffy like; an' then I knew right away it was this car'less fellow that's always singin' an' dancin' and a standin' on his head!"

Mrs. Cummings had to stop because she was out of breath. Joe ducked under the counter, experiencing a strong tendency to fly to fragments.

"I am very sorry," returned Mr. Terry. "It must have been a mistake;" and he tried to steady the corners of his mouth to a becoming sense of gravity.

"No mistake at all!" and she gave her head a violent jerk. "Some of his smart tricks he thought he'd play on me. Didn't I see him a treatin' Dave Downs to loaf-sugar one day; an' bime by he gave him a great lump of salt!"

Mr. Terry had heard the story of the salt, and rather enjoyed it; for Dave was always hanging round in the way.

"And he jest did it a purpose, I know. As soon as ever I tasted that pepper, I knew 'twas one of his tricks. And my whole batch of pies spil't!"

"No," said Joe, in his manly fashion: "I didn't do it purposely, Mrs. Cummings. I must have misunderstood you."

"Pepper an' allspice sound so much alike!" she said wrathfully.

"Well, we will give you a quarter of allspice," Mr. Terry returned soothingly.

"That won't make up for the apples, an' the flour, an' the lard, an' all my hard work!"

"We might throw in a few apples."

"If you're goin' to keep that boy, you'll ruin your trade, I can tell you!"

Still she took the allspice and the apples, though they had plenty at home.

"You must be careful, Joe," said Mr. Terry afterward. "It will not do to have the ill-will of all the old ladies."

Joe told the story at home with embellishments; and Hal enjoyed it wonderfully, in his quiet way.

CHAPTER VII.

THE OLD TUMBLER, AFTER ALL.

Hal's chickens prospered remarkably. Five motherly hens clucked to families of black-eyed chicks; and, out of fifty-eight eggs, he only lost seven. So there were fifty-one left. They made some incursions in his garden, to be sure; but presently every thing grew so large that it was out of danger.

There was plenty of work to do on Saturdays. Picking cherries and currants for the neighbors, and the unfailing gardening. It seemed to Hal that weeds had a hundred lives at least, even if you did pull them up by the roots. Sometimes he managed to get a little work out of Kit and Charlie, but they invariably ended by a rough-and-tumble frolic.

Florence succeeded admirably with her embroidering. She managed to earn some pretty dresses for herself, and added enough to Hal's store to enable him to purchase a suit of clothes, though they were not as grand as Joe's.

Hal and Granny took a wonderful sight of comfort sitting on the doorstep through the summer evenings, and talking over old times. Granny would tell how they did when his father, her own dear Joe, was alive, and how pretty his mother had been.

"Flo's a good deal like her," she would always say; "only Flo's wonderful with her fingers. She can do any thing with a needle."

"Flo's a born genius," Hal would reply admiringly.

"But I'm afraid Charlie'll never learn to sew."

"I can sew better myself," was Hal's usual comment.

And it was true. Hal had a bedquilt nearly pieced, which he had done on rainy days and by odd spells. I expect you think he was something of a girl-boy. But then he was very sweet and nice.

Florence stood by the gate one afternoon, looking extremely lovely in her blue and white gingham, and her curls tied back with a bit of blue ribbon. Dot had been in the mud-pie business; and, if it had proved profitable, she would no doubt have made a fortune for the family.

"Go in the house this minute, and get washed," commanded Florence.

"What a naughty, dirty child you are!"

Then a carriage passed by very slowly. A young man was driving, and two ladies sat on the back seat. They looked as if they were going to halt.

Florence's heart was in her mouth. She drew herself up in her most stately attitude.

The young man turned; and the lady nearer her beckoned.

Florence stepped out slowly. She thought, with some pride, that, if they wanted a drink, she *had* a goblet to offer them.

"My little girl," said the lady, in a soft, clear voice, "can you direct us to a blacksmith's?"

"There is one on this road, rather more than a quarter of a mile farther."

"Thank you."

The other lady leaned over, and studied Florence. She had a worn, faded, and fretful look; but some new expression lighted up her sallow face.

"Oh," she sighed, "what a beautiful girl! Now, if I had a daughter like that! I wonder if she lives in that forlorn old rookery?"

"A princess in disguise;" and the young man laughed.

"She was unusually lovely. At her age I had just such hair. But ah, how one fades!"

The straggling auburn hair, very thin on the top, hardly looked as if it had once been "like fine spun gold."

"The trial of my life has been *not* having a daughter."

Mrs. Duncan had heard this plaint very often from her half-sister, who had married a widower nearly three times her age. He had made a very liberal provision for her during her life, but at her death the fortune reverted to his family again. She had always bewailed the fact of having no children; but boys were her abomination. Mrs. Duncan's house was too noisy, with its four rollicking boys; but now that George was growing to manhood he became rather more endurable.

"I do not believe the child could have belonged there," she commenced again.

"Because she was so pretty?" asked George.

"She doesn't look like a country girl."

"But some country girls are very handsome," said Mrs. Duncan.

"They do not possess this air of refinement generally. And did you observe that she answered in a correct and ladylike manner?"

"Aunt Sophie is captivated. A clear case of love at first sight. Why not adopt *her?*"

"It would be a charity to take her out of that hovel, if it is her home."

"I shouldn't think of such a thing now, Sophie, with your poor health," said her sister.

There are some natures on which the least contradiction or opposition acts instantly, rousing them to a spirit of defiance. For several years Mrs. Duncan had urged her sister to adopt a child; but she had never found one that answered her requirements. She was not fond of the trouble of small children. Now that Mrs. Duncan had advised contrarywise, Mrs. Osgood was seized with a perverse fit.

"I am sure I need a companion," she returned with martyr-like air.

"Take a young woman then, who can be a companion."

"Here is the blacksmith's," announced George. "I suppose you will have to find some place of refuge;" and he laughed again gayly.

"Where can we go?"

George held a short conversation with the smith.

"My house is just opposite, and the ladies will be welcome," the latter said. "It will take me about half an hour to repair your mishap."

George conducted them thither. The good woman would fain have invited them in; but they preferred sitting on the vine-covered porch. Mrs. Osgood asked for a glass of water. O Florence! if you had been there!

It happened after a while, that George and his mother walked down the garden. Mrs. Green felt bound to entertain this stranger cast upon her care, as she considered it.

Mrs. Osgood made some inquiries presently about the house they had passed, with a small stream of water just below it.

"Why, that's Granny Kenneth's," said Mrs. Green.

"And who is the child,—almost a young lady?"

"Why, that must be Florence. Did she have long yeller curls? If she was my gal she should braid 'em up decently. I wouldn't have 'em flyin' about."

"And who is Florence?"

Mrs. Osgood's curiosity must have been very great to induce her to listen to the faulty grammar and country pronunciations. But she listened to the story from beginning to end,—Joe, and Joe's wife, and all the children, figuring largely in it.

"And if Granny Kenneth'd had any sense, she would a bundled 'em all off to the poor-house. One of the neighbors here did want to take Florence; but law! what a time they made! She's a peart, stuck-up thing!"

If Florence had heard this verdict against all her small industries and neatnesses and ladylike habits, her heart would have been almost broken. But there are a great many narrow-minded people in this world, who can see no good except in their own way.

Mrs. Osgood made no comments. Presently the carriage was repaired, and the accidental guests departed. They had a long ride yet to take. George asked if there was any nearer way of getting to Seabury.

"There's a narrer road just below Granny Kenneth's,—the little shanty by the crick. It's ruther hard trav'lin', but it cuts off nigh on ter three miles."

"I think we had better take it," said George. "Even that will give us a five-miles drive."

So they passed the cottage again. This time Hal was feeding the chickens; Kit and Charlie swinging upon an old dilapidated apple-tree; and Florence sat by the open window, sewing.

"There's your princess!" exclaimed George with a laugh.

Florence colored a little at beholding the party again.

Mrs. Duncan had come to Seabury, a rather mountainous place, remarkable for its pure air, for the sake of her youngest son, Arthur, who had been ill with a fever. Mrs. Osgood took an odd fancy to accompany her. The seven years of her widowhood had not been happy years, though she had a house like a palace. When she first laid off mourning, she tried Newport and Saratoga; but somehow she did not succeed in making a belle of herself, and that rather mortified her.

Then she sank into invalidism; which tried everybody's patience sorely.

Leaning back in the carriage now, she thought to herself, "Yes, if I only *had* some one of my own! Sister Duncan never did understand me, or appreciate the delicacy of my constitution. Her nerves have been blunted by those great rude boys. And that girl looks so refined and graceful,—she would make a pleasant companion I am sure. But I should want to take her away from her family: I never could consent to any intimacy with them."

She ventured to broach her subject to Mrs. Duncan the next day. Perhaps Mrs. Duncan had grown rather impatient with her sister's whims and fancies; and she discouraged the plan on some very sensible grounds. Mrs. Osgood felt like a martyr.

Yet the opposition roused her to attempt it. One day, a week afterward perhaps, she hired a carriage, and was driven over to Madison. George had gone back to the city, so there was no question of having him for escort.

Granny Kenneth was much surprised at the appearance of so fine a lady. She seized Dot, and scrubbed her face, her usual employment upon the entrance of any one.

Mrs. Osgood held up her ruffled skirts as if afraid of contamination.

"Is your granddaughter at home?" was asked in the most languid of voices.

"Flo, you mean? No: she hasn't come from school yet. Do walk in and wait—that is—I mean—if you please," said Granny a good deal flustered, while the little gray curls kept bobbing up and down. "Here's a clean cheer;" and she gave one a whiff with her apron.

Poor Flossy. She had tried so hard to correct Granny's old-fashioned words and pronunciations.

"Thank you. Miss Florence embroiders, I believe."

"Yes, she works baby-petticoats, and does 'em splendid."

And then Granny wondered if she, the fine lady, had any work for Florence.

"How glad Flo'll be, and vacation coming so soon," she thought in the depth of her tender old soul.

"And she's a genius at crochetin'! The laces and shawls and hoods she's knit are a real wonder. They didn't do any thing of the kind in my young days."

"You must find it pretty hard to get along," condescended Mrs. Osgood.

"Yes; but the Lord allers provides some way. Joe's gone in a store,—Mr. Terry's. He's next to Florence," went on Granny in sublime disregard of her pronoun.

Mrs. Osgood took an inventory of the little room, and waited rather impatiently. Then she asked for a glass of water.

O Granny! how could you have been so forgetful! To take that old, thick, greenish glass tumbler when Flossy's choice goblet stood on the shelf above! And then to fill it in the pail, and let the water dribble!

Granny wondered whether it would be polite to entertain her or not. But just then there was a crash and a splash; and Dot and the water-pail were in the middle of the floor.

"Here's a chance!" exclaimed Kit, pausing in the doorway. "Give us a hook and line, Granny: Dot's mouth is just at an angle of ten degrees, good for a bite."

"A wail, sure enough!" said Charlie. "Wring her out, and hang her up to dry."

"Oh, dear!" and Granny, much disconcerted, sat Dot wrong side up on a chair, and the result was a fresh tumble.

It was Hal who picked her up tenderly,—poor wet baby, with a big red lump on her forehead, and dismal cries issuing from the mouth that seemed to run all round her head.

"Stay out there till I wipe up," said Granny to the others. "Then I'll get Dot a dry dress. I never did see such an onlucky child—and company too. What *will* Flo say!"

For Florence came tripping up the path, knitting her delicate brows in consternation.

"Never you mind. There's a lady in the parlor who's been waitin'. Oh, my! what did I do with that floor-cloth?"

"A lady?"

"Yes: run right along."

Luckily the door was shut between. Florence gave her curls a twist and a smoothing with her fingers, took off her soiled white apron, pulled her dress out here and there, stepped over the pools of water, and entered.

Mrs. Osgood admired her self-possession, and pitied the poor child profoundly. The flush and partial embarrassment were very becoming to her.

That lady did not mean to rush headlong into her proposal. She broke the ground delicately by inquiring about the embroidering; and Florence brought some to show her.

"Who taught you?" she asked in surprise.

"No one;" and Florence colored a little. "I did not do the first as neatly, but it is quite easy after one is fairly started."

"I really do not see how you find time, with going to school;" and this persevering industry did touch Mrs. Osgood's heart.

"I cannot do very much," answered Florence with a sigh. "But it will soon be vacation."

"How old are you?"

"I shall be fifteen the last of this month."

"What a family your grandmother has on her hands!"

"Yes. If my father had lived, it would have been very different."

A touching expression overspread Florence's face, and made her lovelier than ever in Mrs. Osgood's eyes.

"She certainly *is* very pretty," that lady thought; "and how attractive such a daughter would be in my house! I should live my young life over again in her."

For Mrs. Osgood had found that the days for charming young men were over, and prosy middle-aged people were little to her taste. No woman ever clung to youth with a greater longing.

"What do you study at school?" she asked.

"Only the English branches. I have been thinking of—of becoming a teacher," said Florence hesitatingly.

"You would have a poor opportunity in this little town."

"I might go away;" and Florence sighed again.

"You have never studied music, I suppose."

"No: I have had no opportunity," returned Florence honestly enough.

"Do you sing?"

"Yes. And I love music so very, very much! I do mean to learn by and by, if it is possible."

"I wish you would sing something for me,—a little school-song, or any thing you are familiar with."

Florence glanced up in amazement; and for a few moments was awkwardly silent.

"I should like to hear your voice. It is very pleasant in talking, and ought to be musical in singing."

Florence was a good deal flattered; and then she had the consciousness that she was one of the best singers in school. So she ran over the songs in her own mind, and selected "Natalie, the Maid of the Mill," which she was very familiar with.

She sang it beautifully. Florence was one of the children who are always good in an emergency. She was seldom "flustered," as Granny expressed it, and always seemed to know how to make the best of herself. And, as she saw the pleasure in Mrs. Osgood's face, her own heart beat with satisfaction.

"That is really charming. A little cultivation would make your voice very fine indeed. What a pity that you should be buried in this little town!"

"Do you think—that I could—do any thing with it?" asked Florence in a tremor of delight.

"I suppose your grandmother would not stand in the way of your advancement?" questioned Mrs. Osgood.

"Oh, no! And then if I *could* do something"—

Florence felt that she ought to add, "for the others," but somehow she did not. She wondered if Mrs. Osgood was a music-teacher, or a professional singer. But she did not like to ask.

"There is my carriage," said Mrs. Osgood, as a man drove slowly round. "I am spending a few weeks at some distance from here, and wished to have you do a little flannel embroidery for me. When will your vacation commence?"

"In about ten days,—the first of July."

"I wish to see you when we can have a longer interview. I will come over again then."

Mrs. Osgood rose, and shook out her elegant grenadine dress, much trimmed and ruffled. On her wrists were beautiful bracelets, and her watch-chain glittered with every movement. Then she really smiled very sweetly upon the young girl; and Florence was charmed.

Some dim recollection passed over her mind.

"Oh!" she said, "were you not in a carriage that stopped here some days ago. Another lady and a young gentleman"—

"Yes," answered Mrs. Osgood, pleased at being remembered. "And, my dear, I took a great fancy to you that day. You are so different from the majority of country girls, that it is a pity you should have no better chance."

The longing and eloquent eyes of Florence said more than words.

"Yes. I will see you again; and I may, perhaps, think of something to your advantage."

There was a mode of egress through this "best-room," though Granny had brought her guest in by the kitchen way. Florence opened the door now.

"What a lovely, graceful child!" thought Mrs. Osgood; and she scrutinized her from head to feet.

Florence watched the carriage out of sight in a half-dream. How long she would have stood in a brown study is uncertain; but Granny came in to get some dry clothes for Dot.

"What *did* she want of you?" exclaimed Charlie, all curiosity. "And what were you singing for? Oh, my! wasn't she splendid?"

"You sang like a bird," said Hal in wide-eyed wonder as well. "Did she ask you?"

"Of course. You don't suppose I would offer to sing for a stranger,—a lady too?"

"Did she like it?"

"Yes. She thought I might—that is, if I had any opportunity—oh, I wish we *were* a little richer!" and Florence burst into a flood of hysterical tears.

"I wish we were;" and Hal gave her hand a soft squeeze. "If you could learn to play on the melodeon at church, and give music-lessons"—

The vision called up a heaven of delight to poor Flossy.

"But what *did* she want?" asked Granny in a great puzzle, putting Dot's foot through the sleeve of her dress, and tying the neck-string in garter fashion.

"I do believe she is a singer herself. Maybe she belongs to a company who give concerts; but then she was dressed so elegantly."

"They make lots of money," said Kit with a sagacious nod of the head. "It's what I'm going to be, only I shall have a fiddle."

"And a scalp-lock."

Charlie pulled this ornamentation to its fullest height, which was considerable, as Kit's hair needed cutting.

"Oh! suppose she was," said Hal. "And suppose she wanted to take Flossy, and teach her music,—why, it's like your plan, you know, only it isn't an old gentleman; and I don't believe she has any little girls,—I mean a little girl who died. Did she ask for a drink, Granny?"

"Yes; and then Dot pulled over the water-pail. Oh, my! if I haven't put this dress on upside down, and the string's in a hard knot. Whatever shall I do? And, Flossy, I forgot all about the gobler. I took the first thing that came to hand."

"Not that old tumbler with a nick in the edge? And it is *goblet*. I do wish you'd learn to call things by their right names!" exclaimed Florence in vexation.

"It's the very same, isn't it?" began Charlie, "only, as Hal said, it isn't an old gentleman. Oh, suppose it *should* come true! And if Kit *should* have a fiddle like black Jake."

"And if you *should* run away," laughed Hal. "I don't believe you can find a better time than this present moment. Kit, you had better go after the cows."

Charlie started too, upon Hal's suggestion. Florence gave a little sniff, and betook herself to the next room.

Oh, dear! How poor and mean and tumbled about their house always was! No, not *always*, but if any one ever came. Dot chose just that moment to be unfortunate; and then that Granny should have used that forlorn old tumbler. She doubted very much if the lady would ever come again.

So Flossy had a good cry from wounded vanity, and then felt better. Hal took Dot out with him to feed the chickens, and Granny prepared the table.

Still Florence's lady was the theme of comment and wonder for several days, although the child insisted that she only came to get some embroidering done. All further speculations seemed too wild for sober brains.

"But it is so odd that she asked you to sing," said Hal. "And I do believe something will come of it."

Florence gave a little despairing sniff.

CHAPTER VIII.

FLORENCE IN STATE.

$\mathbf{M}$rs. Osgood leaned back in the carriage,—it was the very best that Seabury afforded,—and, looking out on the pleasant sunshine and waving trees, considered the subject before her. *If* she took Florence, she would have a governess in the house, and go on as rapidly as possible with the finishing process. Music should be the first thing: the child *did* have a lovely voice, and such fair, slender hands! In a year she would be quite presentable. How vexed all the Osgood nieces would be! They were continually hinting at visits, and would be delighted at having Aunt Osgood take them up. But somehow she had a grudge against her husband's relatives, because the property reverted to them in the end.

And then she fancied herself riding out with this beautiful daughter by her side, or stopping at hotels where every one would wonder "who that lovely girl could be!" And Florence would certainly be most grateful for the change. It was a deed of charity to rescue the poor child from the life before her, with no better prospect than that of a school-teacher. She certainly had some ideas and ambitions beyond her sphere.

School closed presently, and the children were wild with delight. They had a great time on examination day, and Florence acquitted herself finely. Mr. Fielder was very proud of her.

"If you can go to school another year, and improve as much," he said, "I can almost promise you a very good situation."

Flossy's dream in respect to her elegant lady was fading, and she came back to humbler prospects quite thankfully.

What Granny was to do with the children through vacation she hardly knew.

"Oh, you needn't worry!" said Charlie consolingly. "Kit and me are going out in the woods; and we'll build a stunning log-hut, or make a cave"—

"O Charlie, if you would be a little more careful! Kit and I."

"I can't be always bothering! Mr. Fielder almost wears me out, so you might let me have a little rest in vacation.

74

'For spelling is vexation,

And writing is bad:

Geography it puzzles me,

And grammar makes me mad.'"

With that Charlie perched herself on the gate-post, and began to whistle.

"If Charlie only *had* been a boy!" groaned Florence.

On Monday of the first week they washed. Florence assisted; but she hurried to get herself dressed in the afternoon, for fear some one *might* come. And then she wondered a little what she ought to do. Embroidering and fancy work appeared to be dull just now; and she would have two months in which she *might* earn considerable money, if it only came. For, with all her small vanities and particular ways, she was not indolent.

On Tuesday they began their ironing at an early hour. There were Florence's pretty dresses and aprons, nothing very costly, but a dainty ruffle here and there added to the general grace. These same ruffles were a great trouble to some of the old ladies in Madison, "who didn't see how Granny Kenneth could let Florence waste her time in such nonsense while *she* slaved herself to death!"

Florence had twisted her hair in a knot, and her dress was rather the worse for wear; but she worked away cheerfully. Her pile of clothes was decreasing very fast.

Suddenly a sound of carriage-wheels startled her; and, glancing up, she uttered a frightened exclamation.

"O Granny! it's the lady again, and I look like a fright! What shall I do? Won't you go and ask her in? and you look dreadful too! Put on your other sacque. There! I'll run and tidy up a bit."

She made a snatch at the brush and comb, and hurried up in the boys' room.

"Oh, dear! How red I am in the face! It's too bad;" and she felt tempted to cry, but she knew that would only make matters worse. So she let down her shining hair, brushed it out, and wound it round her fingers in curls. Then Granny came plodding up stairs.

"I told her you were busy, but that you'd be ready in a few minutes," she explained.

"Why didn't you think to bring up one of my clean dresses?"

"To be sure! which one?"

"The pink calico, I guess. Oh! and the braided white apron."

Down went Granny. Ah! many a step had she taken for these children, weary ones, and yet cheerfully done. Would they ever think of it?

Florence was not long in making herself neat and presentable, but the flushed face still troubled her. She viewed herself critically in the cracked glass, and then ran down, pausing to fan a few moments with the cape of an old sun-bonnet, the nearest thing at hand.

"*Do* I look decent, Granny?" she said apprehensively.

"To be sure you do, and nice too."

Granny's eyes expressed her admiration.

Florence ventured in timidly, and the lady inclined her head.

"I am sorry that I have kept you waiting so long, but it was unavoidable;" and the child made a little halt to wonder if her long word sounded well.

"I suppose I took you somewhat by surprise. Are you very busy to-day?"

"Not very," answered Florence at random, her heart beating violently.

"And quite well? but I hardly need ask the question."

"I am always well, thank you," with a touch of grace.

"How fortunate! Now, I have such wretched health, and my nerves are weak beyond description."

Florence gave a glance of quick sympathy, not unmixed with admiration. There was something very romantic about the languid lady.

"If you are quite at liberty," Mrs. Osgood began, "I should like to have you drive out with me. I have a great deal to say to you, and we shall not be interrupted."

Florence could hardly credit her hearing. To be asked to ride with so grand a lady!

"Oh!" and then she paused and colored.

"Would you like to go?"

"Very, very much indeed;" and the young face was full of pleasure.

"Well, get yourself ready; and, if you will send your grandmother to me, I will explain."

Florence felt as if she were in a dream. Then she wondered what she ought to wear. She had a pretty light gray dress and sacque for "Sunday best," and a new white dress; but her visitor's dress was gray, and that decided her. So she took the articles out of the old-fashioned wardrobe, and summoned Granny.

Granny was dazed. "Where is she going to take you?" she asked in helpless astonishment.

"I don't know. She will tell you, I suppose."

"But, Flo, I have *heerd* of girls being kidnapped or something;" and Granny's face turned pale with fear.

"Nonsense!" returned Flossy with a toss of the curls. She could not even trouble herself about Granny's mispronunciation just then.

"You don't know"—

"I guess she won't eat me up. Any how, I am going."

Florence uttered this with a touch of imperiousness. Granny felt that she would have little influence over her, so she entered the room where the guest was seated.

"Mrs. Kenneth," the lady began in her most impressive and gracious manner, "when I was here a few days ago, I took a great fancy to your granddaughter. My name is Osgood; and I am staying at Seabury with my sister, Mrs. Duncan. And although you may hesitate to trust Florence with a stranger, she will be quite safe, I assure you; and if you are willing, therefore, I should like to take her out for a few hours. I have some plans that may be greatly to the child's advantage, I think."

"You'll be sure to bring her back," asked Granny in a spasm of anxious terror, which showed in her eyes.

"Why, certainly! My poor woman, I cannot blame you for this carefulness;" for the worn face with its eagerness touched Mrs. Osgood. "My brother-in-law, Mr. Duncan, is a well-known merchant in New York; and I think you will confess when I return Florence this afternoon, that the ride has been no injury to her."

Granny could make no further objections, and yet she did not feel quite at ease. But Florence entered looking so bright and expectant, that she had not the heart to disappoint her, so she kept her fears to herself.

"You must not feel troubled," Mrs. Osgood deigned to say, as she rose rather haughtily. "You will find my promises perfectly reliable."

"You needn't finish my pieces," Florence whispered softly to Granny at the door. "I shall be back time enough; and if the fire is out I'll wait till tomorrow They are my ruffled aprons, and"—

Mrs. Osgood beckoned her with a smile and an inclination of the head. Florence felt as if she were being bewitched.

Granny watched her as she stepped into the carriage.

"If she'd been born a lady she couldn't act more like one. It's a great pity"—

A few tears finished Granny's sentence. All the others were more content with their poverty than Florence.

So she went back to her ironing with a heart into which had crept some strange misgiving. Hal was out; Joe never came home to dinner; so Granny gave the children a piece of bread all round, and kept going steadily on until the last ruffled apron had been taken out of the pile.

Very long indeed the hours seemed. Oh, if any harm should befall her beautiful, darling Flossy! Poor Joe, in his grave, had loved her so well!

Flossy meanwhile was having a most delightful time.

"I am going to take you to Salem," Mrs. Osgood said, after Florence had begun to feel quite at home with her. "We will have our dinner at the hotel."

Salem was the county town,—quite a pretentious place, with some broad, straight streets, several banks, and, indeed, a thriving business locality. Florence had been there twice with Mrs. Kinsey.

Mrs. Osgood began to question the child about herself. Florence told over her past life, making the best, it must be confessed, of the poverty and discomforts. And yet she seemed to take rather hardly the fact of such a lot having fallen upon her. Mrs. Osgood was secretly pleased with her dissatisfaction.

"I wonder how you would like to live with me?" she questioned. "I think I should enjoy having some one that I could make a companion of—as one never can of a servant."

Flossy's heart beat with a sudden delight, and for the first moment she could hardly speak.

"I live a short distance from New York, on the banks of the Hudson: at least, my house is there, but I travel a great deal. It would be very pleasant to have a—a friend of one's own,"—Mrs. Osgood was not *quite* sure that it was best or wisest to say child.

"Oh, it would be very delightful! If I could"—and the child's eyes were aglow with delight.

"There are so many of you at home, that your grandmother would not miss one. Besides, I could do a great many nice things for you."

"It is like a dream!" and Flossy thought of her wild day-dream. "And I could sew as well as embroider; and oh! I *would* try to make myself useful," she said eagerly.

Mrs. Osgood smiled. She had taken a strange fancy to this child, and enjoyed her look of adoration.

They talked it over at some length, and Flossy listened with delight to the description of the beautiful house. This was altogether different from Mrs. Van Wyck's affair.

Presently they arrived at the hotel. Mrs. Osgood ordered the horses to be cared for, and then entered the parlor.

"Can we have a private room?" she asked with an air that Florence thought extremely elegant. "And then our dinner"—

"Will you have it brought up to your room?"

"Oh, no! Perhaps I had better give my order now," and there was a languid indifference in her tone.

"Yes, it would be better," replied the brisk waitress.

"Well, we will have some broiled chicken, I think—are you fond of that, Florence? and vegetables—with some lobster salad and relishes."

Florence had a wonderful deal of adaptiveness, and she almost insensibly copied Mrs. Osgood. They went up to the room, and refreshed themselves with a small ablution, for the riding had been rather dusty. Florence shook out her beautiful curls, and passed her damp fingers over them.

"What lovely hair!" exclaimed Mrs. Osgood with a sigh: it was a habit of hers, as if every thing called up some past regret. "When I was a young girl, mine was the admiration of everybody. You would hardly think it now."

"Were you ill?" asked Florence, feeling that she was expected to say something sympathizing.

"My health has been wretched for years. Mr. Osgood was sick a long while, and I had so much trouble! His people were not very kind to me: they tried to make him leave the property away from me, and then they attempted to break the will. There's so much selfishness in this world, my dear!"

Florence experienced a profound sympathy for Mrs. Osgood, and was quite ready to espouse her cause against any one. Already she felt in some way constituted her champion.

But, as Mr. Osgood left no children, he thought it quite just that his property should go back to his own family after Mrs. Osgood's death. And, to confess the truth, he had not found his wife quite perfection.

There were not many people in the dining-room when they entered. They had one end of the long table, and the colored waiter was most polite and solicitous. One by one their little dishes came on, and the broiled chicken had a most appetizing flavor.

Florence acquitted herself very creditably. She was not awkward with her silver fork, and allowed herself to be waited upon with great complacency. Mrs. Osgood was wonderfully pleased, for she was watching every action. How had the child acquired so many pretty ways?

By the time they reached home again it was agreed, if grandmother made no objection, that Florence should spend a month at Seabury with Mrs. Osgood. This was the better arrangement the lady thought; for, if she changed her mind, in that case she could draw back gracefully.

Granny was much relieved to see them return. Mrs. Osgood deigned to enter the cottage again, and explained the matter to old Mrs. Kenneth. Florence seconded the plan so earnestly, that it was quite impossible to refuse. And somehow Granny felt very much bewildered.

"Can you be ready next week?" asked Mrs. Osgood.

Florence questioned Granny mutely with her eyes; but, seeing that her senses were going astray, answered for herself.

"Monday, then, I will come over for you. And now, my child, good-by. I hope you have had a pleasant day."

Florence thanked her again and again. Mrs. Osgood's heart was really touched.

"What does she want you to do?" asked Granny, absently trying to thread the point of her darning-needle.

"Why,—I'm sure I don't know;" and Flossy fell into a brown study. "To wait upon her, I suppose, and sew a little, and—I like her so much! We had an elegant dinner at Salem, and ice-cream for dessert. O Granny, if one only *could* be rich!"

"Yes," rejoined Granny with a sigh.

"Tell us all about it," said open-mouthed Charlie. "Mrs. Green saw you riding by; and maybe she didn't make a time! She said you put on more airs than all Madison."

"It is nothing to her," bridled Flossy.

"But what *did* you have? Lots of goodies?"

"Yes, indeed. Silver forks and damask napkins and finger-bowls."

"Finger-bowls?"

That grandeur was altogether above Charlie's capacity.

"You need not look so amazed."

"What do you do with 'em."

"Why, there's a piece of lemon floating round on the top; and you dip in the ends of your fingers, and wipe them on the napkin."

"But can't you eat the lemon? That's what I'd do."

"It would be very ill-bred."

"Hum!" and Charlie's nose was elevated. "As if I'd care!"

"You would if you were out with refined people."

"Oh, my! How aristocrockery you are getting!" and Charlie gave a prolonged whistle, and stood on one foot.

Flossy sighed a little over the supper-table. How nice it would be to live at a hotel, and have a servant to wait upon one! But every thing here was so dreadfully common and poor. And, though Flossy would have scorned the idea of living out as a servant, she fancied a position of companion or ladies' maid would be rather agreeable than otherwise.

Hal was very much interested in her day's adventure. He seemed to understand it better than any of the others, and she could talk to him without the fear of being laughed at. They still sat in the moonlight, when suddenly a sharp click was heard, and a report that made them all scream.

Joe, the good-for-nothing, laughed.

"Wasn't that gay? Hurrah for Fourth of July!"

"Is it you?" asked Granny, who had thrown her apron over her head to keep her from being shot. "And is it a musket, or a cannon?"

"Why don't you frighten us all to death?" said Florence indignantly.

"Oh, it's a pistol!" exclaimed Hal.

"O Joe! and you'll be shot all to pieces before to-morrow night," bewailed Granny. "I'm so afraid of guns and fire-crackers! I once knew a little boy who had his hand shot off."

"If he could only have had it shot on again. I mean to try that way, like the man who jumped into the bramble-bush. Or wouldn't it do to shoot the pistol off instead of my fingers."

"Is it yours for good, Joe?" and Charlie's head was thrust over Hal's shoulders. "A real pistol! Let me see it."

"Yes, it's mine. I bought it to keep Fourth of July with."

"Why, I forgot all about Fourth of July," said Charlie in an aggrieved tone. "And I haven't a cent!"

"Bad for you, Charlie."

"Won't you let me fire off the pistol?"

"Oh, don't!" implored Granny.

"Just once more. It was splendid! I was fast asleep on the floor, and it woke me up."

"Good for the pistol," said Joe. "I'll try it in the morning when you are asleep."

They all had to handle the pistol, and express their opinions. Joe had bought it of Johnny Hall, for a dollar, as Johnny, in turn, wanted to buy a cannon. And the remaining half-dollar of his week's wages had been invested in fireworks.

Granny sighed. But boys would be boys, and Fourth of July only came once a year.

"There's to be an oration on the green, and the soldiers will be out, and it'll be just jolly! Hurray! And a holiday in the middle of the week! Mr. Terry said I needn't come to the store at all."

"There'll be some music, won't there?" asked Kit.

"A drum and a bass-viol, I guess. But it would be royal to go over to Salem, and hear the brass band."

"What's a brass band?" was Kit's rather puzzled inquiry.

"What a goose! Why, a brass band is—horns and things."

"What kind of horns?" for Joe's explanation lacked lucidity.

"Oh, bother! Kit, you'll burn up the ocean some day with your brightness."

"Cornets," said Hal; "and something like a flute, and cymbals, and ever so many instruments."

"Did you ever see 'em?"

"No, but I've read about them."

Kit chewed his thumb. It was one of his old baby habits.

"Now I am going to load her again," said Joe, in a peculiarly affectionate tone. "It's as light as day out here."

"But, Joe, if you *should* shoot some one, or your fingers, or put your eyes out!"

"Never you mind, Granny. Boys go ahead of cats for lives."

Granny put her apron over her head again, and then ran in to Dot.

"Bang!"

"Nobody wounded," laughed Joe, "and only two or three slightly killed. The country is safe, Granny, this great and *gelorious* country, over which the eagle waves his plumes, and flaps his wings, and would crow if he could. My soul is filled with enthusiasm,—I feel as if I should *bust*, and fly all round! There's that miserable Dot lifting up her voice."

The racket had broken her slumbers, and then the children were implored to be quiet. Joe went to bed, in order to be able to get up good and early. Charlie thought she should sleep with her clothes on, so as to save the trouble of dressing. Kit sat in the moonlight chewing his thumb, and wondering if he could manage to get over to Salem to-morrow. If he could only hear that music!

CHAPTER IX.

FOURTH OF JULY.

The children were up at the peep of dawn. Granny was awakened by something that seemed not unlike the shock of an earthquake; but Flossy, rubbing her eyes, said with a sigh,—

"Oh, dear! Joe has begun with his pistol the first thing! What does possess boys to be so noisy!"

Charlie, perched astride the gate-post, her clothes considerably tumbled, and her hair unkempt, thought it splendid. "If Joe would only let her fire *once!* Just as soon as she had a dollar she meant to buy a pistol of her own. It would always be good to keep away robbers!"

Joe laughed uproariously.

"Robbers indeed! There's nothing to steal here, unless it's some of the youngsters. You'd be sure to go first, Charlie!"

"I shall be thankful when Fourth of July is over," said Granny in a troubled voice, while Joe was singing,—

"But children are not pigs, you know,

And cannot pay the rint;"

but at that remark so derogatory to patriotism, he bridled up at once.

"Fourth of July's as good as Saint Patrick, or any other man. Who would be so base and ignoble of soul, and stingy of powder, as not to celebrate his birthday! when the country stretches from the north pole to the south, and is kept from bursting only by the centrifugal forces of the equator"—

Hal's rooster finished the speech by his longest and loudest crow.

"Good for you! You've some patriotism, I see. You are not craven of soul, if powder doesn't come in your way. Granny, when can we have breakfast? I'm about famished with all my speech-making."

Hal fed his crowd of chickens, and amused Dot, who did not quite enjoy being deprived of her morning nap. Presently they were summoned to their meal.

"I'm going over to the store," announced Joe. "I want to see the Declaration of Independence read by the American eagle, and the salute fired by the Stars and Stripes, while the militia climb up their muskets and give three cheers."

"Are they going to do that?" asked Charlie. "Granny, can't I go too?"

"You must put on a clean dress."

"Oh, dear! when I slept in mine too, so as to be ready," Charlie exclaimed, broken-hearted. "Won't you wait, Joe?"

"I can't bother with girls," returned Joe.

Charlie lamented her hard fate, but emerged from the hands of Florence quite a respectable looking child. Kit spent some time in adorning himself, and trying to smooth his refractory scalp-lock. He had been very quiet all the morning.

"Now that they are off we can have a little peace," said Florence.

Granny sighed. They were a great bother and torment, to be sure; but, after all, it was good to have the merry, noisy crew, safe and sound, and she should be glad when they returned.

Hal's tastes inclined neither to fire-crackers nor sky-rockets. So he went into the garden, and began to look after his rather neglected vegetables. The chickens made bad work, it must be confessed, though the attractions of their buckwheat field were pretty strong, and Hal ingeniously repaired the fence with brush; but now and then there would be a raid. The Lima beans were doing beautifully, the corn looked promising; and, altogether, he thought the prospect was fair. Then he met with a delightful surprise.

"O Granny!" and he rushed into the house. "Just think,—three of my grape-vines have beautiful long shoots on them. I haven't looked in ever so long, for I thought they didn't mean to grow. Come and see."

There they were, sure enough. Hal had set out some cuttings from the neighbors, but he had been almost discouraged with their slow progress.

"That's a Concord, and that's a Hartford Prolific. Don't they look lovely in their soft, pinkish green! Why, I feel as if I could give them all a hug. I'll have to put a lattice round, for fear of the chickens."

So he went to work. Dot wanted to help, and brought him useless sticks, while she carried off his hammer and lost his nails. But when she looked up at him with the sweetest little face in the world, and said, "Ain't Dotty 'mart? Dotty help 'ou," he could not scold her.

The dinner was rather quiet. None of the stray youngsters made their appearance. Afterward Florence dressed herself, and went to see Netty Bigelow, her dearest school-friend, and imparted to her that she was going to Seabury next Monday, to stay a month with a very elegant lady, and that she would live at a hotel. Then she described her ride to Salem, and the dinner.

"Oh, how nice it must have been!" said Netty. "You are the luckiest girl I ever did know, Florence Kenneth."

"I just wish I was as rich as Mrs. Osgood. It seems to me that poor people cannot be very happy."

"I don't know," Netty returned thoughtfully. "The Graysons do not seem *very* happy."

"But I never saw such mean, disagreeable girls; and they are not dressed a bit pretty. If there's any thing in school they always want their share, but they never treat."

"And we are poor," continued Netty; "but I'm sure we are happy."

Florence felt that her friend could hardly understand the degree of happiness that she meant. She was rather out-growing her youthful companions.

About mid-afternoon Hal took a walk over to the store. The old rusty cannon of Revolutionary memory had been fired on the green, the speeches made, and the small crowd dispersed. Nearly everybody had gone to Salem; but a few old stagers still congregated at the store, it being general head-quarters.

Hal picked Charlie out of a group of children, in a very dilapidated condition. Her once clean dress was soiled, torn, and burned; her hands gave the strongest evidence that dust entered largely into the composition of small people; and her face was variegated by perspiration and dabs from these same unlucky hands.

"O Charlie! you look like a little vagabond!" exclaimed Hal in despair. "I'm ashamed of you!"

"But I've had such fun, and cakes and candies and fire-crackers and torpedoes! I wish Fourth of July would keep right straight along. I burned one of my fingers, but I didn't mind," declared the patriotic girl.

"Where's Kit?"

"I don't know. Joe was round this morning, but I guess he went to Salem."

"You must come home with me now."

"O Hal! we haven't found all the 'cissers' yet. They're almost as good as fire-crackers."

Several of the children were burrowing in the grass and sand for "fusees,"—crackers that had failed to explode to the full extent of their powder. They broke them in two and relighted them.

Hal was inexorable; so Charlie cried a little, and then bade her dirty companions a sad farewell.

"Oh!" exclaimed Granny, as they came marching up the path, "what a sight! And your Sunday best dress, Charlie!"

"Well," sniffed Charlie with a crooked face, though there were no tears to give it effect, "I'm sure I didn't want to put it on. I hate to be dressed up! Something always happens to your Sunday clothes. I couldn't help tearing it, and Jimmy Earl set off a cracker right in my lap"—

"Well, I'm glad it wasn't your eyes," said Granny thankfully. And then she took the forlorn pyramid of dirt and disorder up stairs, where she had a good scrubbing, and was re-arrayed in a more decent fashion. Anybody else would have scolded, but Granny was so glad to have her back safe and sound.

Her heart was sorely anxious about Kit and Joe. She let the supper stand on the table, and they all sat on the doorstep in the moonlight; for Dot had taken a nap in the afternoon, and was bright as a new penny.

And she fancied, as many mothers and grandmothers have before now, that shocking accidents had happened, and maybe they would be maimed and crippled for life.

Presently they came straggling along, and Granny uttered a cry of relief.

"Oh!" she said, "are you all here? Haven't you lost your hands, nor your fingers, nor"—

"Nor our noses, and not even our tongues," laughed Joe. "Here we are, pistol and all."

"O Kit! where have you been? I was a most worried to death; and you look tuckered out."

For Kit was pale to ghostliness as he stood there in the moonlight.

"Where do you think I found him,—the small snipe? Way over to Salem!"

"O Kit! did you see the fireworks and the soldiers?" exclaimed Charlie breathlessly.

Kit sank down on the doorstep.

"Walked all the way over there, and hadn't a penny!"

"How could you Kit, without saying a word?" exclaimed Granny in a tone of mild reproach.

"I could have given you a little money," said Hal tenderly.

"And it's a mercy that you didn't get run over, or shot to pieces, or trampled to death in the crowd"—

"O Granny! don't harrow up our feelings," said Joe.

"I was afraid you wouldn't let me go," began Kit, at the first available opportunity for slipping in a word. "And I didn't walk quite all the way there, —a man came along, and gave me a ride. I wanted to hear the music so much! The soldiers were splendid, Charlie; some of 'em with great white feathers in their hats and swords and beautiful horses and coats all over gold"—

"Wonderful hats," suggested Joe with a twinkle; for Kit had gone on with small regard to commas or accent.

"They all know what I mean!" said Kit rather testily.

"Don't plague him," interposed Hal. "About the music, Kit?"

"Oh! I can't half tell you;" and Kit gave a long sigh. "There were drums and fifes, and those clappers—I don't remember what you called 'em, but I liked it best when the men were horning with their horns"—

Joe gave a loud outburst, and went over on his head.

"Well," said Kit much aggrieved, "what are you laughing about?"

"Horning! That is good! You had better write a new dictionary, Kit. It is a decided improvement upon 'toot,' and must commend itself to Flossy's attention for superior elegance. There, my dear, give me a vote of thanks;" and Joe twitched Flossy's long curls.

"I don't know what you call it, then," said Kit rather sulkily.

"They blew on the horns," Hal rejoined in his soothing tone, that was always a comfort in times of disturbance; "and the cornets, wind-instruments, I believe, though I don't know the names of them all. It must have been delightful."

"Oh, it was! I shut my eyes, and it seemed as if I was floating on a sea, and there were all the waves beating up and down, and then a long soft sound like the wind blowing in and shaking it all to echoes. I was so sorry when they stopped. They all went into the hotel, I guess it was. By and by I wandered off a little ways, and sat on a stoop; and some one was playing on a piano. That was beautiful too. I'd like to crawl inside of something, as the fairies do, and just live there and listen forever."

"And then I found him, hungry and tired, and bought him some cake," interrupted Joe. "We waited to see the fireworks, and rode home in Mr. Terry's wagon. But for that I guess he'd been sitting on the stoop yet."

"And you haven't tasted a mouthful of supper!" exclaimed Granny; "and I a listenin' here, and never thinkin' of it."

"I'm not much hungry," said Joe. "I was treated a time or two by the boys."

But he thought he wouldn't tell that he had taken up his week's wages in advance, and spent it all. Fourth of July did not come but once a year, and a body ought to have a good time.

Poor Joe had discovered, much to his chagrin, that a dollar and a half would not work wonders. It seemed to him at first that he never could get his suit of clothes paid for; then it was a hat, a pair of shoes, some cheap summer garments; and he never had a penny for Hal or any one else. In fact, he began to think that he would make more money working round for the farmers. But then the store was steady employment.

He gave Charlie a glowing account of the fireworks, while Kit was eating a bowl of bread and milk; then they were glad to tumble into bed.

"I'm thankful it's all over, and their arms and legs are safe, and their eyes not blown out," said Granny with fervent gratitude.

Kit was pretty tired the next day, and Joe found it rather hard to make all things work together for good. Granny shed a few tears over Charlie's "best dress," and wondered how she could patch it so as to look decent.

Florence, in the mean while, was much occupied with her own plans. She could hardly wait for Monday to come, and proposed to do the usual washing on Saturday, so there wouldn't be any "muss" around when Mrs. Osgood called.

She was neat as a new pin as she sat awaiting her visitor. Her clothes had been looked over, and the best selected. There was nothing to pack them in, however, except a small, moth-eaten hair trunk, or a dilapidated bandbox; and the latter was Florence's detestation.

"I can do them up in a paper," she said; and Charlie was sent to scour the neighborhood for the required article.

Mrs. Osgood and Mrs. Duncan came together. The latter lady had laughed a little at her sister's plan at first; but, when she found it was really serious, thought it would be as well for her to try it a month.

Mrs. Duncan was rather exclusive, and had a horror of crowds of poor people's children.

"It would be so much better to take some one who had no relatives," she said.

"I shall not adopt the whole family, you may be sure," was the response.

Some of Mrs. Duncan's prejudices were surmounted by the general order and tidiness to which Florence had reduced matters; and she was wonderfully well-bred, considering her disadvantages.

"I shall keep her for a month, while I remain at Seabury; and, if I should want her afterward, we can make some new arrangements," Mrs. Osgood explained. "I shall see, of course, that she has ample remuneration."

Florence colored. Living with such a grand lady seemed enough, without any pay.

"What are you crying for, Granny?" she asked as she followed her into the kitchen. "How ridiculous! Why, it is just as if I were going away upon a visit; and you wouldn't be sorry then."

"It isn't because I'm sorry;—but—none of you have ever been away afore"—

Florence knitted her brows. How foolish to make such a fuss!

"There are so many of us, that we're like bees in a hive. You ought to be glad to have me go. And I dare say I shall ride over some day"—

"To be sure. But every one is missed."

Florence kissed the children all round, and was much mortified at the bundle tied up in a newspaper.

"If I get any money, I mean to buy a travelling-bag," she commented internally.

"Tate me too," exclaimed Dot, clinging to Florence's dress: luckily her hands were clean.

"Oh! you can't go, Dotty: Charlie will show you the beautiful chickens."

Dot set up a fearful cry, and wriggled herself out of Charlie's arms, and Granny took her. Florence hurried through her good-bys, and was glad to leave the confusion behind.

Granny indulged in a little cry afterward, and then went to her ironing. Of course they must all flit from the old hive some time. She could hardly persuade herself that Florence was fifteen,—almost a young lady.

Joe and Hal wanted to hear all the particulars that evening. Charlie dilated grandly on the magnificence of the ladies.

"It's real odd," said Joe. "Flossy always wanted to be a lady; and maybe this is a step towards it. I wonder if I shall ever get to sea!"

"Oh, don't!" exclaimed Granny in a pitiful voice.

When Mrs. Green heard the news, she had to come over.

"I don't suppose they'd ever thought on't, if it hadn't been for me," she exclaimed. "They stopped to my house while their wagon was bein' mended, and the sickly lookin' one seemed to be terribly interested in your folks; so, thinks I, if I can do a good turn for a neighbor it's all right; and I spoke a word, now and then, for Florence,—though it's a pity her name hadn't been Mary Jane. I never did approve of such romantic names for children. And I hope Florence will be a good girl, and suit; for the Lord knows that you have your hands full!"

Charlie ran wild, as usual, through vacation. In one of her long rambles in the woods she found a hollow tree with a rock beside it, and her fertile imagination at once suggested a cave. She worked very industriously to get it in order; brought a great pile of leaves for a bed, and armsful of brush to cook with, and then besought Kit to run away and live in the woods.

Kit tried it for one day. They had some apples and berries, and a piece of bread taken from the pantry when Granny wasn't around. They undertook to fish, but could not catch any thing; though Charlie was quite sure, that, if Joe would lend her his pistol, she could shoot a bird.

"Anyhow, we'll have a fire, and roast our apples," said Charlie, undaunted.

"But it's awful lonesome, I think. S'pose we don't stay all night: Granny'll be worried."

"Pooh!" returned Charlie with supreme disdain.

So she lighted her fire. The twigs crackled and blazed, and the flame ran along on the ground.

"Isn't it splendid!" she exclaimed, "Why, it's almost like fireworks! Oh, see, Kit! that dead tree has caught. We'll have a gay old time now."

Alas! Charlie's "gay old time" came to an ignoble end. Some one rushed through the woods shouting,—

"Hillo! What the mischief are you at? Don't you know any better than to be setting the woods on fire?"

It was Mr. Trumbull, looking angry enough. He bent the burning tree over, and stamped out the blaze; then poked the fire apart, and crushed the burning fragments into the soft ground. A dense smoke filled the little nook.

"Whose work is this? You youngsters deserve a good thrashing, and I've half a mind to take your hide off."

With that he caught Kit by the arm.

"He didn't do it," spoke up courageous Charlie. "He never brought a leaf nor a stick; and you sha'n't thrash him!"

"What's he here for, then?"

"I brought him."

"And did you kindle the fire?"

"Yes," said Charlie, hanging her head a little.

"What for? Didn't you know that you might burn the woods down, in such a dry time? Why, I could shut you up in jail for it."

That frightened Charlie a good deal.

"I didn't mean to—do any harm: we thought—we'd have a little fun"— came out Charlie's answer by jerks.

"Fine fun! Why, you're Granny Kenneth's youngsters! I guess I'll have to march you off to jail."

"Oh, let Kit go home!" cried Charlie with a great lump in her throat. "It wasn't his fault. He didn't even want to come."

Something in the child's air and frankness touched Mr. Trumbull's heart, and caused him to smile. He had a houseful of children at home, every one of whom possessed a wonderful faculty for mischief; but this little girl's bravery disarmed his anger.

"I want to explain to you that a fire like this might burn down a handsome piece of woodlands worth thousands of dollars. All these large trees are sent to the sawmill, and made into boards and shingles and various things. So it would be a great loss."

"I'm very sorry," returned Charlie. "I didn't know it would do any harm."

"If I don't take you to jail this time, will you promise never to do it again?"

Charlie shivered a little at her narrow escape.

"I surely wouldn't," she said very soberly.

By this time Mr. Trumbull had the fire pretty well out.

"Well, don't ever let me catch you at it again, or you will not get off so easily. Now trot home as fast as you can."

Charlie paused a moment, tugging at the cape of her sun-bonnet.

"I'm glad you told me about burning up the woods," she said. "I didn't think of that."

Mr. Trumbull laughed pleasantly.

So the two walked homeward, Charlie in a more serious frame of mind than usual.

"I tell you, Kit," she began at length, "out West is the place to have a cave, and fires, and all that Hal had a book about it. Sometimes children are kidnapped by Indians, and live in their tents, and learn how to make bead-bags and moccasins"—

"I don't want to go;" and Kit gave his slender shoulders a shrug. "They scalp you too."

"But they wouldn't me. I should marry one of the chiefs." Then, after a rather reflective pause, "I'm glad we didn't burn down Mr. Trumbull's woods: only I guess he wasn't in earnest when he said he would put me in jail."

But for all that she begged Kit not to relate their adventure to Granny, and perplexed her youthful brain for a more feasible method of running away.

The house seemed very odd without Florence. The children's small errors passed unrebuked; and they revelled in dirt to their utmost content. For what with working out a day now and then, getting meals, patching old clothes, and sundry odd jobs, Granny had her poor old hands quite full. But she never complained.

CHAPTER X.

WHICH SHOULD SHE CHOOSE?

The reality at Seabury far exceeded Florence Kenneth's expectations. The hotel was really finer than that at Salem. And then, instead of being maid, she found here a woman who waited upon Mrs. Osgood, arranged her hair, kept her dresses in order, and did the small errands. What was she to do, then?

Not very much, it seemed. She read aloud, and Florence was an undeniably good reader; she embroidered a little, went every day for a ride, and absolutely sat in the parlor. It was rather embarrassing at first.

"I have decided," Mrs. Osgood said to her sister, a few days afterward. "The child has a very sweet temper, and a most affectionate nature; and then she is so lovely. A perfect blonde beauty! In two years she will be able to enter society. Mrs. Deering declared yesterday that her voice was remarkable."

"I hope you will not spoil her completely. She has a good share of vanity, I perceive."

"It is only proper pride: the child is well-born. I know her mother must have been a lady, and Kenneth is not a common name."

"I am sure I hope your *protégée* will prove a comfort."

Then Mrs. Osgood announced her plans to Florence, who was literally overwhelmed. To be adopted by so rich a lady, to have an elegant home, and become skilled in all accomplishments—was it not a dream,—her wild, improbable dream?

To Florence Mrs. Osgood was an angel. True, she had seen her rather pettish, and sometimes she scolded Martha, and gave way to hysterical spasms; but these were minor faults. She drew the child to her with the sweet and not-forgotten arts of her faded girlhood, and was pleased with the sincere homage that had in it so much of wonder. Florence would love her like a daughter.

"I cannot promise to leave you a fortune," she said, "but while I live you shall have every thing. I was treated very unjustly by Mr. Osgood's will; though I know he was influenced by his relatives, who grudge me every penny. They would be very glad to have some of their children live at

Roselawn: I christened the place myself on account of the roses."

"How beautiful it must be!" exclaimed Florence, enchanted.

"It *is* a handsome place. You would have a governess, and be taught music and French and drawing, and be introduced everywhere as my daughter. If I had one, I fancy she would look something like you, for I was called very pretty in my younger days;" and Mrs. Osgood sighed.

"I can never be grateful enough," said Florence.

"I shall want you to love me a great deal,—just as if I were your own mother. And when you are grown you must make me your confidant. You will marry brilliantly, of course; but you must promise that it will not be without my consent."

"I shall never want to leave you!" declared Florence impulsively, kissing the thin hands.

"It will be such a luxury to have your affection. My life has always been so lonely. Very few people can understand my sensitive nature, but I trust you will be able to."

There was some other points not so congenial. When they came to these, Florence's heart shrank a little.

For, if she chose Mrs. Osgood, the group at home must drop out of her life completely. There could be no visiting, no corresponding.

Poor Florence! This was a cloud upon her bright visions.

"I shall write to your grandmother occasionally to let her know that you are well; but, as my daughter, you will be in such an entirely different sphere, that the slightest intimacy would be unwise."

What should she do? Would Granny think her cruel and ungrateful?

Mrs. Osgood proposed to take her back to Madison to spend a few days in which to decide. As for her, it hardly appeared possible to her that the child could hesitate. And now that she had enjoyed this little taste of luxury, poverty would seem all the more repulsive.

They drove over one morning. Luckily, Granny was in very tolerable order; but, oh the difference! She was so glad to see Florence, that she kissed and cried over her a little.

"I want to have a talk with your grandmother," Mrs. Osgood said; and Florence betook herself to the kitchen. How dreadfully poor and mean every thing looked!

Mrs. Osgood went straight about the business in hand. She described her offer in the most glowing terms, and held out all its advantages. It would relieve Mrs. Kenneth from much care and anxiety, give her one less to struggle for; and then Florence would have the position for which Nature had fitted her. Not one thing was forgotten.

Granny listened like one in a dream. Flossy to be a rich lady's daughter,— to ride in a carriage, to have a piano, and be dressed in silk! Could it be true?

"But oh! I can't give her up," moaned Granny. "She was poor Joe's first-born, and such a sweet, pretty baby! There never was one on 'em that I could spare."

"I wish you would take counsel with some friend. I think this opportunity for Florence is too good to be thrown away."

"I don't know, I'm sure. You are very kind and generous. But to part with my poor darling."

The lady rose at length.

"I shall leave Florence here for three days," she said. "In the mean while consider the subject well, and do not stand in the way of the child's welfare."

Florence was very sorry to part with Mrs. Osgood. She walked out to the gate, and lingered there, clinging to the slender hand, and at last being kissed tenderly.

"Think earnestly of my proposal. On Saturday I shall come for my answer," said Mrs. Osgood.

The lady had not much fear. She knew that money was all-potent in this world; and it was quite absurd to suppose that a pretty girl would prefer toil and poverty in this hovel, to luxury and ease with handsome surroundings.

"Oh dear!" and Granny's arms were around Flossy's neck. "I can't let you go away forever. And I am sure you don't want to," scanning the fair face with her fond and eager eyes.

"Granny, I don't know what to say. I should so like to have an education, and to be—oh! don't cry so. If every one thinks I ought not to go,"—and Flossy's lip quivered.

"I am a foolish old body," sobbed Granny. "I'm not worth minding, my dear."

"Fossy tum home. What 'ou ky?" said Dot, tugging at Granny's dress.

"If we could see you once in a while."

Florence felt the last to be an impossibility. She had a keen perception of the difference in station, and the nameless something that Granny could not be brought to see.

"You would hear about me," she said softly.

Granny went back to her ironing. Florence offered to help, and arranged her own light table. But it was uncomfortable this hot summer day, and her tender hand felt as if it was blistered. She consoled herself by relating the experiences of the past month, and inwardly sighing for the luxurious life. Granny was not so stupid but that she could see the direction of the child's desires.

"I don't wonder that you liked it; and she couldn't help loving you, even if I do say it. Why, a queen might be proud of you! If we knew some one to ask."

"There is Mr. Howard," Florence suggested.

"Sure enough. He would see all sides of it. We'll go over after the work is done;" and Granny tried to smile a little lightness into her sad face.

Charlie had gone to pull weeds for a neighbor, Hal was out also, so there was only Kit to dinner. After that was out of the way, and Dot had her nap, they made themselves ready for their call.

Florence tried her best to make a lady out of Granny. A queer little old woman she was, and would be to the end of the chapter. Her bonnet was dreadfully old-fashioned, and her gingham dress too short for modern requirements. Her wrinkled hands were as brown as berries, and she never *would* wear gloves in the summer. Then, after she was all ready, she surreptitiously tied on her black alpaca apron; at which Flossy gave a sigh of despair.

The parsonage was a pretty little nest, half-covered with vines, and shaded by a great sycamore. Dolly and Fred Howard were playing on the grass, and Dot started for the small group instantly.

"O Mrs. Kenneth! how do you do? What a stranger you are! And here is Florence, fresh as a rose! I heard that you had run away, my child. Come and sit in the shade here: it is cooler than within doors. Mary, here are some visitors."

Mrs. Howard gave them a cordial welcome, and insisted that Granny should lay aside her bonnet. She inquired if Florence had enjoyed her month at Seabury, and if she was not glad to get back again.

Granny twisted her apron-strings, and glanced at the young girl uneasily.

Of course she must begin somehow, but there was a great sinking at her heart.

"Flossy's had a chance," she began; and then the strings were untied. "We thought we'd come and ask a little advice. It's hard tellin' what's for the best;" and Granny looked as if she might break down into a cry.

"A chance for an education?" asked Mrs. Howard.

"No: it's—to go for good. Flossy, you tell. I am not much of a hand at getting things straight," murmured Granny.

Florence told the story in a very ladylike fashion, giving it the air of a romance.

"Why, Florence, that is quite an adventure. And she wants to adopt you?" Mrs. Howard exclaimed, much interested.

"Do you know any thing about this Mrs. Osgood?" asked Mr. Howard.

Florence used her limited knowledge to its fullest extent.

"Oh! I believe I know something about Mrs. Duncan. Dr. Carew was attending the boy. I have heard him speak of them all. Isn't Mrs. Osgood something of an invalid,—rather full of whims?"

"She is not very strong," Florence admitted.

"But it is a remarkable offer," rejoined Mrs. Howard. "And to have one of the family so well provided for, seems like an especial providence."

"But to have her go away," said Granny. "To give her up, and never see her again!"

"That does seem unkind. Perhaps it would not be quite as bad as that."

Mr. Howard studied Florence attentively for a few moments. He had always considered her rather above her station.

"It certainly is a generous proposal, granting every thing to be as represented. Florence will receive a superior education, and be raised above the care and drudgery of life. Yet she may have to devote many of her best years to Mrs. Osgood; and ministering to an invalid is wearisome work. It is taking her entirely away from her family, to be sure; but, putting aside love, she might never be able to help along much. Women are not extravagantly remunerated; and, if she went away to teach school, she could not do much more than take care of herself. And there would be a partial separation."

Florence gave Mr. Howard a look of relief and thankfulness.

"I don't want to keep her from doing whatever will be best," said Granny tremulously.

"There are Joe and Hal to help along,—smart boys both. And though your strong and tender arms have kept the little flock together these many years, they will wear out by and by. And, if any accident befell you, it would be well to have some of them provided for. The important question seems to be whether what Florence can do at home will compensate for what she must relinquish. The entire separation appears to me rather unjust. You said that Mrs. Osgood proposed that you should take counsel of some one: suppose I should go to Seabury, and talk the matter over with her?"

"Oh, if you would!" said Florence beseechingly. She felt that Mr. Howard was on her side, though she did not quite understand why.

"Yes," rejoined Granny, catching at a straw. "You could tell her how it is, —poor Joe's children, every one on 'em so precious to me. I never had much learnin'; but I love 'em for father and mother both, and I can't bear to think of their going away. Ah, well! it's a world full of trouble, though they've always been good to me, poor dears."

Mrs. Howard turned away her face to hide her tears, and presently left them to get a slice of nice fresh cake and a glass of milk for her guests. Her heart really ached for Granny.

So it was settled that Mr. Howard would go over to Seabury, and learn all the particulars of the offer. Granny was very thankful indeed. Soon after, they picked up Dot, and started homeward.

"You rather approve of it," Mrs. Howard said to her husband, watching the retreating figures, and smiling at Dot, who pulled at every wayside daisy-head.

"Florence has her heart set upon it, that is plain to see."

"And yet it seems ungrateful in her."

"It would be nobler for her to stay with Granny, and help rear the others. Yet that is more than one can reasonably expect of pretty young girlhood."

"She is industrious, and has many excellent points but she is a good deal ashamed of the poverty."

"I wonder whether she would be any real assistance? She has a good deal of vanity, and love of dress; and no doubt she would spend most of her money upon herself. Then, in some mood of dissatisfaction, she might marry unwisely, and perhaps be more trouble than comfort to Granny. If Mrs. Osgood is in earnest, Florence would at least receive an education that might fit her for a nice position in case Mrs. Osgood tired of her."

"And the life at home is not a great delight to her," said Mr. Howard with a smile. "But whether I would like to give up my brothers and sisters"—

"Florence is peculiar. Ten years from this time she may love them better than she does now."

There was a noisy time in the "Old Shoe" that night. They were all so glad to have Flossy back again. Kit played on imaginary fiddles; Charlie climbed on her chair, and once came tumbling over into her lap; Hal watched her with delight, and thought her prettier than ever; Joe whistled and sang, and told her all that had occurred in the store, pointing his stories with an occasional somerset, or standing on his head to Dot's great satisfaction.

"Well, that is really margaret-nificent," declared Joe, flourishing Granny's old apron on the broomstick. "Flossy, you are in luck! It is all due to your winning ways and curly hair."

"If I go"—with a sad little sigh.

"Go? why, of course you will! She'd be a great goose; would she not, Granny?

'Washing and ironing I daily have to do;

Baking and brewing I must remembertoo;

Three small children to maintain:

Oh, how I wish I was single again!'"

sang Joe with irresistible drollery.

Granny laughed; but she winked her eyes hard, and something suspicious shone in them.

"It would be splendid, and no mistake! To think of having a piano, and learning French, and riding in a carriage—'A coach and four and a gold galore!' And then pretty Peggy we should"—

Joe made a great pause, for something stuck in his throat.

"But couldn't we ever see you?" asked Charlie.

An awesome silence fell over the little group.

"If you could come and see us once in a while," said Hal softly. "We would not so much mind not going *there*"—

"I'd run away and visit her," announced daring Charlie. "I'd hide about in the woods until I saw her some day, and then"—

"They'd set the dog on you."

"Hum! As if I was afraid of a dog, Joe Kenneth! I'd snap my fingers in his face, and ask him what he had for breakfast. Then I'd come back home and tell you all about it."

"The breakfast, or the dog?"

"Joseph, I am afraid you are getting in your dotage," said Charlie with a shake of the head. "But, if I started to, I know I'd find Florence."

"It is rather cruel," said Joe sturdily. "I don't see why she should want to take you entirely away from us."

"We cannot look at it just as the lady does," said Hal's mild voice. "I suppose she thinks, if she does so much for Flossy, that she ought to have a good deal of love in return."

"She is ashamed of us because we are poor. But maybe if we managed to get along, and grow up nicely—she wouldn't feel so—so particular about it."

"I don't believe she would," exclaimed Florence. "You see, people are so different; and—I'm sure I've always wanted you to have nice manners."

"So you have, Flossy," declared Joe. "And you were meant for a lady."

Hal and Granny sat on the doorstep after the rest had gone to bed, crying a little, and yet finding some comfort.

"It would be so nice for Florence!" Hal said in his pleading tone. "She would always have to work here, and not learn music and all those lovely things. And she has such a beautiful voice, you know, and such pretty hands, and nice, dainty ways"—

"But never to see her again!" groaned Granny.

"I think we shall see her,—some time. Perhaps Mrs. Osgood might die: she is not very well, and Flossy might come back to us. Oh, yes, Granny, I do believe we shall see her again!"

"I've loved you all so much!"

"And we should always love you, even if we went to Japan. Then, if Flossy should have to work hard, and be unhappy, we might be sorry that we kept her out of any thing so nice."

"I do believe you are right, Hal; only it's so hard to think of not seeing her again."

"I'll try to make it up, dear. You will always have me."

The soft young lips kissed those that quivered so piteously, and smoothed the wet, wrinkled cheek.

"We'll pray about it, Granny. Somehow it seems as if God made these things plain after a while; and it is in his hands. He hears the ravens cry, poor, hungry little birdies; and he must care for us. He will watch over Florence."

"O Hal, you talk like a minister! Maybe you will be one some day. And it is so sweet to have you, dear boy!"

"I shall never be half good enough," he said solemnly.

He crept up to his room, but laid awake a long while, watching the stars, and thinking.

Florence resolved the next day that she would not go, and braced herself to martyr-like endurance. But oh, how mean and poor every thing appeared by contrast! Charlie in rags,—you never could keep Charlie in whole clothes; Dot playing in the dirt, for, though you washed her twenty times an hour, she would not stay clean; the shabby, old fashioned, tumble-down cottage,—no, Mrs. Osgood never would want any of these wild Arabs visiting her.

So she shed many quiet tears. Perhaps it would be best to make the sacrifice, hard as it was.

Granny saw it all. Her old eyes were not blind, and her heart smote her for something akin to selfishness. Poor, aching heart.

"Flossy," she said, over her heart-break, "if Mr. Howard is satisfied, I think you had better go."

"I have about decided to give it up. Perhaps it is my *duty* to stay."

Granny scanned the face eagerly, but found there no cheerful and sweet self-denial.

"I've been thinking it over"—her voice broken and quavering. "Perhaps it will be best. Though I don't like to part with you, for your poor father"—and Granny's inconsequent speech ended in tears.

"I'll stay home then, and do what I can; only it seems as if there were so many of us,—and the place so little, and I can't help being different, and liking music and education, and a nice orderly house"—

"No, you can't help it. Poor Joe—your father I mean—liked 'em all too. I've sometimes thought that maybe, if he'd gone away, he might have been a gentleman. He'd a master voice to sing. And God will watch over you there, and not let you come to harm. Oh, dear!"

Granny covered her face with her apron, and cried softly.

Mr. Howard called that evening. He had been quite favorably impressed with Mrs. Osgood's proposal.

"Her connections are all reputable people," he said; "and I think she means to treat Florence like a daughter. She can give her many advantages, and she is strongly attached to her already. But she *is* exclusive and aristocratic. She wants Florence all to herself. Still, she has made one concession: she will allow her to write home once a year."

"And then I could tell you every thing!" exclaimed Florence overjoyed.

"But she is resolved not to permit any visiting. To be sure, time may soften this condition; yet, if Florence goes, she ought to abide by her promise."

"Yes," answered the child meekly.

"It does seem a remarkable opportunity. I do not know as it would be wise to refuse."

Ah, if one *could* know what was for the best! The days flew by so rapidly, there was so much talking, but never any coming to a conclusion. Joe was loudly on Florence's side. So was Hal, for that matter; but from more thoughtful motives. And Granny was too conscientious to stand in the way of the child's advancement, much as she loved her, and longed to keep her.

Then, on Friday evening they sat on the old stone doorstep, a sad group, going over the subject in low, sad tones, the pain of parting already in their voices. Granny's vehemence had subsided. Hal had Florence's soft hand in his, Kit's head was in her lap, and Charlie sat at her feet.

Should she go? When all the mists and glamor of desire cleared away, as they did now in the calm star-light, with God watching up above, she felt that it would be nobler and truer to remain with them, and share the poverty and the trials. For to have them ill, dying perhaps, without looking upon their dear faces, with no last words or last kisses to remember, was more than she could bear. Would it not seem selfish to go off to luxury and indolence, when they must struggle on with toil and care and poverty?

"Oh!" she exclaimed, going to Granny's arms, with a sob. "I believe I cannot leave you when it comes to absolute parting. We have been happy, in spite of the troubles and wants. I should miss you all so much! And, if I could get to be a teacher, I might help a little."

Granny held her to her heart, and kissed the wet face again and again.

"My dear darling, God bless you!" she said brokenly.

Flossy thought herself a very heroic girl. There was a great lump in her throat, and she could not utter another word. It was a born princess turning her back on the palace.

Hal and Joe eyed each other inquisitively. It was the noblest thing she could do, but would it be the wisest?

CHAPTER XI.

OUT OF THE OLD HOME-NEST.

But then it all looked so different by daylight! The old rickety house, the noisy children, the general shabbiness, and the life of hard work and dissatisfaction, stretching out interminably. For, to the eyes of fifteen, it seems a long way to fifty; and roses are so much more tempting than thorns!

Hal found her out in the garden crying.

"Dear Flossy," he began tenderly, "I think you had better go, after all. When the parting is over, Granny will be reconciled, and understand that it is for the best."

"But I ought to stay at home and help," she sobbed. "If I could do both"—

"That is not possible;" and Hal tried to smile away the tears in his eyes.

"It looks so—so foolish not to be able to make up one's mind."

"It is a hard case, and there is so much on Mrs. Osgood's side."

"Hal, what would you do?" and Florence glanced up earnestly.

"My darling, I think you want to go, and that you would always be unhappy and regretful if you staid. We can't help all our feelings and wants and tastes; and it seems as if you were born for a lady. That is natural too."

"But I do love you all, and dear Granny"—

"We shall never doubt that," he answered re-assuringly. "We shall often sit on the old doorstep, and talk about you, and try to imagine you in the beautiful house, with the pictures and the piano, and all the nice things you will be learning. It will be just lovely for us too. Then you can write every summer."

"And perhaps I shall come back when I am a woman!"

At this Florence brightened wonderfully, but after a moment said, "You don't think it very selfish, Hal?"

"My dear, no," replied brave little Hal. "I am sure it would be a great trial for me to give up any thing so splendid."

"If you would only tell Granny—again."

Hal nodded; for he couldn't say any more just then.

Granny wiped the tears out of her old eyes with the corner of her checked apron, and trod upon the cat, stretched out upon the floor, who added her pathetic howl to the fund of general sorrow.

So it came to pass, when Mrs. Osgood made her appearance, Florence was quite elegant and composed. The lady was very, very gracious. She expatiated on the great advantage this step would be to Florence, the pleasure to *her*, and the relief to Granny to know that one of her flock was provided for. Of course, she understood it was hard to part with her; but they had so many left, that in a little while they would hardly miss her. Then they *would* hear about her, and no doubt come to rejoice in her good fortune.

Indeed, by the time Mr. Howard arrived, she had talked them into quite a reasonable frame of mind. She promised to treat her like a daughter, educate her handsomely; so that, in case of her death, Florence would be able to take care of herself. If, at the end of the first year, she should feel unwilling to remain, Mrs. Osgood would not oppose her return.

Granny was calm, but very grave, while these preliminaries were being discussed. Hal kept swallowing over great sobs that wrenched his heart at every breath. The agreement was concluded and signed.

"Now, my dear, put on your hat," said Mrs. Osgood in her sweetest tone. "Brief partings are the kindest; are they not, Mr. Howard? I am much obliged for your assistance in this matter; and you must permit me to offer you a small donation for your pretty little church."

Granny's tears streamed afresh; but Hal managed her with delicate tenderness. Florence kissed them all many times. Dot wanted to go in the "boofer wagon;" while Kit and Charlie looked on, with tearful, wondering eyes, not half understanding the importance of the step.

Then—she was driving away. One last, long look. Was that the waving of her pretty white hand? Their eyes were too dim to see.

"It seems to me that she will come back to the old house some time," said Hal, breaking the sad silence.

Granny turned away, and shut herself in the best room. For a long while they heard nothing of her. But God was listening to the heart-broken prayer, which he answered in his own time and his own way.

"So Flossy's gone!" exclaimed Joe soberly that night. "I can't make it seem a bit real. Air-castles don't generally turn into the substantial. After the king's ball I guess she will come home in glass slippers, and we will have her giving us loads of good advice. It is so sure to be true, Granny, that we can afford to take a little comfort meanwhile."

Granny did not laugh as usual. Kit chewed his thumb vigorously, and saw piles of violins in the distance.

But they confessed to being very lonesome on Sunday. Charlie declined wearing Flossy's second-best hat; for she insisted that she "felt it in her bones" that Florence would return, which Joe declared was incipient rheumatism, and that she must take a steam-bath over the spout of the tea-kettle. Yet secretly in his heart he had greater faith in the mythical sea-captain who was to take him off with flying colors.

About a month afterwards they received a letter from Mrs. Osgood. Joe displayed the handsome monogram in great triumph, and begged Mr. Terry to let him run home with it at noon. They all crowded round him with eager eyes.

"It's Granny's letter," he said, handing it to her.

"Read it, Hal," she rejoined tremulously.

Mrs. Osgood gave a delightful account of Florence; declaring that she already loved her as a mother, and, the homesickness being over, she was studying industriously. There was no doubt but that she would make a very fine musician; and it was extremely fortunate that such talent could be rescued in time to make the most of it. Then Florence added a few words, to say that she was very happy, and that it seemed like fairy-land, every thing was so beautiful. She enclosed a gift for them all, and said good-by until next year.

They felt then how surely they were divided; yet they all rejoiced in Flossy's good fortune. Mr. and Mrs. Howard were very kind; but I think Hal's tender love did more towards comforting Granny than all the rest. She kept telling herself that it was foolish to grieve; yet there was a dumb ache way down in the poor old heart, an empty corner where one birdling had flown out of the home-nest.

The affair had created quite an excitement in Madison. Joe pictured it in the most gorgeous style, and made Mrs. Osgood an actual fairy godmother. Mrs. Van Wyck, who still held a little grudge against her, insisted that it was not half as grand as the Kenneths represented it.

"Now, Mr. Howard," she said at one of the parsonage gatherings, "is it really true? Did this woman adopt that flyaway Kenneth girl, or only take her as a sort of servant? And is she so very rich?"

"Mrs. Osgood is a lady of means and position, and is connected with some of the most reliable people in New York. She has legally adopted Florence, and I was a witness to the agreement. It certainly was a rather remarkable event."

"Well, she's nothing but a bunch of vanity, anyhow. She'll make one of the high-flyers, without a grain of sense, and I dare say elope with the coachman. I wish the woman joy of her bargain;" and Mrs. Van Wyck set her cap-streamers in violent motion.

Autumn came on apace. Poor Granny was grievously perplexed when she entered the clothing-campaign. Florence's fertile brain and handy fingers were sorely missed. Granny did her best; but the tasty touches the child was wont to add, that transformed the commonest garb into certain prettiness, were lacking now. Still, Charlie thought it a godsend to have so many clothes all at once, having fallen heir to Flossy's discarded heritage.

"Granny!" exclaimed Hal, rushing in breathless one afternoon, "Mr. Kinsey says he will take all my chickens to market! Isn't that splendid? He is going on Friday, and again next Tuesday; and he showed me how to make a crate to pack them in. Now is the very time, he says."

"But we'll have to kill 'em, Hal!" exclaimed Granny aghast.

"To be sure: that's the hard part of it, isn't it;" and Hal looked sober.

"They seem a'most like human beings. They patter round after Dot, and talk to her in their queer fashion, and eat out of her hand. But, then, we couldn't keep them all through the winter."

"We shall save the pets. There are some that I could not spare. But you must not grow chicken-hearted, Granny;" and he laughed softly at her.

"Deary me! Somehow I can't bear to part with any thing any more. What a foolish old cretur!"

"The dearest old creature in the world!" and Hal kissed her. "I wouldn't have you changed a mite, except, that, when you were almost a hundred, I'd like to set you back so that we could keep you always."

"I sha'n't be worth it, Hal;" and she shook her head.

"I shall have to stay home from school on Tuesday. I am quite anxious to know what our fortune will be, and whether it has paid."

For Hal had gone back to school, as there seemed no business opening for him. Mr. Terry had raised Joe's wages; and, one way and another, they managed to get along quite comfortably. Hal tried to make up for the absence of Florence, and comforted Granny in many tender, girlish ways. He would pull her cap straight, and find her glasses and her thimble, two things that were forever going astray. Then he borrowed books from one and another to read aloud evenings; and, though Granny sat in the chimney-corner and nodded, she always declared that it was the loveliest thing in the world, and that she didn't believe but Hal would write a book some day himself, he was so powerful fond of them.

To Charlie and Kit this was a great enjoyment. Indeed, it seemed as if in most things they listened more readily than they ever had to Florence. Dear, sweet-souled Hal! Your uses and duties in the world were manifold. And yet it tries our faith to see such fine gold dropped into the crucible. Is it those whom the Lord loveth?

They had a great time on Thursday. Joe was up early in the morning, as he thought there was some fun in making an onslaught upon the army of chickens; so when Hal and Granny stepped over the threshold, they saw a great pile of decapitated fowls.

"Why, Hal, you'll make a mint of money!" exclaimed Joe. "I suppose you mean to put it in government bonds."

Hal only laughed.

But he and Granny were busy as bees all day. About four o'clock Mr. Kinsey came over to see how the packing progressed.

"There are just two dozen," said Hal; "and I shall have two dozen again next week."

"They're beauties too! Why, I believe they go ahead of mine. You've plucked them nicely. Poultry's pretty high this year; retailing at twenty-five and twenty-eight, I heard."

They weighed them, and then laid them snugly in the crate; plump and yellow, looking almost good enough to eat without a pinch of salt, Mr. Kinsey said.

"Now I shall send them all over to the station, and they'll go through in the freight-train. Jim will soon be here with the wagon."

Joe and Hal counted up the possible profit that evening. They had raised, with all their broods, sixty-five chickens. The actual outlay for food had been seventeen dollars; and Hal had sold eggs to the value of two dollars and a half.

"It's better than keeping store, I do believe!" ejaculated Joe. "Hal, you have a genius for farming."

"Does raising chickens prove it?"

"If a hundred of corn-meal costs two fifty, what will the biggest chanticleer in the lot come to? There's a question for you, Granny."

"Why, it would depend on—how much he weighed," said Granny cautiously.

"Oh, no! it would depend on how you cooked him. In my kitchen he'd come to pot-pie, according to the double rule of a good hot fire."

"You won't sell 'em all, Hal?" said Charlie anxiously.

"No: we will have a little Thanksgiving for ourselves."

Granny sighed. They all knew of whom she was thinking,—a sweet, fair face dropped out of the circle. Now that Flossy was gone, they remembered only her pleasant qualities; and it seemed as if Joe did not care half so much for making a noise when she was not here to be teased.

Mr. Kinsey did not return until Saturday, but he came over with a smiling face.

"Royal luck for you, Hal!" he said in his hearty tone. "I've half a mind to make you guess, and keep all that is over."

"But I might guess high;" and a bright smile brought sunshine into the boy's face.

"Try it, then."

"Thirty dollars," ventured Hal, rather hesitatingly. "Though I don't believe it *is* as much as that."

"Thirty-two dollars; and the same man has spoken for your next lot. They were about the handsomest chickens in the market."

"Oh! isn't that splendid?" said Hal. "Why, I can hardly believe it!"

"There's the money. I've always observed that there's no eye-salve like money;" and Mr. Kinsey laughed.

"You ought to have something for your trouble."

"No, my fine little fellow. I shall only take out the freight. I'm glad to see you so energetic; and I do hope you will prosper as well in every thing you undertake."

Hal thanked Mr. Kinsey again and again, and insisted that he should come over and do some work for the farmer; but that gentleman only laughed.

"Have your second lot ready on Tuesday evening," said he, as he wished them good-day.

The next was still more of a success, for they netted thirty-four dollars. Hal was overjoyed.

"That certainly is 'bully!' our dear Flossy to the contrary," declared Joe. "Why, I'm so glad that I could stand on my head or the tip of my little finger. What *will* you do with it all? Granny, was there ever so much money in this old house? It's lucky that I have a pistol to keep guard."

Granny smiled, but a tear crept to the corner of her eye.

"Now let us reckon it all up," said Hal. "Here is my book."

Every item had been put down in the most systematic manner. They made a list of the expenses, and added the column, then subtracted it from the whole sum.

"Forty-seven dollars!"

"All that clear!" asked Granny in amaze.

"Yes. Isn't it wonderful?"

Joe could hold in no longer; but took a tour over the chairs, as if they had been a part of the flying trapeze. Hal's eyes were as large as saucers,—small ones.

"I wouldn't a' believed it! But you've been very ekernomical, Hal, and used every thing, and raised so much corn"—

"And the buckwheat-field was so nice for them! If we can only keep them comfortable through the winter, and have them lay lots of eggs!"

"It's astonishing how contrary they are when eggs are scarce," said Joe gravely. "What do you suppose is the reason, Charlie?"

"Forty-seven dollars!" said Charlie, loftily ignoring the last remark.

"Enough to buy me a fiddle," Kit remarked.

"It will have to buy a good many things," said Hal. "I am so very, very thankful for it."

Granny insisted that Hal should have a suit of clothes, and finally persuaded him into buying a complete outfit. That took twenty-three dollars. Then some boots for Kit, shoes for Charley, a pretty dress for Dot, a barrel of flour, and there was very little of it left.

"But it was really magnificent!" said Hal with a sigh of pleasure. "I shall try it again next year, if you don't mind the trouble, Granny."

Granny said that she should not.

Their Christmas festival was quiet compared to the last one. Flossy had helped make them gay then, and there had been the wonderful shoe. Would any thing ever be quite as brilliant again?

"It almost seems as if Flossy was dead, doesn't it?" Hal said softly to granny. "And yet I suppose she has had lots of presents, and is—very—happy."

"God keep her safely," answered Granny.

Before spring some changes came to Madison. Grandmother Kinsey died, having reached a good old age; and Mr. Kinsey resolved to put his pet project into execution,—removing to the West, and farming on a large scale. Everybody was very sorry to have them go. It seemed to Granny as if she were losing her best friend. Ah! by and by the world would look very wide and desolate.

But the Kenneths had a little recompense for their loss. In casting about for a parting gift to Hal, fortune seemed to put an excellent one right in his way. In having some dealings with Farmer Peters, he took the small piece of land that Hal had made so profitable, and deeded it to the boy.

"It is not much," he said; "but it may help along a little. I only wish you were going out West with me. That's the place for boys!"

Hal almost wished that he could.

"But you will come and visit us some day, I know. You are a brave, ambitious little chap, and deserve to prosper. I hope you will, indeed."

Hal was a good deal astonished, and wonderfully thankful for his gift. To think of being actual owner of some land!

"You beat the Dutch for luck, Hal! I never did see any thing like it," was Joe's comment.

All Madison bewailed the Kinseys. They were some of the oldest settlers, and it was like removing a landmark. Mrs. Kinsey did not forget Granny, but sent her many useful articles in the way of old clothes, and some furniture that would have brought but a trifle at auction, yet served to quite renovate the little cottage. But when Granny tried to thank her kind friend, Mrs. Kinsey said,—

"I've always been glad to do what I could; for when I thought of you at your age, taking charge of all those little ones, it seemed as if every one ought to stand by you. And they will be a comfort to you, I know. God will not let you go without some reward."

Granny wiped the tears from her eyes, and answered brokenly. One and another were dropping out of her world.

She had hardly recovered from this blow when one night Joe came home in high glee.

"The luck's changed, Hal!" he said in his laughing, breezy voice. "Just guess"—

"More wages?"

"No indeed! Better still, a great sight. If you have tears, please wring out your pocket-hand*kerchers*, and prepare to shed 'em! Slightly altered from Shakspeare. I'm going to sea! Hip, hip, hurrah!"

Joe swung his old hat so hard that crown and brim parted, the crown landing on the mantle-piece.

"Couldn't have done better if I'd tried. I'm a dead shot, for certain!"

"Going to sea?"

Granny came out at that.

"Yes. A cousin of Mr. Terry's has been visiting there; and we have struck up a friendship and a bargain,—Cap'n Burton. He owns a sloop that goes to Albany and around, and wants a boy who can keep books a little, and all that. It's just as jolly as a lark!"

It was plain to be seen that Joe no longer stood in awe of Florence's ladylike reprimands.

Granny's eyes grew larger and larger. She fairly clutched Joe's arm as she gasped,—

"Going—to sea!"

"Yes, Granny. Don't get solemn new, as if you thought a shark would devour me the first thing,—body and boots. You know it always *was* my idea, and this is real splendid! And there's no more danger than driving Mr. Terry's grocery-wagon."

"But you might get drownded," Granny said awesomely.

"Tell you what I'll do, Granny. Tie a rope to my leg, and fasten it to the mast. Then you know, if I fall overboard, I can haul in. There isn't a bit of danger. Why, Capt. Burton's been all his life. There, don't cry. You are the dearest old grandmother that ever was; but we can't stay under your wing forever."

"You have not made your bargain?" asked Hal, surprised that another dream should come true.

"Well,—almost. He's coming down here in the morning to have a talk with Granny. He will give me ten dollars a month and found, which mean, tea and fish and baccy."

"Oh!" said Hal, "you won't chew tobacco?"

"Sailors always do. But ten dollars a month *is* better than eight, and my board thrown in. I'm going, Granny."

Granny sighed. It was useless to endeavor to talk Joe out of his project; and so she might as well keep silence.

Capt. Burton came the next morning. He had taken a wonderful fancy to Joe, and was very anxious to engage him.

"He's just the kind of lad that I need," exclaimed the captain. "I want some one who is handy, and quick in figgers; who can keep my accounts for me, as my eyes are getting rather poor; and do arrants; and I've taken a 'mazing liking to him. I'll keep a good watch over him; and he can come home once in a while."

"How far do you go?" asked Granny.

"To Albany, mostly. Now and then I take a trip around Long Island, or up the Sound. Your boy has taken a 'mazing fancy to the sea; and he will never be satisfied until he's had a taste of salt water, in my 'pinion."

"No, that I won't!" declared Joe stoutly.

"We haul off in the winter 'bout three months; which'll give him a holiday. Sence he hankers after it so, you better consent, I think. Cousin Terry will tell you that I ain't a hard master."

What could Granny say? Nothing but cry a little, look up Joe's clothes, and kiss him a hundred times, or more, after the fashion of Mrs. Malloy and her dear Pat. Joe was so delighted, that he could hardly "hold in his skin," as he said to Kit, who sagely advised him not to get into a cast-iron sweat,— Kit's chronic fear on remarkable occasions.

There was not much time for consideration. In two days Joe was off, bag and baggage, whistling, "The girl I left behind me."

And so the gay household thinned out. They missed Joe terribly. To be sure, vacation commenced after a while; and Kit and Charlie were in mischief continually, or in rags: Granny hardly knew which was worse.

They had some glowing letters from Joe, who didn't believe there was any thing finer in Europe than New York and the Hudson River. Capt. Burton was a "jolly old tar;" and nautical phrases were sprinkled about thick as blackberries.

Mr. Terry offered the place in the store to Hal, who consulted awhile with Granny.

"I think I could make as much money by working round, and raising chickens, and all that; and then I could go to school. I believe I should like it better; and there is so much that I want to learn!"

"But you know a master sight now, Hal," said Granny in admiration.

So the proposal was very kindly declined.

Charlie thought Fourth of July was "awful dull" this year. She lamented Joe loudly.

"If she had only been a boy!" said Hal regretfully.

The latter part of July, Joe came home for a flying visit. It seemed as if he had grown taller in this brief while. His curly hair had been cropped close; and he was brown as an Indian. Charlie made herself a perpetual interrogation-point; and Joe told her the most marvellous yarns that ever were invented. She soon learned every thing about the sloop, and wished that she could be a sailor, but finally comforted herself by thinking that she *might* marry a sea-captain.

Then, to crown all, they had a letter from Florence. It was written on tinted paper, and had a beautiful monogram in green and gold. She was very well, very happy; had grown a little taller than Mrs. Osgood; and was studying every thing. She could play quite well, and read French, and went to dancing-school, besides lovely little parties. Then the house was so elegant! She had never been homesick at all.

Perhaps she thought it would be wrong to wish to see them; for that was never once expressed.

"But I am glad she is happy," said Granny, striving to be heroic.

CHAPTER XII.

JOE'S FORTUNE.

Hal's chickens were a success again, though it cost more for him to get them to market this fall. And, since eggs seemed to be a very profitable speculation, they concluded to winter over quite a number, mostly spring broods. Hal enlarged their house; as he had a wonderful gift, Granny declared, for building. And a very nice place it was, I can assure you.

Granny still wove rag-carpets and the like, and now and then helped a neighbor at house-cleaning; but she had not worked out so much since the Kinseys went away. It troubled Hal to have her do it at all.

"When I get a little older, you never shall, Granny," he would say, giving her a fond hug; and she would answer,—

"You're a great blessing, Hal. Whatever should I have done without you?"

Dot grew nicely, though she was still "small for her size." Joe said. But now she kept quite well; and she was as fair as a lily, with tiny golden curls that never seemed to grow long. There the resemblance to Florence ceased. She was such an odd, old-fashioned little thing! and reminded Hal more of Granny than any one else.

"It would be sweet to have her a baby always, now that she is well, and doesn't cry all the time," said Hal. "I'm sorry to have her lose all her crooked baby words. Joe use to laugh so over 'pety poket,' and 'poky hontis,' and 'umbebella tause it wained.' Dear, dear! shall we ever have such nice, gay times again, Granny, when there wasn't any thing but mush and molasses for supper, and a crowd of hungry children?"

Granny sighed at the remembrance.

"And yet it is a comfort to grow up, and be able to do something for you."

Hal studied hard, and spent much of his leisure time in reading. Charlie was wilder than a hawk, combining Joe's love of mischief with perfect lawlessness. Mr. Fielder tried every motive of reward, and every method of punishment; and Charlie cried one moment, but laughed the next, and, what was infinitely more aggravating, made all the children laugh. If every thing else failed her, she could draw funny faces on her slate, that set every one in a titter. And then she climbed trees, jumped fences, or perched herself on a post, and made Fourth-of-July orations. She could talk Irish with a true national screech and whoop, or broken German as if she had just come over; she could make "pigs under the gate," cats in a terrible combat, and a litter of puppies under your feet that would absolutely frighten you.

Nobody could see what Granny Kenneth would do with Charlie. Florence, now, had been a lady; but Charlie was a regular wild Indian. She could work like a Trojan, but she did not like it; and as for sewing—well, there was no word that could describe the performance. With all her faults, she had a warm, tender side to her character. She fought Kit's battles, and always came off triumphant. She was never cruel to any thing smaller and weaker than herself; and I think no one ever could remember her telling a lie. But as Dot said in her sage way, with a solemn shake of the head,—

"She was the worstest child we had."

Joe came home the latter part of December as important as the Great Mogul himself. We had been selling out the old craft, and were bargaining for a regular little beauty,—a trading-vessel to make trips between New York and the West Indies, Cuba, and all those places. The boys opened their eyes at that. Joe Kenneth actually going to Havana, to be feasted continually upon oranges, figs, cocoanuts, and bananas!

Why, it was wonderful! incredible! There *was* nothing like being a sailor, and travelling all over the world. Joe took upon himself the tallest kind of airs, confused the boys with his flying-jib and spanker and mizzen-mast and capstan and larboard and starboard, and forty other things that he knew all about, and they didn't. And then the frolics and tricks, the sailors' yarns, the storms and dangers, held them all spell-bound. Indeed, I don't believe Joe ever knew so much again in all his life.

Capt. Burton followed him about a week later. "The Morning Star" had been purchased, and was being repaired a little.

The captain's principal errand in Madison was to see Granny Kenneth.

"Joe and me gets along tip-top," he said. "He's a sailor all over: there isn't a hair in his head but loves salt water. And I'm as glad to have him as he is to go; but, as we were making a new bargain all round, it wouldn't 'a been the thing not to come here and have a talk with you."

"Yes," replied Granny with a bob of her curls, though for her life she could not have told to what she was assenting.

"It's just here, you see. If the lad means to be a sailor, he can't have a much better chance. He's smart and quick in figgers, which suits me to a shaving; and I'd like to take him for the next two years. I'll give twelve dollars a month, beginning now, and look after him as if he'd a been my own son. I had a lad once,—about like him. It all came back when I was at Cousin Terry's last winter, watching him, so full of pranks and tricks, and with a smile and a pleasant word for everybody. My Dick was jest so. I took him on a trip with me, for he had a hankerin' after the sea; but his poor mother she most grieved herself sick. There wa'n't no gals to comfort her. He was all we had. So I left him home next time. I can jest see him, with the tears shining in his eyes, and a' choking over his good-by; and then how he turned round and put his face right between his mother's neck and shoulder, so's I shouldn't see him cry. Well, when I came back my poor Dick was dead and buried."

Granny gave a little sob, and Capt. Burton drew the back of his hand across his eyes.

"Yes, 'twas a fever. His poor mother was 'most crazy. So I tried to comfort her. 'Sweetheart,' said I, 'God is all over, on the sea as well as the land, and he's brought our Dick into a better port, though we can't understand it jest now in our grief. If we didn't know there was a wiser hand than ours in it, we couldn't bear it; but that will help to cheer a bit. But it was a hard blow."

Capt. Burton wiped his eyes, and cleared the huskiness from his voice.

"So I took a 'mazing fancy to this lad; and I'm proud to say I like him better'n better. He's trusty, for all his fun and nonsense, and bright as steel. So, if you'll agree, I will promise to do my best, and put him along as fast as I can, so that by the time he's a man he will be able to manage a craft of his own. He's a smart lad."

Granny was glad to hear the good report; and as for the bargain,—why, there was nothing to do but to consent. She did not know as it would be any worse to have Joe go to Cuba than to Albany.

"It won't be as bad," said he. "Why, I can come home every time that we're in port unloading. It's the most splendid streak of luck that I ever heard of. And, Granny, I'm bound to go to China some day."

Granny consented inwardly, with a great quaking of the heart.

"And you'll have the green-house, Hal! Wasn't it funny that we should plan it all up in the old garret?"

Hal's eyes sparkled with a distant hope.

"Can't girls *ever* go to sea?" asked Charlie.

"Oh, yes! they can go to see their friends and take tea, or go to Europe if they have money enough."

"I did not mean that!" she said with contempt.

"Tell you what, Charlie," and there was a sly twinkle in Joe's eye: "there is something that you can do if you would like to be a boy."

"What?" and Charlie was on tiptoe.

"Why, there's a kind of mill somewhere; and they put girls in it, and grind 'em all up fine, and they come out boys!"

"O Joe!"

"Fact," said Joe solemnly.

"I wonder—if—'twould—hurt much?" and Charlie considered on her powers of endurance.

That was too much for Joe, and even Hal joined the laugh.

"I knew it wasn't true," said Charlie, red with anger and disappointment. "But I do hate to be a girl, and you having all the fun and going everywhere."

"Well, you can run away. There is a bright opening for your future."

"You see if I don't!" returned Charlie.

So Joe went off again in capital spirits. At Capt. Burton's suggestion he told Granny that he meant to give her half his pay; which she, simple soul, thought the noblest thing in the world.

"I mean to do a good deal for you by and by, Granny. I'll be a captain some day, and make oceans of money."

"It is nice to have Joe settled and in good hands," Hal said after he was gone. "And I hope we'll all be an honor to you, Granny."

"You've been a comfort since the day you were born," was Granny's tremulous answer.

They found Joe's six dollars a month a great help; and then the two were missed out of the dish, as well as the household circle. Hal still kept to his thoughtful ways, reading and studying, and planning how he should make his wants and his opportunities join hands. For somehow he did mean to compass the green-house.

Joe's letters and stories were wonderfully entertaining. He began to lose the boy's braggadocio: indeed, the facts themselves were interesting enough, without much embellishment. One by one the islands came in for a share. Moro Castle and all the old Spanish fortifications, the natives who were so new and peculiar, the different modes of life, the business, the days and nights of listless, lovely sailing, the storms and dangers, gave a great variety to his life.

Now and then he brought them some choice fruits; and, while Charlie and Kit devoured them, Hal used to sit and listen to the description of orange-groves, and how pine-apples and bananas grew. It was something to have been on the spot, and looked at them with your own eyes,—ever so much better than a book.

Thus the months and years ran on. Joe was past sixteen, tall, and, though not thin, had a round, supple look, and could dance a break-down to perfection. He did not practise standing on his head quite so much, but I dare say he could have done it with equal grace. He was just as droll and as merry as ever; and you would always be able to tell him by the twinkle in his fun-loving eye. In fact, Joe Kenneth was "somebody" at Madison.

Hal was much smaller of his age. Charlie began to evince symptoms of shooting up into a May-pole, and being all arms and legs. She was still thin, lanky indeed, and always burned as brown as a berry, except a few weeks at mid-winter; and her eyes looked larger than ever; while her hair was cropped close,—she would have it so, and, to her great disgust, it seemed as if it was actually turning red.

"Because you always ran in the sun so much," Hal would say.

They heard from Flossy, who was happy and prosperous,—a great lady indeed. She had elegant dresses, and went to grand parties, had created a sensation at Saratoga, been to Niagara Falls, and expected to spend the winter at Fifth-avenue Hotel.

Ah, how far she had drifted beyond them! They could not cross the golden river that flowed between. Did she ever long for them a little? Would she be glad to drop down upon them in all her glory and beauty, and be kissed by the dear old lips that prayed daily and nightly for her welfare?

There came some quite important changes to Madison. A new railroad was projected, that would shorten the distance to the intervening cities, and bring it within an hour's ride from the great emporium, New York. Then began a great era of activity. Streets were laid out around the station; quite an extensive woollen-mill was put in operation, which caused an influx of population. The old sawing-mill was enlarged, so great became the demand for lumber; the Kinsey farm was divided into building-lots, some rather elegant mansions were raised, and a new church erected.

The Kenneth place was rather out of range of all this.

"But our little farm may be quite valuable by and by," declared Hal. "It would be astonishing, Granny, if you were to become a rich woman before you died."

"I'll have to live a good long while;" and Granny gave her cracked but still pleasant little laugh.

Joe remained nearly two years and a half with Capt. Burton, when the crowning good fortune of his life, as he thought it, occurred. This was nothing less than an opportunity to go to China, his great ambition.

It almost broke Granny's heart. To have him away two or three months had appeared a long while; but when it came to be years—

"Of course I shall return," declared Joe. "Did you ever hear of a fish being drowned, or a bad penny that didn't come back? And then for a silk gown, Granny, and a crape shawl! You shall have one if you are a hundred years old, and have to hobble around with a crutch."

"I'd rather have you than a hundred silk gowns."

"And I expect you to have me. The very handsomest grandson in the family. If you are not proud of me, Granny, I shall cut you off with a shilling, and wear a willow garland all the days of my life, in token of grief."

So he kept them laughing to the latest moment; and, after all, it was not so very different from the other partings. But he declared, if Granny didn't live to see him come home, he never should be able to forgive her.

Hal actually went down to New York to see him off, and had a pleasant visit with Mrs. Burton. It was a great event in the boy's life.

"I didn't think there ever could be quite such a splendid place!" he said on his return. "And the great beautiful bay, with its crowds and crowds of shipping, looking like flocks of birds in the distance; but the people almost frightened me, for it seemed as if one could never get out of the tangle. Then the park is just like fairy-land. And I found a place where a man buys cut-flowers, especially all kinds of beautiful white ones. And, Granny, one *could* make a good deal of money with a hot-house."

"I hope you'll have it," Granny answered; though, truth to tell, she had no very clear ideas upon the subject, except that Hal of all others deserved to have his dream come true.

Hal had treated himself to a book on gardening, and another on floriculture. He was fifteen now,—a steady, industrious little chap; and the farmers round were very glad to have him when they were in a hurry or ran short of help. For Hal had a good many very sensible ideas, and sometimes quite astonished the country people who went on in the same groove as their fathers and grandfathers. To be sure, they laughed and pooh-poohed a little;

but, when his plans proved more fortunate in some respect, they admitted that he had an old head on young shoulders.

"I'm going to have some nice hot-beds for next spring," he said to Granny. "I'm sure I can sell early lettuce and radishes, and some of those things."

So he worked on, spending his leisure days in improving his own little garden-spot. The place had begun "to blossom like a rose," dear Joe said. There were honeysuckle and roses trained over the house, making it a pretty little nest, in spite of want of paint and a general tumbling into decay. Over the kitchen part crept clusters of wisteria; and in front there were two mounds of flowers, making the small dooryard bright and attractive.

The chickens had to be kept by themselves, on Hal's farm. Every day he felt thankful for that little plot of ground. Mr. Terry was glad to take all their eggs, for Hal managed that they should be large and choice.

"And if I should have a hot-house by the time Joe comes back, it will be just royal!"

Granny smiled.

Poor dear Hal! One day he was working out in the hayfield, gay as a lark; and Farmer Morris said his boys did as much again work when Hal was there. The last load was going home. Hal mounted to the top, calling merrily to the group, when the horses gave a sudden start. It seemed as if he only slid down, and the distance was not very great; but he lay quite still. They waited for a laugh or a shout, and then ran; but Hal's face was over in the grass.

Great brawny Sam lifted him up, uttering a sharp cry; for Hal was deathly white, and could not stand. A deep groan escaped the lips that had laughed with gladness only a moment ago, and were now drawn to a thin blue line.

They crowded round with awe-stricken faces.

"Oh, he isn't dead!"

"No, I guess not;" and Sam's voice had a quiver in it, as if tears were not far off. "O father, father!"

Mr. Morris hurried to the spot.

"Poor Hal! Let's take him home, and send for a doctor. I wouldn't had it happen for a hundred dollars! It'll about kill his grandmother."

Hal gave another groan, but did not open his eyes.

"Can't we rig up some kind of a litter? for, if he's hurt much, it will never do to carry him by hand. Run get a shutter, Sam. Dick, go and bring a hatful of water. Poor boy! I'd rather it had been one of my own."

Dick flew to the brook, and brought back some water, with which they bathed the small white face. Then Sam made his appearance, with a shutter on his shoulder.

"Raise him softly, so. Dick, run after Dr. Meade as fast as you can go. We'll take him home."

They lifted him with tender hands; but both soul and body were unconscious of pain. Sam brushed away some tears with his shirt-sleeve, and Farmer Morris spread his linen coat over the silent figure. It was some distance to Mrs. Kenneth's.

Charlie was firing stones at a mark; but she rushed to the gate and screamed, "Granny, Granny!"

When Granny Kenneth saw them with their burden, a speechless agony seized every pulse. She could not even utter a cry.

"He isn't dead," Farmer Morris hurried to say. "But it's a sad day's work, and I'd a hundred times rather it had been my Dick."

"O Hal, my darling! The greatest comfort your poor old Granny had! No, I can't have him die. Oh! will God hear us, and pity me a little? I've had a sight o' troubles in my day, but this"—

They laid him on Granny's bed, and washed his face with camphor, feeling of the limp wrists, and chafing the cold hands.

A little quiver seemed to run along the lips, deepening into a shudder, and then a groan which they were thankful to hear.

"No, he isn't dead. Thank God for that!"

Fortunately Dr. Meade was at home, and he lost no time in coming over immediately.

Mr. Morris and the doctor stripped off Hal's clothes, and began to examine the limbs. The arms were all right,—ankles, knees, ah, what was this!

Hal opened his eyes, and uttered an excruciating cry.

Granny rocked herself to and fro, her poor old brain wild with apprehension, for his pain was hers.

"The trouble's here,—in the thigh. Not a break, I hope; but it's bad enough!"

Bad enough they found it,—a severe and complicated fracture, and perhaps internal injuries.

"Do your best, doctor," said Mr. Morris. "I'm going to foot this bill; and if any thing'll save him"—

He sent Sam back for some articles that they needed, and tried patiently to understand the full extent of the injury. Part of the time Hal was unconscious. And after a long while they laid him on his back, bandaged, but more dead than alive.

"My wife will come over and stay with you," Mr. Morris said to Granny. "She's a master hand at nursing."

Dot hid herself in the shadow of Granny's skirts, clinging fast with her little hands; and Kit and Charlie huddled in the corner of the kitchen window-sill, crying softly. No one wanted any supper, except the chickens, who asked in vain.

All night Granny prayed in her broken, wandering way. God had her own dear Joe up in heaven. Flossy was gone; little Joe was on the wide ocean; and how could she live without her precious Hal! Not but what he was good enough to be an angel, only—only—and the poor heart seemed breaking.

God listened and answered. The August weather was hot and sultry; and Hal had to battle with fever, with dreadful languor and mortal pain. He used to think sometimes that it would be blessed to die, and have a little rest, but for Granny's sake!—

After the first fortnight the danger was over, and the case progressing fairly. Hal's back had received some injury, that was evident, and recovery would be tedious. But Granny was so thankful to have him any way.

Everybody was very kind. Mr. and Mrs. Howard came often; the Terrys sent in many luxuries; Sam Morris drew a cord of wood, sawed, split, and piled it; and there was nothing wanting. But Hal lay there white and wan, his fingers growing almost as thin as Dot's little bird's claws.

"I can't understand why it had to happen to you, Hal," Granny would exclaim piteously. "Now, if it had been Charlie, who is always sky-larking round; but you, the very best one of 'em all!"

Hal would sigh. He couldn't exactly understand it, either. But somehow— God was so much greater than them all; and he *did* keep watch, for it was better to be lying here than in the churchyard yonder.

Mr. Fielder had gone away, and Hal felt the loss sorely. He was a little afraid of Mr. Howard, and could not seem to talk of his plans and his flowers, and ask any question that puzzled him; though Mr. Howard kindly sent him entertaining books, and used to drop in for a chat now and then.

September passed. Hal was still unable to sit up, and he began to grow weary of the confinement.

"Granny," he said one day, "I believe I'll have to be a girl, and learn to make myself useful. I could knit a little once, or I might sew patchwork. There is no one to laugh at me."

"Dear heart, so you shall," replied Granny.

So she cut him out a pile of pretty bright calicoes begged of the dressmaker. And then he knit Charlie a pair of yarn mittens, and crocheted some edging for Dot's white apron.

Indeed, Dot was a great comfort to him. She used to climb up on his bed with her "Red Riding Hood," or "Mother Goose Melodies," and read him stories by the hour. Then she would twine her fingers in his soft brown hair to make him "pretty," as she said, and cuddle him in various ways, always ending with a host of kisses and, "Dotty so sorry for you, Hal!"

For she was still a little midget, and cried so dreadfully the first day she went to school that they let her stay home. Hal had taught her a great deal; but she was so shy that she would hardly say a word to a stranger.

Charlie began to improve a little, it must be confessed; though she had fits of abstraction, when she salted the pan of dish-water in the closet, and threw the knives and forks out of doors, and one day boiled the dish-cloth instead of the potatoes, which Hal fancied must be army-soup; and sometimes, without the slightest apparent cause, she would almost laugh herself into hysterics.

"What *is* the matter?" Granny would ask. "Are you out of your head?"

And Charlie would answer, "I was only thinking."

"I'd like to get inside of her brain, and see what was there," Hal would sometimes remark.

The chickens had to be made ready and taken to market this year without any of Hal's assistance. And then he began to wonder if he ever would get well? Suppose he did not?

CHAPTER XIII.

FROM GRAY SKIES TO BLUE.

They were pretty poor, to be sure,—poor as in the hardest of times. There were the chickens, and Granny could make a bit of broth for Hal; but Kit and Charlie raced like deers, and had appetites. After Granny bought them clothes and shoes, the funds were rather low. Hal guessed at it all, but Granny never made any complaints.

He had begun a tidy in red-and-white diamond-shaped blocks; but it seemed to grow upon his hands; and one day when Dot called it a beautiful *bedcrilt*, for her tongue still had a few kinks in it, a new idea crept into his brain.

"Do you think it would make a pretty spread?" he asked Mrs. Howard rather timidly, during a call.

"Why, it would, to be sure, and so serviceable! It is a bright idea, Hal."

"Do you suppose I could sell it?"

"If you want to—yes."

"I can't do any thing else," said Hal with a sigh; "and if I have to stay here all winter."

For Hal's back was so weak that he could only be bolstered up in the bed, and he had not walked a step yet.

Mrs. Howard thought a moment, then said,—

"Finish it Hal, and I will see that it is sold."

So Hal went on hopefully. Granny bewailed the fact that she had done nothing all the fall to help along. They missed their allowance from Joe; but they had heard from him in his usual glowing and exuberant fashion.

Mrs. Howard took a trip around Madison one morning, and held sundry mysterious conferences with some of her neighbors, returning home quite well pleased.

"I am so glad I thought of it!" she said to her husband; and he answered, "So am I, my dear."

One afternoon early in December she went over to Mrs. Kenneth's. Dot had been clearing up under Hal's instructions, and they looked neat as a pin. After she found that her visitor intended to remain, Granny put on a fresh calico dress and a clean cap; and they had a nice old-fashioned time talking, which Hal enjoyed exceedingly.

Mrs. Howard had brought a basket full of various luxuries,—some nice cold tongue, and part of a turkey, besides jellies and cake. Quite a little feast, indeed.

Hal begged them to have tea in the best room, where he lay; and he enjoyed it almost as much as if he could have sat up to the table. Kit and Charlie were delighted with the feast.

Then they settled every thing again, and Granny stirred the fire. The wind whistled without, but within it was bright and cheerful. Hal felt very happy indeed. It seemed as if God's strong arms were about him, helping him to bear the weariness, as he had been strengthened to bear pain.

Presently there was a tramping up the path, and a confusion of voices.

"Some one is coming;" and Hal raised himself. "I am almost sorry—we were having such a nice, quiet time."

A knock at the door, which Granny opened. Kit, in the glowing chimney-corner, rubbed his eyes; and it would have been hard to tell which was the sleepiest, he or the old gray cat.

"O-o-h!" exclaimed Charlie; and then she darted to Hal. "A whole crowd of 'em!"

A crowd, sure enough. It was something of a mystery to know how they were going to get in that small place. There was Dr. and Mrs. Meade, Mr. Howard, Mr. and Mrs. Morris, and the boys, all the Terrys,—indeed, half Madison, Hal thought.

Mrs. Howard laughed a little at Hal's puzzled face.

"Oh!—I guess"—

Granny in the other room was quite overcome. Parcels and bags and boxes, shaking of hands, and clattering of tongues.

"It isn't exactly Christmas, Hal," began Mr. Morris; "but Santa Claus does sometimes lose his reckoning. So we thought we'd all drop in."

"And give me a surprise-party," said Hal.

"Exactly. Why, you look quite bright, my boy!"

Hal was bright enough then, with cheeks like roses, and lustrous eyes.

Dr. Meade sat him up in the bed. One and another came to shake hands, and say a pleasant word; and in a few moments the whole group were laughing and talking. There was skating already over on the pond, the boys told him; they were going to have a Christmas exhibition; Jim Terry had received a letter from Joe; and all the small gossip that sounds so pleasant when one is shut within doors.

Then Mrs. Howard brought out the bedspread. None of the boys laughed at Hal, you may be sure; and the older people thought it quite wonderful. Mrs. Morris declared that she'd really like to have it.

"It is for sale," said Hal with a little flush.

"Let's take shares!" exclaimed Sam. "Now's your chance, mother: how much will you give?"

"A right good plan," returned Mrs. Meade.

After a little discussion they adopted it. There were twenty-six people who subscribed a dollar; and then the slips of paper were arranged for drawing. The younger portion were considerably excited; and Hal's face was in a glow of interest.

So they began. One after another took his or her chance; and, when it was through, they all opened their slips of paper, looking eagerly at each other.

Clara Terry blushed scarlet; and Sam's quick eyes caught the unusual brilliancy. For the cream of the affair was, that Clara expected to be married in a few weeks.

Dr. Meade guessed also, and then they had a good laugh. Hal was delighted.

"It went to the right one," said Mr. Morris. "So much towards housekeeping, Clara."

"I shall always think of Joe as well as you," she said in a soft whisper to Hal, holding the thin fingers a moment.

After that they had a pleasant time singing. Hal was very fond of vocal music. It seemed to him about the happiest night of his life. Then the crowd began to disperse.

"I have thought of something new, Hal," said Dr. Meade. "I sent to New York this morning for a small galvanic battery, to try if electricity will not help you. We shall have you around yet: do not be discouraged."

"Everybody is so kind"—and Hal's voice quivered. "This has been a lovely surprise party."

After they were gone Charlie began to count up the spoils; and every exclamation grew longer and louder. There was a large ham, a fine turkey, tea and coffee and butter, flour, rice, farina, cake and biscuit, a bag of apples, and some cans of fruit.

"We shall live like kings," said Granny, with a little sound in her voice that might have been a sob or a laugh. "And only this morning I was a wondering how we *should* get along."

"And twenty-six dollars. Why, it is almost as good as being a minister, and having a donation-party."

"God doesn't forget us, you see," said Hal with great thankfulness.

He finished the spread a few days afterward, and sent it to Miss Clara; and then Mrs. Meade brought him the materials to make her one.

The fracture had united; but there seemed such a terrible weakness of the muscles in Hal's back, that Dr. Meade had become rather apprehensive. But, after using electricity a few weeks, there *was* an improvement. And one day Hal balanced himself upon two crutches.

"That's red hot!" ejaculated Charlie.

"O Charlie! worthy follower of Joe, what will you do when you get to be a young lady?"

"Oh, dear! I wish I didn't have to be one;" and Charlie began to cry. "I'll wear a big stone on top of my head."

"I am afraid it is too late. You are as tall as Granny now."

Hal gained slowly. All this time he was thinking what he should do? for he had a presentiment that he might never be very strong again. No more working around on farms; and, though there were some sedentary trades in cities, he would meet with no chance to attain to them. So he must have the green-house.

By spring he was able to go about pretty well. But he looked white as a ghost, quite unlike the round rosy Hal of other days.

"Kit," said he, "you'll have to be my right-hand man this summer. Maybe by another Christmas we might have the violin."

"O Hal! I'd work from morning till night," and the eager eyes were luminous.

"Well, we'll see."

Charlie was seized with a helpful fit also. After the garden was ploughed, they all planted and hoed and weeded; and, as it was an early season, they had some quite forward vegetables.

One day Hal went over to Salem, and invested a few dollars in tuberoses, besides purchasing some choice flower-seeds. Then he stopped into a small place where he had noticed cut-flowers, and began to inquire whether they ever bought any.

"All I can get," said the man. "Flowers are coming to be the rage. People think they can't have weddings or funerals without them."

"But you want white ones mostly?"

"White ones for funerals and brides. There are other occasions, though, when colored ones are worth twice as much, and as much needed."

"You raise some?" said Hal.

"All I can. I have a small green-house. Come in and see it. Did you think of starting in the business?"

Hal colored, and cleared his voice of a little tremble.

"I believe I shall some time," he said.

The green-house was not very large, to be sure, now quite empty, as the flowers were out of doors.

"I wonder how much such a place would cost?" Hal asked with some hesitation.

"About a thousand dollars," replied the man, eying it rather critically. "Have you had any experience with flowers?"

"Not much;" and Hal sighed. A thousand dollars! No, he could never do any thing like that.

"The best way would be to study a year or two with a florist."

"I suppose so."

Hal was quite discouraged, for that appeared out of his power as well.

"There is not so great a demand for flowers in summer, you know; but in winter they are scarce, and bring good prices. Still, some of the choicer kinds sell almost any time; fine rosebuds, heliotrope, and such things."

After a little further talk, Hal thanked the man, and said good-by with a feeling of disappointment. A hot-house was quite beyond his reach.

However, he did mean to have some early vegetable beds for another spring—if nothing happened, he said to himself, remembering his last summer's plans.

Not that he was idle, either. He did a good deal in the lighter kinds of gardening. The new houses required considerable in the way of adornment; and Dr. Meade spoke a good word for him whenever opportunity offered. He had so much taste, besides his extravagant love for flowers; and then he had studied their habits, the soil they required, the time of blossoming, parting, or resetting. And it seemed as if he could make any thing grow. Slips of geranium, rose-cuttings, and indeed almost every thing, flourished as soon as he took it in hand.

The new railroad brought them in direct and easy communication with another city, Newbury. Hal took a journey thither one day, and found a florist and nurseryman who conducted operations on quite an extensive scale. But still it was expensive in the start. He had thought of mortgaging the place; but the little money he could raise in that way would hardly be sufficient; and then, if he was not prosperous, they might lose their little home.

At midsummer they heard some wonderful news about Florence. Mrs. Osgood wrote that she was going to marry very fortunately, a gentleman of wealth and position. She sent love to them, but she was very much engrossed; and Mrs. Osgood said they must excuse her not writing. She enlarged considerably upon Florence's brilliant prospect, and appeared to take great pleasure in thinking she had fitted her for the new position.

"Oh!" said Granny with a sigh, "we've lost her now. She will be too rich and grand ever to come back to us."

"I don't know," returned Hal. "She did owe Mrs. Osgood a good deal of gratitude; and it was right for her to be happy and obedient when she was having so much done for her. But now she may feel free"—

"She has forgotten us, Hal: at least, she doesn't want to remember;" and Granny wiped her eyes.

"I can't quite believe it. She had a good heart, and she did love us. But maybe it's best anyway. We have been unfortunate"—

Hal's voice trembled a little. Granny rocked to and fro, her old method of composing her mind when any thing went wrong. And, though she could not bear to blame Flossy, there was a soreness and pain in the old heart,—a little sting of ingratitude, if she had dared to confess it.

"Hal," said Dr. Meade one day, "they are going to start a new school over at the cross-roads. It's a small place, and probably there will not be more than twenty or thirty scholars,—some of the mill-children. If you would like to teach it, I am pretty sure that I could get it for you."

"Oh, if I could!" and Hal's eyes were all alight.

"To be sure you can. The salary is very small"—and Dr. Meade made a long pause.

"Even a little would help along," was Hal's reply, his heart beating with a strange rapidity.

"There can't be any appropriation made for it, you see, as there will be no election till spring. But four hundred dollars have been subscribed, and the committee had a fancy that they might get a lady for that."

"I'd take it," said Hal. Four hundred dollars looked like quite a fortune to him.

"It may get up to four hundred and fifty, though I would not like to promise. It *is* a small sum."

"But there's always Saturday to yourself, and nights and mornings," was Hal's hopeful reply.

"Well, I will propose you, then. I shall be on the examining committee."

"How kind you are!" and Hal's smile was most grateful.

Still Hal was in so much doubt about his good fortune that he didn't say a word to Granny until the examination was over and he was sure of the appointment.

"It's just royal, isn't it?" and his eyes danced with delight. "I was wondering what we should do this winter, when there would be no gardening, unless I went to work in one of the mills."

"And you'd like this better? O Hal! it does seem as if the good God was watching over us, and always sent something along in the right time."

"He does, Granny, I am sure."

"For, when we were nearly out last winter, there was that splendid surprise-party. I never can get over it, Hal. And your *bew*tiful quilt, that I don't believe another boy in the world could have done. O Hal! you're such a comfort!"

And Granny wiped her poor old eyes.

The first pea-vines were pulled up; and then Hal began to prepare for his spring bed. It was vacation; and Charlie and Kit went into the experiment with a great deal of zeal. First Hal dug two trenches about twelve feet long, and four feet apart. He laid in these the stones the children brought in a wagon that he had manufactured for Dot a long while before. He piled them up like a wall, sifted sand between them, and then banked up the outside, making one edge considerably higher than the other. Around it all, at the top, he put a row of planking about twelve inches high, and fixed grooves for the sashes to slide across. Then he lowered the ground inside, and enriched it with manure, making quite a little garden-spot.

Charlie wanted to have something planted right away; and she did put in surreptitiously some peas, morning-glories, and a few squash-seed.

"I don't know but we might make another," said Hal, surveying it with a good deal of pride.

"Oh, do!" exclaimed Charlie. "It's such fun!"

Kit didn't mind, if Hal would only tell him a story now and then. Mozart's childhood that he had read in a stray copy of an old magazine, fragments of Mendelssohn, and all the floating incidents he could recall of Ole Bull. When these were exhausted, Hal used to draw a little upon his imagination. They had a wonderful hero named Hugo, who was stolen by gypsies when he was a little boy, and wandered around in the German forest for years, meeting with various adventures, and always playing on a violin to solace himself when he was cold, or tired, or hungry, or beaten.

And, though Hal often declared that he couldn't think of any thing more, Kit pleaded so wistfully with his luminous blue eyes and soft voice, that Hugo would be started upon his travels again.

When the frames were done, Hal went to see Mr. Sherman, the carpenter at Madison, to find what the sashes would cost.

"There's an odd lot up in the loft," he said to the boy. "They are old-fashioned; and nobody seems to want any thing of that kind, except now and then for a kitchen. I'll sell 'em cheap, if you can make 'em answer."

So they were sent down to the Kenneths. Hal worked over them a few days, and found that he could make them serviceable, only there would not be quite enough. He was very handy; and soon fitted them in theirplaces.

"Now, that's what I call smart," exclaimed Mr. Sherman. "Why, Hal! you'd make a good carpenter. Tell you what I'll do. I'm in an awful hurry; and, if you'll come over and work for me a spell, we will quit square."

Hal was delighted, and accepted at once.

"How lucky it all comes round, Granny!" he said in a gratified tone. "And I've been thinking"—

"I'll be bound it's a bright idea;" and Granny gave her little chirruping laugh.

"I was considering about the loom-room, Granny. You'll never weave any more carpets; it's too hard work: and then Mr. Higgins wants to set up in the business. He asked me about our loom the other day."

"No, I sha'n't never weave no more;" and Granny sighed, not at the confusion of negatives, but at the knowledge that old things were passing away.

"And it would make such a beautiful flower-room, lying to the south and west!"

Joe would have said, "What! the loom?" But dear, rollicking Joe was not there to catch anybody tripping in absence of mind.

"So it would. Yes, you shall have it, Hal."

For Granny would have given him her two eyes, if it would have done him any good, and been satisfied to be led about by a dog and a string all the rest of her life.

They ran up stairs to survey. The afternoon sun was shining in at the windows, covering half the floor.

"Oh, it *would* be splendid! We can put up a little stove here; and I can have it for a kind of study besides. And a room full of flowers!"

The tears fairly stood in Hal's eyes.

There was not much time to lose; for in ten days school would begin. And now Hal considered what he must do.

The windows came almost down to the floor, the ceiling being low. But it would not do to have all the flowers stand on a level, as the sun would not reach them alike. And then a brilliant idea occurred to Hal.

He went over to Mr. Sherman's, and gathered some pieces of joist that had been sawed off, and thrown by as nearly useless. He found eight that he made of a length, about three feet high, and bespoke a number of rough hemlock-boards. Out of these he made a sort of counter, with the joists for support; and then, nailing a piece all round, he had quite a garden-bed. This was to stand back from the windows, and have slips and various seeds planted in it. Charlie and Kit helped bring up the soil to fill it.

Then Hal bought, for a trifle, a lot of old butter-tubs and firkins that Mr. Terry was not sorry to be rid of. He sawed them down just the height he wanted; and they made very good flower-pots for some of the larger plants. They were so beautiful, that it would be a shame to leave them out to perish in the cold blasts.

"And somehow they seem just like children to me," he said, his brown eyes suffused with tenderness.

On the last Saturday he cast up his accounts, and took a small inventory.

"We shall have potatoes and vegetables for winter; and we have a barrel of flour, and a hundred of meal, besides lots of corn for the chickens; then my salary will be a little more than thirty-six dollars a month, counting eleven months; and fifty dollars for our poultry."

"Why, we'll be as rich as kings!" was Granny's delighted reply. "You're a wonderful boy, Hal!"

"And if I could sell some flowers! Anyhow, there will be the spring things. It does look a little like prosperity, Granny."

"I'm so thankful!" and Granny twisted up her apron in pure gratitude.

"Charlie had better go to school again. I wish she could learn to be a teacher; for she never will like to sew."

"No," replied Granny, with a solemn shake of the head.

"And she is getting to be such a large girl! Well, I suppose something will come. It has to all of us."

CHAPTER XIV.

A FLOWER-GARDEN IN DOORS.

Hal went to school bright and early the first Monday in September. It was about a mile to the place called the "Cross-roads," because from there the roads diverged in every direction. An old tumble-down house had been put in tolerable order, and some second-hand desks and benches arranged in the usual fashion. Just around this point, there was quite a nest of cottages belonging to the mill workmen.

The children straggled in shyly, eying the new master. Rather unkempt, some of them, and with not very promising faces, belonging to the poorer class of German and English; then others bright and tidy, and brimming over with mirthful smiles.

By ten o'clock sixteen had assembled. Hal gave them a short address, made a few rules, and attempted to classify them. They read and spelled a little, at least those who were able, when the bell on the factory rang out the hour of noon.

Three new ones came after dinner. Hal labored faithfully; but it *was* a relief to have the session close.

Before the week ended, however, the prospect became more inspiriting. There were twenty-three scholars, and some whom it would be a pleasure to teach. But, after all, it was not as delightful as working among the flowers,— the dear, beautiful children who gave only fragrance and loveliness continually.

He had been so tired every night, that he could do nothing but rest; and so he was glad to have Saturday come.

"It seems early to take them in," he said, surveying the garden so full of glory. "But there is a good deal to do; and I shall have only one day in the week."

Kit took the wheelbarrow, and trundled off to the woods for some more good soil; for Hal had to be economical, since he could not afford to buy every thing. They were out of debt, and had a little money,—very little indeed; but there were some pears and grapes to sell. Hal's Concord and Rogers hybrid had done beautifully; and two of the new-comers in Madison had offered to take all he had, at ten cents a pound.

"I could get more in the city," he said; "but there would be the time and trouble of going. And grapes are heavy too: it doesn't take many bunches to weigh a pound; and ten pounds come to a dollar."

But on this day he went at his roses. He had obtained quite a number of slips of hybrid monthlies, mostly tea-roses; and they were doing nicely. Some had blossomed once, and others were just showing bud. These he meant to transplant to his bed up stairs. Careful and patient, he took up the most of them so nicely, that I don't believe they knew they were moved, until they began to look around for their companions.

Dot ran up stairs and down, and was most enthusiastic.

"It will be *so* lovely to have a garden in the house!" was her constant ejaculation.

By noon he had all the small roses in,—five white ones, four pink, and about a dozen of different shades of deep velvety red. In this soil he had used an abundance of powdered charcoal. Then came half a dozen young heliotropes.

"Now, I am going to save the rest of the space, and shall plant sweet-alyssum and candytuft, and some mignonette. I guess we have done about enough for one day," he said to Granny and Dot.

Charlie and Kit were lolling under the trees, resting from their labors. Now and then they had a merry outburst; but Charlie had grown strangely quiet. She would sit lost in thought for hours together, unless some one spoke to her; and then she would take to reading in the same absorbed manner.

"Hal," she said one evening, "what do you know of drawing?"

"A little more than the old woman who could not tell a cow from a rosebud;" and Hal smiled with quiet humor.

"I wish some one would teach me!"

"They do not have any drawing at school?"

"No, only at the academy. Belle Hartman is learning; but I don't care any thing about flowers and such."

Faces and grotesque situations were Charlie's passion. She could see the ludicrous side so quickly!

"You might practise at home, evenings."

"But paper costs a good deal. Oh, I wish I had some money!"

"Well Charlie, be patient. Something may come around by and by."

"Oh, dear!" and Charlie sighed. "I wish some one would come along and adopt me; but then I'm not handsome, like Flossy. I suppose she is having a splendid time. It seems to me that she might write just a little word."

Hal thought so too. As the months went on, he began to feel bitterly disappointed. Ah! if they could but see her once,—their beautiful Florence.

Through the course of the month Hal managed to get his flowers in very nice order,—several fuchsia that were in splendid bloom, two large heliotropes, an elegant and thrifty monthly carnation, and a salvia that was a glory in itself. But alas! that drooped and withered: so Hall trimmed it down. Besides this, some rose and balm geraniums, a tub full of callas, and ten of his tuberoses, that he had saved for winter blossoming. The other two had been a source of untold comfort to him. Then he had an exquisite safrano, and two chromatilla roses.

"Why it's quite a green-house," he said delightedly. "Now, if I can only make them blossom all winter!"

The first spare Saturday he went over to Salem to see Mr. Thomas. He was rather diffident, and did not like to explain his economical arrangements, but said that he was likely to have some flowers for sale. Mr. Thomas took him through his green-house again; and, though there were a great many more plants, Hal thought he could show almost as much bloom.

"I'll take your flowers," he promised, "provided you do not have too many, and if we could manage it this way: sometimes I receive a large order nearly a week beforehand, and I could let you know, in order that you might bring me all you had which were really fine. And, to be frank with you, I cannot afford to pay as much as you might get at Newbury or New York."

"I should like to know some of the prices," Hal remarked.

"It depends a good deal upon the demand and the season; but prices never vary a great deal."

They went round, and Hal learned a good deal in the course of his tour.

"Do you know of any place in Newbury where I could dispose of flowers?" he asked.

"There is a Mr. Kirkman,—one brother keeps a confectionery, and the other supplies flowers. But perhaps I may be able to do as well by you. However, I will give you his card."

Hal and Mr. Thomas parted very good friends; and the florist gave him some valuable advice.

"That fellow will succeed," he said to himself, watching Hal's retreating

139

figure. "His whole soul is in the flowers; and he blushes over them as if they were a sweetheart. Looks pale and delicate, though."

Truth to tell, Hal had been working pretty hard. The school *was* a great tax upon him; and the labor with his plants had been severe. Kit and Granny tried to save him all they could in the way of getting in winter vegetables, and looking after the chickens.

Ten days after his visit to Salem, he received a little note from Mr. Thomas on this wise.

"Bring me on Thursday morning, if you have them, three dozen roses, assorted colors, heliotrope, and fine sprays of fuchsia, if yours are still in bloom."

"F. Thomas."

Hal was delighted. Through September they had managed to get along on the proceeds of their garden, and the fruit; but his first month's pay had to go for clothes. It almost broke Granny's heart to take it.

"Why, I shall earn some more!" Hal exclaimed with his gay laugh. "It is just what it is for, Granny, to spend. I'm thankful to be able to earn it."

It was the middle of October now; and there had been some severe frost already. Tender out-doors plants were a mass of blackened ruins.

"You will have to go over for me, Charlie," said Hal, "because I cannot leave school. The stage starts at nine."

Charlie was in ecstasies. She rose by daylight on Thursday morning, to curl her hair, Kit said; and could hardly wait for Hal to cut and pack the flowers.

"I am sure I shall be left!" she declared twenty times at least.

Hal thought of it all the way to school. It seemed different from any other earnings, and gave him an exquisite pleasure. His own lovely darlings, his dream actually coming to pass.

Charlie was superbly generous, and left the stage at the Cross-roads, when she might have ridden half a mile farther.

The children were just being dismissed: so she rushed in full of excitement.

"O Hal! he said they were lovely, and the carnations magnificent. He wondered how you raised them. They were a great deal prettier than his."

Hal blushed like a girl. He had sent the carnations at a venture.

"And here's the bill and the money."

Charlie was as proud as if it had been her own. Hal's fingers trembled as he opened it. There they all were:—

> Three dozen Roses $1.50
> Two dozen Heliotrope .75
> Fuchsias   .75
> One dozen Carnations.48
>   ——
> $3.48

"Oh!" exclaimed Hal with a glad cry: "it's just splendid! And he liked them all?"

"Yes. There's going to be a great wedding in Salem. Such hosts and hosts of flowers! And Jim Street took me for fifteen cents!"

"So there's more than three dollars profit," Hal returned. "Now you must run home, Charlie, and get some dinner. I have not enough for two."

"I don't see why I can't stay. I should like to see your school, Hal, when all the children are in."

"But Granny will be troubled. Yes, you had better go, Charlie. You have been so good this morning, that you must not spoil it all. And then she'll be glad to hear."

Charlie went reluctantly. Granny was overjoyed The three dollars looked as large to her as a hundred would have to many a one.

Hal could hardly wait until four o'clock. He hurried home, and ran up stairs; but the poor flowers had been shorn of their crown of glory.

"I can't bear to look at 'em," said Granny with a quiver in her voice. "The poor dear things, that seemed jest like human creeturs! I used to talk to 'em every time I came in."

"But they'll soon be lovely again; and it pleases me so much to think that I can make a little money. I shall have the green-house some day; and you won't have any thing to do but walk round in it like a queen."

Granny smiled. Every plan of Hal's was precious to her.

The heliotrope appeared to be the better for the pruning; and some of the tuberoses shot up a tall spike for buds.

Then Hal had a few demands from the neighbors round. Mr. Thomas's next call was early in November, when he asked Hal to bring all the flowers that were available. It being Saturday morning, he went in with them himself, and became the happy recipient of five dollars and a quarter. Then he took a ramble in a bookstore, and, being attracted by the first few pages of "Charles Auchester," purchased the book.

Kit went nearly wild over it. Hal read it aloud; and he held his breath at the exquisite description of Charles's first concert, and the tenderness and sweetness of the Chevalier. Though part of it was rather beyond their comprehension, they enjoyed it wonderfully, nevertheless.

The little room up stairs became quite a parlor for them. The stove kept it nice and warm; and they used to love to sit there evenings, inhaling the fragrance, and watching the drowsy leaves as they nodded to each other: it seemed to Hal that he had never been so happy in the world. He ceased to long for Florence.

They did very well on their chickens this year, clearing forty dollars. Granny thought they were quite rich.

"You ought to put it in the bank, Hal! it's just a flow of good luck on every side."

And, when he received his pay for November, he actually did put fifty dollars in the bank, though there were a hundred things he wanted with it.

The latter part of December Hal's flowers began to bloom in great profusion. The alyssum and candytuft came out, and the house was sweet with tuberoses. There being more than Mr. Thomas wanted, he took a box full to Newbury one Saturday morning, and found Mr. Kirkman, to whom the flowers were quite a godsend. Eight dollars! Hal felt richer than ever.

He had set his heart upon buying some Christmas gifts. At first he thought he would break the fifty dollars; but it was so near the end of the month that he borrowed a little from Dr. Meade instead. He came home laden with budgets; but both Kit and Charlie were out, fortunately.

"Now, Granny, you *will* keep the secret," he implored. "Don't breathe a hint of it."

Very hard work Granny found it. She chuckled over her dish-washing; and, when Dot asked what was the matter, subsided into an awful solemnity. But Wednesday morning soon came.

They all rushed down to their stockings, which Kit and Charlie had insisted upon hanging up after the olden fashion. Stockings were empty however, as Santy Claus' gifts were rather unwieldy for so small a receptacle.

Kit started back in amazement. A mysterious black case with a brass handle on the top.

"O Hal! you are the dearest old chap in the world; a perfect darling, isn't he Granny? and I never, never can thank you. I've been thinking about it all the time, and wondering—oh, you dear, precious fiddle!"

Kit hugged it; and I am not sure but he kissed it, and capered around the room as if he had lost his senses.

Charlie's gift was a drawing-book, a set of colored pencils, and a new dress; Granny's a new dress; and Dot's a muff and tippet, a very pretty imitation of ermine. How delighted they all were! Kit could hardly eat a mouthful of breakfast.

Granny gave them a royal dinner. Altogether it was almost as good as the Christmas with "The old woman who lived in a shoe."

Yet there were only four of them now. How they missed the two absent faces!

Shortly after this they had a letter from Joe. He had actually been at Canton, seen John Chinaman on his native soil in all the glory of pigtail and chop-stick. Such hosts of funny adventures it would have been hard to find even in a book. He meant to cruise around in that part of the world until he was tired, for he was having the tallest kind of sport.

February was very pleasant indeed. Hal stirred up the soil in his cold frames, and planted some seeds. His flowers were still doing very well, the slips having come forward beautifully. On the whole, it had proved a rather pleasant winter, and they had been very happy.

Granny declared that she was quite a lady. No more weaving carpet, or going out to work,—nothing but "puttering" about the house. She was becoming accustomed to the care of the flowers, and looked after them in a manner that won Hal's entire heart.

Easter was to fall very early. Mr. Thomas had engaged all Hal's flowers, and begged him to have as many white ones as possible. So he fed the callas on warm water, with a little spirits of ammonia in it, and the five beautiful stalks grew up, with their fairy haunt of loveliness and fragrance. Dot used to look at them twenty times a day, as the soft green turned paler and paler, bleaching out at last to that wonderful creamy white with its delicate odor.

Outside he transplanted his heads of lettuce, sowed fresh seeds of various kinds, and began to set slips of geranium. On cold or stormy days they kept the glass covered, and always at night. It was marvellous, the way everything throve and grew. It seemed to Hal that there was nothing else in the world so interesting.

Kit had begun to take lessons on his violin; but he soon found there was a wide difference between the absolute drudgery of rudiments, and the delicious dreams of melody that floated through his brain. Sometimes he cried over the difficulties, and felt tempted to throw away his violin; then he and Hal would have a good time with their beloved Charles Auchester, when he would go on with renewed courage.

After Easter the flowers looked like mere wrecks. Hal cut most of the roses down, trimmed the heliotrope and fuchsias, and planted verbenas. His pansies, which had come from seed, looked very fine and thrifty, and were in bud. So he mentioned that he would have quite a number of bedding-plants for sale.

Indeed, the fame of Hal's green-house spread through Madison. It was a marvel to everybody, how he could make plants grow in such a remarkable fashion, and under not a few disadvantages. But he studied the soil and habits minutely; and then he had a "gift,"—as much of a genius for this, as Kit's for music, or Charlie's for drawing.

But with these warm spring days Hal grew very pale and thin. It seemed to him sometimes as if he could not endure the peculiar wear and anxiety of the school. There were thirty-five scholars now; and, although he tried to keep respectable order, he found it very hard work. He had such a tender, indulgent heart, that he oftener excused than punished.

His head used to ache dreadfully in the afternoon, and every pulse in his body would throb until it seemed to make him absolutely sore. The gardening and the school were quite too much.

"Granny," said Charlie one evening, "I am not going to school any more."

Granny opened her eyes in surprise.

"I am going to work."

"To work?"

It was astonishing to hear Charlie declare such sentiments.

"Yes,—in the mill."

"What will you do?"

"Sarah Marshall began last fall: it's cleaning specks and imperfections out of the cloth; not very hard, either, and they give her four and a half a week."

"That's pretty good," said Granny.

"Yes. I shall have to do something. I hate housework and sewing, and—I want some money."

"I'm sure Hal's as good as an angel."

"I don't want Hal's. Goodness knows! he has enough to do, and it's high time I began to think about myself."

Granny was overwhelmed with admiration at Charlie's spirit and resolution, yet she was not quite certain of its being proper until she had asked Hal.

"I wish she wanted to learn dressmaking instead, or to teach school; but she isn't proud, like Flossy. And now she is growing so large that she wants nice clothes, and all that."

Yet Hal sighed a little. Charlie somehow appeared to be lacking in refinement. She had a great deal of energy and persistence, and was not easily daunted or laughed out of any idea.

"Though I think she will make a nice girl," said Hal, as if he had been indulging in a little treason. "We have a good deal to be thankful for, Granny."

"Yes, indeed! And dear, brave Joe such a nice boy!"

Hal made a few inquiries at the mill. They would take Charlie, and pay her two dollars a week for the first month, after that by the piece; and, if she was smart, she could earn three or four dollars.

So Charlie went to work with her usual sturdiness. If they could have looked in her heart, and beheld all her plans, and known that she hated this as bitterly as washing dishes or mending old clothes!

On the first of June, Hal took an account of stock. They had been quite fortunate in the sale of early vegetables. The lettuce, radishes, and tomato-plants had done beautifully. For cut-flowers he had received fifty-two dollars; for bedding-plants,—scarlet and other geraniums, and pansies,—the sum had amounted to over nine dollars; for vegetables and garden-plants, eleven. They had not incurred any extra expense, save the labor.

"To think of that, Granny! Almost seventy-five dollars! And on such a small scale too! I think I could make gardening pay, if I had a fair chance."

Dr. Meade admitted that it was wonderful, when he heard of it.

"I'm not sure that a hot-house would pay here in Madison, but you could send a great many things to New York. Any how, Hal, if I were rich I should build you one."

"You are very kind. I shouldn't have done as well, if it had not been for you."

"Tut, tut! That's nothing. But I don't like to see you growing so thin. I shall have to prepare you a tonic. You work too hard."

Hal smiled faintly.

"You must let gardening alone for the next six weeks. And the school isn't the best thing in the world for you."

"I've been very thankful for it, though."

"If you stay another year, the salary must be raised. Do you like it?"

"Not as well as gardening."

"Well, take matters easy," advised the good doctor.

The tonic was sent over. Hal made a strong fight against the languor; but the enemy was rather too stout for him. Every day there was a little fever; and at night he tossed from side to side, and could not sleep. Granny made him a "pitcher of tea," her great cure-all,—valerian, gentian, and wild-cherry,—in a pitcher that had lost both handle and spout; and, though he drank it to please her, it did not appear to help him any.

It seemed to him, some days, that he never could walk home from school. Now and then he caught a ride, to be sure; but the weary step after step on these warm afternoons almost used up his last remnant of strength.

"Now," said Dr. Meade when school had ended, "you really must begin to take care of yourself. You are as white as if you had not an ounce of blood in your whole body. No work of any kind, remember. It is to be a regular vacation."

Hal acquiesced from sheer inability to do any thing else. The house was quiet; for Dot never had been a noisy child since her crying-days. She was much more like Florence, except the small vanities, and air of martyrdom, that so often spoiled the elder sister's sacrifices,—a sweet, affectionate little thing, a kind of baby, as she would always be.

Her love for Hal and Granny was perfect devotion, and held in it a strand of quaintness that made one smile. She could cook quite nicely; and sewing appeared to come natural to her. Hal called her "Small woman," as an especial term of endearment.

But they hardly knew what to make of Charlie. Instead of launching out into gayeties, as they expected (for Charlie was very fond of finery), she proved so economical, that she was almost stingy. She gave Granny a dollar a week; and they heard she was earning as much as Sarah Marshall already. In fact, Charlie was a Trojan when she worked in good earnest.

"What are you going to do with it all?" Hal would ask playfully.

"Maybe I'll put it in the bank, or buy a farm."

"Ho!" said Kit. "What would you do with a farm?"

"Hire it out on shares to Hal."

"You are a good girl, Charlie; and it's well to save a little 'gainst time o' need."

Which encomium of Granny's would always settle the matter.

Hal did not get better. Dr. Meade wanted him to go to the seaside for a few weeks.

"I cannot afford it," he said; "and I shouldn't enjoy it a bit alone. I think I shall be better when cool weather comes. These warm days seem to melt all the strength out of me."

"Well, I hope so."

Hal hoped so too. He was young; and the world looked bright; and then they all needed him. Not that he had any morbid thoughts of dying, only sometimes it crossed his mind. He had never been quite so well and strong since the accident.

For Granny's sake and for Dot's sake. He loved them both so dearly; and they seemed so peculiarly helpless,—the one in her shy childhood, the other on the opposite confine. He wanted to make Granny's life pleasant at the last, when she had worked so hard for all of them.

But God would do what was best; though Hal's lip quivered, and an unbidden tear dropped from the sad eye.

O Florence! had you forgotten them?

CHAPTER XV.

HOW CHARLIE RAN AWAY.

"Where is Charlie?" asked Hal as they sat down to the supper-table one evening.

"She didn't go to work this afternoon, but put on her best clothes, and said she meant to take a holiday."

"Well, the poor child needed it, I am sure. To think of our wild, heedless, tomboy Charlie settling into such a steady girl!"

"But Charlie always was good at heart. I've had six of the best and nicest grandchildren you could pick out anywhere, if I do say it myself."

Granny uttered the words with a good deal of pride.

"Yes," said Kit: "we'll be a what-is-it—crown to your old age."

Granny laughed merrily.

"Seven children!" appended Kit. "You forgot my fiddle."

"Eight children!" said Dot. "You forgot Hal's flowers."

Hal smiled at this.

"I may as well wash the dishes," exclaimed Dot presently. "I guess Charlie will stay out to tea."

After that they sat on the doorstep in the moonlight, and sang,—Dot with her head in Hal's lap, and Hal's arm around Granny's shoulder. A very sacred and solemn feeling seemed to come to them on this evening, as if it was a time which it would be important to remember.

"I do not believe Charlie means to come home to-night," Hal said when the clock struck ten.

"But she has on her best clothes. She wouldn't wear 'em to the mill."

So they waited a while longer. No Charlie. Then they kissed each other good-night, and began to disperse.

Hal looked into the deserted flower-room, which was still a kind of library and cosey place. The moonlight lay in broad white sheets on the floor, quivering like a summer sea. How strange and sweet it was! How lovely God had made the earth, and the serene heaven above it!

Something on the table caught his eye as he turned,—a piece of folded paper like a letter. He wondered what he had left there, and picked it up carelessly.

"To Granny and Hal."

Hal started in the utmost surprise. An unsealed letter in Charlie's handwriting, which had never been remarkable for its beauty. He trembled all over, and stood in the moonlight to read it, the slow tears coming into his eyes.

Should he go down and tell them? Perhaps it would be better not to alarm them to-night. Occasionally, when it had rained, Charlie spent the night with some of the girls living near the mill: so Granny would not worry about her.

O brave, daring, impulsive Charlie! If you could have seen the pain in Hal's heart!

He brought the letter down the next morning.

"How queer it is that Charlie stays!" said Dot, toasting some bread. "O Hal! what's the matter?"

"Nothing—only— You'll have to hear it sometime; and maybe it will all end right. Charlie's gone away."

"Gone away!" echoed Granny.

"Yes. She left a letter. I found it last night in the flower-room. Let me read it to you."

Hal cleared his throat. The others stood absolutely awe-stricken.

"DEAR GRANNY AND HAL,—You know I always had my heart set on running away; and I'm going to do it now, because, if I told you all my plans, you would say they were quite wild. Perhaps they are. Only I *shall* try to make them work; and, somehow, I think I can. I have sights of courage and hope. But, O Granny! I couldn't stay in the mill: it was like putting me in prison. I hated the coarse work, the dirt, the noise, and the smells of grease, and everybody there. Some days I felt as if I must scream and scream, until God came and took me out of it. But I wanted to earn some money; and there wasn't any other way in Madison that I should have liked any better. I've had this in my mind ever since I went to work.

"I can't tell you all my plans,—I don't even know them myself,— only I am going to try; and, if I cannot succeed, I shall come back. I have twenty-five dollars that I've saved. And, if I have good luck, you'll hear that too. Please don't worry about me. I shall find friends, and not get into any trouble, I know.

"I am very sorry to leave you all; but then I kissed you good-by,— Hal and Kit this morning, when I said it softly in my heart; and Dot and you, dear Granny, when I went away. I had it all planned so nicely, and you never suspected a word. I shall come back some time, of course. And now you must be happy without me, and just say a tiny bit of prayer every night, as I shall for you, and never fret a word. Somehow I feel as if I were a little like Joe; and you know he is doing beautifully.

"Good-by with a thousand kisses. Don't try to find me; for you can't, I know. I'll write some time again. Your own queer, loving.

"CHARLIE."

"Well, that's too good!" said Kit, breaking the silence of tears. "Charlie has the spunk—and a girl too!"

"Oh!" sobbed Granny, "she don't know nothing; and she'll get lost, and get into trouble."

"No, she won't, either! I'll bet on Charlie. And she was saving up her money for that, and never said a word!"

Kit's admiration was intense.

"It's about the drawing; and she has gone to New York, I am almost sure," said Hal. "Don't cry, Granny; for somehow I think Charlie will be safe. She is good and honest and truthful."

"But in New York! And she don't know anybody there"—

"Maybe she has gone to Mrs. Burton's. I might write and see. Or there is Clara Pennington—they moved last spring, you remember. I'm pretty sure we shall find her."

Hal's voice was strong with hope. Now that he had to comfort Granny, he could see a bright side himself.

"And she has some money too."

"She'll do," said Kit decisively. "And if that isn't great! She coaxed me to run away once and live in the woods; but I think this is better."

"Did you do it?" asked Dot.

"Yes. We came near setting the woods on fire; and didn't we get a jolly scolding! Charlie's a trump."

So they settled themselves to the fact quite calmly. Charlie had taken the best of her clothes, and would be prepared for present emergencies.

Before the day was over, they had another event to startle them.

Dr. Meade tied his old horse to the gate-post, and came in. Granny was taking a little rest in the other room; and Dot was up stairs, reading.

"Better to-day, eh?" said the doctor.

"I believe I do feel a little better. I have not had any headache or fever for several days."

"You'll come out bright as a blue-bird next spring."

"Before that, I hope. School commences next week."

"Then you have heard—nothing?"

"Was there any thing for me to hear?"

Hal looked up anxiously; and the soft brown eyes, in their wistfulness, touched the doctor's heart.

"They've served you and me a mean trick, Hal," began the doctor rather warmly. "Some of it was my fault. I told the committee that you would not take it next year under five hundred dollars."

"It's worth that," said Hal quietly.

"Yes, if it is worth a cent. Well, Squire Haines has had a niece staying with him who has taught school in Brooklyn for eight or ten years,—a great, tall sharp kind of a woman; and she was willing to come for the old salary. She's setting her cap for Mrs. Haines's brother, I can see that fast enough. The squire, he's favored her; and they've pushed the matter through."

"Then Miss Perkins has it!" Hal exclaimed with a gasp, feeling as if he were stranded on the lee-shore.

"Exactly. And I don't know but it is best. To tell the truth, Hal, you are not strong, and you did work too hard last year. You want rest; but you'll never be able to go into the battle rough and tumble. I may as well tell you this."

"Do you think I shall never"—Hal's lip quivered.

"The fall gave you a great shock, you see; and then the confinement in school was altogether wrong. You want quiet and ease; and I do think this flower-business will be the very thing for you. I've been casting it over in my mind; and I have a fancy that another spring I'll be able to do something for you. Keep heart, my boy. It's darkest just before the dawn, you know."

"You are so kind!" and the brown eyes filled with tears.

"It will all come out right, I'm pretty sure. This winter's rest will be just the thing for you. Now, don't fret yourself back to the old point again; for you have improved a little. And, if you want any thing, come to me. We all get in tight places sometimes."

Hal repeated this to Dot and Granny; and when Kit came home he heard the "bad news," over which he looked very sober.

"But then it might be worse," said Hal cheerily; for he was never sad long at a time. "We have almost a hundred dollars, and I shall try to make my flowers more profitable this winter."

And the best of all was, Hal *did* begin to feel better. The terrible weakness seemed to yield at last to some of the good doctor's tonics, his appetite improved, and he could sleep quite well once more.

At this juncture Kit found an opening.

"They'll take me in the melodeon-factory over at Salem," he announced breathlessly one evening. "Mr. Briggs told me of it, and I went to see. I can board with Mr. Halsey, the foreman; and oh, can't he play on the violin! He will go on teaching me, and I can have my board and four dollars a month."

"Well, I declare!" ejaculated Granny. "What next?"

"Then you won't have me to take care of this winter. I'm about tired of going to school, and that's nice business. I can come home every Saturday night."

"Yes," said Hal thoughtfully.

"I do believe Mr. Halsey's taken a great liking to me. He wants you to come over, Hal, and have a talk."

So Hal went over. The prospect appeared very fair. Kit had some mechanical genius; but building melodeons would be much more to his taste than building houses.

"It has a suggestion of music in it," laughed Hal.

So the bargain was concluded. About the middle of September, Kit started for Salem and business.

But oh, how lonely the old house was! All the mirth and mischief gone! It seemed to Granny that she would be quite willing to go out washing, and weave carpets, if she could have them all children once more.

There was plenty of room in the Old Shoe now. One bed in the parlor held

Dot and Granny. No cradle with a baby face in it, no fair girl with golden curls sewing at the window. Tabby sat unmolested in the chimney-corner. No one turned back her ears, or put walnut-shells over her claws; no one made her dance a jig on her hind-legs, or bundled her in shawls until she was smothered, and had to give a pathetic m-i-a-o-u in self-defence.

Oh, the gay, laughing, tormenting children! Always clothes to mend, cut fingers and stubbed toes to doctor, quarrels to settle, noises to quell, to tumble over one here and another there, to have them cross with the measles and forlorn with the mumps, but coming back to fun again in a day or two,—the dear, troublesome, vanished children!

Many a time Granny cried alone by herself. It was right that they should grow into men and women; but oh, the ache and emptiness it left in her poor old heart! And it seemed as if Tabby missed them; for now and then she would put her paws on the old window-seat, stretching out her full length, and look up and down the street, uttering a mournful cry.

One day Dot brought home a letter from the store directed to Hal.

"Why, it's Charlie!" he said with a great cry of joy and confusion of person. "Dear old Charlie!"

He tore it open with hasty, trembling fingers.

"DEAR HAL AND GRANNY,—I'm like Joe, happy as a big sunflower! I can't tell you half nor quarter; so I shall not try, but save it all against the time I come home; for I *am* coming. Every thing is just splendid! It wasn't so nice at first, and one day I felt almost homesick; but it came out right. Oh, dear! I want to see you so, and tell you all the wonderful things that have happened to me,—just like a story-book. I think of you all,—Hal in his school, Granny busy about the house, Dot, the little darling, sweet as ever, and a whole roomful of flowers up-stairs, and Kit playing on his violin. Did you miss me much? I missed the dear old home, the sweet kisses, and tender voices; but some day I shall have them again. I never forget you a moment; but oh, oh, oh! That's all I can say. There are not words enough to express all the rest. Don't forget me; but love me just the same. A thousand kisses to all you children left in the old shoe, and another thousand to Granny.

"Your own dear

CHARLIE."

Hal's eyes were full of tears. To tell the truth, they had a good crying-time before any of them could speak a word.

"Dear, brave Charlie! She and Joe are alike. Granny, I don't know but they are the children to be proud of, after all."

"Where is she?" asked Granny, wiping her nose violently.

"Why, there isn't a bit of—address—to it; and the post-mark—begins with an N—but all the rest is blurred. She means to wait until she comes home, and tell us the whole story; and she will not give us an opportunity to write, for fear we will ask some questions. She means to keep up her running away."

They were all delighted, and had to read the letter over and over again.

"She must be in New York somewhere, and studying drawing. I've a great mind to write at a venture."

"And she will come home," crooned Granny softly.

"I'm glad she thinks us all so happy and prosperous," said Hal.

I shall have to tell you how it fared with Charlie and not keep you waiting until they heard the story.

She had indeed followed out her old plan. Child as she was, when she went to work in the mill she crowded all her wild dreams down in the depths of her heart. No one ever knew what heroic sacrifices Charlie Kenneth made. She was fond of dress, and just of an age when a bright ribbon, a pretty hat, and a dozen other dainty trifles, seem to add so much to one's happiness.

But she resolutely eschewed them all. Week by week her little hoard gained slowly, every day bringing her nearer the hour of freedom. She planned, too, more practically than any one would have supposed. And one evening she smuggled a black travelling-bag into the house, hiding it in a rubbish-closet until she could pack it.

She seized her opportunity at noon, to get it out unobserved; and, putting it in an out-of-the-way corner, dragged some pea-brush over it, that gave it the look of a pile of rubbish. Then she dressed herself, and said her good-bys gayly, but with a trembling heart, and went off to take her holiday.

Charlie tugged her bag to the depot, and bought a ticket for Newbury. Then she seated herself in great state, and really began to enjoy the adventure. She wondered how people could spend all their lives in a little humdrum place like Madison.

At Newbury she bought a ticket for New York. Then she sat thinking what she should do. A family by the name of Wilcox had left Madison two years before, and gone to New York. The mother was a clever, ignorant, good-hearted sort of woman, of whom Charlie Kenneth had been rather fond in her childish days. Mary Jane, the daughter, had paid a flying visit to Madison that spring, and Charlie had heard her describe the route to her house in Fourteenth Street. This was where she purposed to go.

The cars stopped. The passengers left in a crowd, Charlie following. If they were going to New York, she would not get lost. So the ferry was crossed in safety. Then she asked a policeman to direct her to City Hall. A little ragged urchin pestered her about carrying her bag, but it was too precious to be trusted to strangers.

She saw the Third-avenue cars; but how was she to get to them? The street seemed blocked up continually. By and by a policeman piloted her across, and saw her safely deposited in the car.

Charlie paid her fare, and told the conductor to stop at Fourteenth Street; but, after riding a while, she began to look out for herself. What an endless way it was! and where *did* all the people come from? Could it be possible that there were houses enough for them to live in? Ah! here was her corner.

She turned easterly, watching for the number. There was Mrs. Wilcox's frowsy head at the front basement window; and Charlie felt almost afraid to ring at the front-door, so she tried that lowly entrance.

"Come in," said a voice in response to her knock.

It was evident she had grown out of Mrs. Wilcox's remembrance, so she rather awkwardly introduced herself.

"Charlie Kenneth! The land sakes! How you have growed! Why, I'm right glad to see you. How is Granny and all the children, and all the folks at Madison?"

Charlie "lumped" them, and answered, "Pretty well."

"Did you come down all alone? And how did you find us? Mary Jane'll be powerful glad to see you. Ain't you most tired to death luggin' that heavy bag? Do take off your things, and get rested."

Charlie complied. Mrs. Wilcox went on with her endless string of questions, even after she rose to set the supper-table.

"And so Florence is married. Strange you've never heard about her. She's so rich and grand that I s'pose she don't want to remember poor relations. And Hal's been a teachin' school! Why, you're quite gettin' up in the world."

Mary Jane soon made her appearance. A flirting, flippant girl of sixteen, rather good-looking, and trimmed up with ribbons and cheap furbelows. She appeared glad to see Charlie, and all the questions were asked over again. Then Mr. Wilcox came in, washed his hands and face, and they sat down to supper. Before they were half through, Tom and Ed came tumbling in, full of fun and nonsense.

"Boys, be still!" said their father; which admonition they heeded for about the space of ten seconds.

Mary Jane rose from the table as soon as she had finished her supper.

"Charlie'll sleep with me, of course," she said. "Bring your bag and your things up stairs, Charlie."

Charlie followed her to the third story,—a very fair-sized room, but with an appearance of general untidiness visible everywhere.

"You can hang up your clothes in that closet," indicating it with her head. "Did you go to work in the mill, Charlie?"

"Yes."

"Didn't you like it?"

"Not very much," slowly shaking out her clean calico dress.

"I shouldn't, either. What did you earn?"

"Sometimes four dollars and a half."

"I earn six, week in and week out. Then I do a little overwork every day, which gives me Saturday afternoon. Charlie, why don't you stay?"

Mary Jane was taking down her hair, and turned round suddenly.

"I thought I would;" and Charlie blushed. "I've saved up a little money, enough to pay my board for a few weeks, until I can find something to do."

"Flower-making is first-rate. Some of the girls earn ten dollars a week. I've only been at it a year, you see. They pay a dollar a week while you're learning. Shall I try to get you in?"

"I don't know yet," was the hesitating answer.

"What makes you wear your hair short, Charlie?"

"Why—I like it so. It's no trouble."

"But it's so childish!"

Mary Jane was arranging a wonderful waterfall. On the top of this she hung a cluster of curls, and on the top of her head she tied in a bunch of frizettes with a scarlet ribbon.

"Now, that's what I call stylish;" and she turned round to Charlie. "If I was you, I'd let my hair grow; and, as soon as it is long enough to tie in a little knot, you can buy a waterfall."

Charlie was quite bewildered with these manifold adornments.

Then Mary Jane put on a white dress, a red carved ivory pin and ear-rings, and presented quite a gorgeous appearance.

"Charlie, I've been thinking—why can't you board here? I pay mother two dollars a week, and you could just as well have part of my room. Mother wanted me to let the boys have it, because there were two of them; but I wanted plenty of room. Yes: it would be real nice to have you here. I'll ask mother. I know you can find something to do."

A great load seemed lifted from Charlie's heart.

Then they went down to the next floor. The boys had the hall bedroom, and the back room was used by the heads of the family. There were two large pantries between, and then a front parlor. Charlie was quite stunned; for the place appeared fully as gorgeous as Mary Jane. A cheap Brussels carpet in bright colors, the figure of which ran all over the floor; two immense vases on the mantle, where grotesque Chinese figures were disporting on a bright green ground; a rather shabby crimson plush rocker; and some quite impossible sunsets done in oil, with showy wide gilt frames. Mrs. Wilcox had purchased them at auction, and considered them a great bargain.

Then Mary Jane, with a great deal of giggling and blushing, confessed to Charlie that she had a beau. "A real nice young man," clerk in a dry-goods store, Walter Brown by name, and that he came almost every evening.

"You can't help liking him," was the positive assertion. "I wish you didn't have short hair, nor look so much like a little girl; for you are as tall as I am."

Which was very true; but Charlie felt herself quite a child, and very much startled at the idea of beaux.

Mary Jane took out some embroidery, and did not deign to revisit the kitchen. A trifle after eight Mr. Brown made his appearance, looking neat as a pink, and nearly as sweet with perfume. For the first time in her life, Charlie was painfully bashful. When he proposed a walk to an ice-cream saloon, she would fain have remained at home; but Mary Jane over-ruled.

The walk was quite pleasant, and the cream a positive treat. Charlie said some very bright things, which Mr. Brown appeared to consider exceedingly funny. Then they rambled around a while; and when they returned, Mary Jane lingered at the hall-door to have a little private talk, while Charlie ran up stairs. Mrs. Wilcox sat in the parlor fanning herself, and eagerly questioned the child as to where they had been, and how she liked New York.

Tired and excited, Charlie went to bed at last; but she could not sleep. The strange place, the tinkle of the car-bells, the noises in the streets, and, most of all, her own thoughts, kept her wakeful. She could hardly believe that she had achieved her great ambition, and actually run away. On the whole, it was rather comical.

Had they found her letter yet? What did Hal and Granny think? Would they be very much worried?

And if she only *could* find out something about pictures, and begin to work in good earnest at the right thing. It was as much to her as the flowers were to dear Hal. God bless and keep them all!

CHAPTER XVI.

ALMOST DISCOURAGED.

Charlie was really tired on Friday, and did not feel equal to making any effort; so she assisted Mrs. Wilcox with the housework, and tidied up Mary Jane's room until one would hardly have known it. But every thing seemed so strange and new.

Late in the afternoon she gained courage to say,—

"Did Mary Jane tell you, Mrs. Wilcox, that—I'd like to stay?"

"Yes. And so you *really* came to York to get something to do! I s'pose there's such a host of you at home!"

Charlie swallowed over a lump in her throat. Perhaps she was not a little glad that Mrs. Wilcox did not suspect her unorthodox manner of leaving Madison.

"I mean to find something to do. And if you would board me"—

"Now, Charlie Kenneth! first you stay and make a visit, and see what you can find, before you talk of payin' board. Thank Heaven! I never begrudged any one a meal's vittles or a night's sleep. Your poor old grandmother's slaved herself half to death for you, and I'm glad to see you have some spunk."

"Then, you'll let me stay?" and a soft flush of relief stole over Charlie's face.

"Stay!" rather indignantly. "No one ever heard of Hannah Wilcox turnin' people out o' doors. Your Granny has done more than one good turn for me."

"But I've saved some money to pay my board"—

"I won't take a cent of it till you get to work, there, now! Jest you never fret yourself a word. It'll all come right, I know."

"I'm very much obliged," said Charlie, feeling as if she would like to cry.

"Mary Jane spoke of a chance of getting you at the flowers. It's light, easy work,—I tell her jest like play. But you must have a visit first."

On Saturday Mary Jane came home at noon.

"I do think Charlie Kenneth's earned a holiday," said Mrs. Wilcox. "I couldn't begin to tell the things that girl's done this mornin'. Swept and dusted, and helped me clean the closet"—

"Then you're in clover, mother;" and Mary Jane laughed. "I never could bear to do housework."

"A great kind of a wife you'll make."

"That will be some one else's look out;" and Mary Jane tossed her head in a curiously satisfied manner.

They took a promenade on Broadway in the afternoon. Charlie was delighted; and the shop-windows entertained her beyond description. They bought some trifles,—a pair of gloves, a collar, and a ribbon or two,—and Charlie found that money absolutely melted away. She had spent four dollars.

She summoned courage to question Mary Jane a little, but found her exceedingly ignorant on the great topic that absorbed her.

"I believe girls do color photographs in some places, but then you'd have to know a good deal to get a situation like that. I guess only rich girls have a chance to learn drawing and painting."

"But when it comes natural," said Charlie slowly.

"Well, I'll ask *him*;" and Mary Jane smiled, and nodded her head. "*He* knows most every thing."

"Are you going to marry him?" Charlie asked innocently, understanding the pronoun.

"Oh, I don't know!" with a toss of the head. "I mean to have some fun first. Some girls have lots of beaux."

Charlie colored. She had not the judgment or the experience to assist her in any sort of analysis; but she *felt* that these Wilcoxes were very different from their household. They had always been poor, lived in an old tumble-down cottage, with a bed in the parlor; were a noisy, frolicksome, romping set; given to slang, Flossy's great abhorrence; and yet—there was a clean, pure element in them all,—a kind of unconscious refinement. Florence's fine-ladyisms had not been entirely useless or wasted.

Refinement was the idea floating so dimly through Charlie's brain. In after years she understood the force of Hal's example, and the many traits Joe had laughed at as being girlish. But now she could only feel that there was a great gulf between her and Mary Jane; that the latter could *not* enter into her hopes and ambitions.

However, Charlie's drawings were brought to Mr. Brown for inspection.

160

"Why, you're a regular genius!" he exclaimed in surprise.

Charlie colored with delight, and every nerve seemed to expand with precious hope.

"It is a great pity that you are not a man."

"Why?" and Charlie opened her large eyes wonderingly.

"Because then you could do something with your talent. All these comic pictures in papers are designed by men; and they sometimes travel about, writing descriptions of places, and drawing little sketches to go with them. It is capital business."

"That is what I should like;" and Charlie's face glowed.

"But girls and women never do it. It's altogether out of their sphere. You see, that is one of the disadvantages."

Mr. Brown uttered this dogmatically.

"But if they know how, and can do it"—

"They couldn't travel about alone, running into dangers of all kinds. And it is just here. Now, some of these sketches are as good as you see in the papers; but no one would think of buying them of a woman, because it is men's work."

Charlie winked the tears out of her eyes. The argument was crushing, for she could not refute the lameness of the logic; and she had always felt sore about being a girl.

"They teach women to draw and paint down here at Cooper Institute," he said presently.

"But I suppose it costs a good deal?" and Charlie sighed.

"Yes."

"These things are for rich people," said Mary Jane with an air of authority.

Charlie could not summon heart to question further: besides, she had some ideas in her brain. Maybe she *might* sell her pictures to some newspaper. Any how, she would try.

She began the week with this determination. On Monday she dressed herself carefully, and gave her face a rather rigorous inspection. It *did* look very little-girlish. And somehow she wished her hair wasn't short, and that she could be handsome. Who ever heard of such dark eyes and light hair, such a peculiar tint too,—a kind of Quaker-drab; not golden nor auburn nor chestnut. Well, she was as she grew, and she couldn't help any of it.

By dint of inquiring now and then, she found her way about pretty well. Her first essay was in the office of an illustrated paper.

The man listened to her story with a peculiar sharp business air, and merely said,—

"No: we don't want any thing of the kind."

Charlie felt that she could not say another word, and walked out.

She stood a long while looking in the window of a print-shop, and at last ventured again.

This person was less brusque.

"My little girl," he said, "we never do any thing with such matters. We buy our pictures, printed or painted, or engravings, as the case may be, from all parts of the world. Many of them are copies from different artists well known to fame. It costs a great deal for the plate of a picture."

Which explanation was quite unintelligible to Charlie.

She rambled on until she came to a bookstore. There being only a boy within, she entered.

"Do you ever buy any pictures for books?" she asked.

"Books allus have pictures in 'em," was the oracular reply.

"But who makes them?"

"Why, engravers, of course;" with supreme astonishment at her ignorance.

"And they—do the thinking,—plan the picture, I mean?"

"What?" asked the boy, as if Charlie had spoken Greek.

"Some one must have the idea first."

He could not controvert it, and stared about helplessly.

"Are there any lady engravers?"

"No, I guess not;" scratching his head.

"And who makes these little pictures of children like this girl teaching the dog to read, and this one with the flowers?"

"Oh, I know what you want!" exclaimed the boy. "We gets 'em down in Ann Street. There's some girls working in the place. Do you know where Ann Street is?"

Some of Charlie's old humor cropped out.

"No, nor Polly Street, nor Jemima Street."

The boy studied her sharply, but preserved a sullen silence, strongly suspecting that he was being laughed at.

"Will you please tell me?" quite meekly. "And—the man's name."

The boy found a card, and directed her. Charlie trudged on with a light heart.

The place was up two flights of very dirty steps. Mr. Balcour had gone out to dinner, and she was rather glad of an excuse to rest. In the adjoining room there were three girls laughing and chatting. Now, if she could come here to work!

When Mr. Balcour entered, Charlie found him a very pleasant-looking man. She made known her errand with but little hesitation.

"It is something of a mistake," was the smiling answer. "My business is coloring prints, flower-pieces, and all that. Sometimes they are sent to me, but these little things I buy by the hundred or thousand, and color them; then picture-dealers, Sunday-schools, &c., come in here to purchase."

With that he displayed cases of birds, flowers, fancy scenes, and tiny landscapes.

"Oh, how beautiful they are!" and she glanced them over with delight. "I should like to do them!"

"Do you know any thing about water-coloring?"

"No;" rather hesitatingly, for she was not at all certain as to the precise nature of water-coloring.

"I keep several young ladies at work. It requires taste, practice, and a certain degree of genius, artistic ability."

"I meant the first thought of the picture," said Charlie, blushing. "Some one must know how it is to be made."

"Yes, certainly."

"If you would look at these"—

She opened her parcel, and spread them before him.

"Did you do them?"

He asked the question in astonishment.

"Yes," was Charlie's simple reply.

He studied her critically, which made her warm color come and go, and she interlaced her fingers nervously.

"My child, this first thought, as you call it, is designing. You have a very remarkable genius, I should say. How old are you?"

"Fifteen."

"You have had some instruction!"

Charlie concluded it would be wiser to say that she had, for there was the drawing-book and Hal.

"You wish to do this for a living?" he asked kindly.

"Oh, if I could! I like it so much!" and there was a world of entreaty in Charlie's tone.

Mr. Balcour had to laugh over some of the drawings, for the faces were so spirited and expressive.

"I will tell you the very best thing for you to do. Enter the School of Design for women. The arrangements, I believe, are very good; that is, there is a chance to earn something while you are studying."

"Oh!"

Charlie's face was fairly transfigured. Mr. Balcour thought her a wonderfully pretty girl.

"It is at Cooper Institute, Third Avenue and Seventh or Eighth Street. I really do not know any thing about it, except that it does profess to assist young students in art."

"I am so much obliged to you;" and Charlie gave him a sweet, grateful smile.

"I should like to hear a little about you!" he said; "and I hope you will succeed. Come in some time and let me know. Do you live in the city?"

"No; but I am staying with some friends on Fourteenth Street."

"Not far from Cooper Institute, then."

"No, I can easily find it."

They said good-by; and Charlie threaded her way up to City Hall with a heart as light as thistle-down, quite forgetting that she had missed her dinner. Then, by car, she went up to Cooper Institute.

And now what was she to do? I told you that Charlie had a great deal of courage and perseverance. And then she was so earnest in this quest! She inquired in a china-store, and was directed up stairs.

It was very odd indeed. First she stumbled into a reading-room, and was guided from thence to the art-gallery by a boy. The pictures amused and interested her for quite a while. One lady and two gentlemen were making copies.

By and by she summoned courage to ask the lady which was the school, or study-room.

"School of Design?"

"Yes," timidly.

"It is closed."

Charlie's countenance fell.

"When will it be open?"

"About the first of October."

The child gave a great sigh of disappointment.

"Were you thinking of entering?"

"I wanted to see—if I could."

"Have you painted any?"

"No: but I have been drawing a little."

"You are rather young, I think."

Then the lady went on with her work. Charlie turned away with tears in her eyes. A whole month to wait!

Mrs. Wilcox plied her with questions on her return, but Charlie was not communicative.

After a night's rest she felt quite courageous again. She would see what could be done about engraving.

Poor Charlie! There were no bright spots in this day. Everybody seemed cross and in a hurry. One man said coarsely,—

"You needn't tell me you did them things by yourself. You took 'em from some picturs."

So she came home tired and dispirited. Mary Jane had a crowd of gay company in the evening, and Charlie slipped off to bed. Oh, if she could only give Dot a good hug, and kiss Hal's pale face, and hear Granny's cracked voice! Even the horrible tuning of Kit's fiddle would sound sweet. But to be here,—among strangers,—and not be able to make her plans work.

Charlie turned her face over on the pillow, and had a good cry. After all, there never could be anybody in this world half so sweet as "The old woman who lived in a shoe!"

On Wednesday it rained. Charlie was positively glad to have a good excuse for staying within doors. She helped Mrs. Wilcox with her sewing, and told her every thing she could remember about the people at Madison.

"How strange it must look,—and a railroad through the middle of it! There wa'n't no mills in my time, either. And rows of houses, Mary Jane said. She'd never 'a' known the place if it hadn't been for the folks. Dear, dear!"

Mary Jane came home in high feather that night.

"I found they were taking on some girls to-day, Charlie; and I spoke a good word for you. You can come next Monday. I don't believe you'll make out much with the pictures."

"You were very good;" but Charlie's lip quivered a little.

"It will be ever so nice to have company up and down! and you'll like it, I'm sure."

Mary Jane, being of a particularly discursive nature, was delighted to have a constant listener.

"Well, that was better than nothing," Charlie thought. She might work a while, and perhaps learn something more definite about the School of Design.

"For I'll never give it up, never!" and Charlie set her resolute red lips together, while her eyes glanced into the future.

The following morning was so lovely, that she felt as if she must have a walk. She put on her white dress and sacque, and looked as fresh as a rose. She would go over on Broadway, where every thing was clean and lovely, and have a delightful time looking at the shop-windows and the beautiful ladies.

It was foolish to take her pictures along, and yet she did it. They really appeared a part of her life. On and on she sauntered, enjoying every thing with the keenest relish. The mellow sun, the refreshing air that had in it a crisp flavor, the cloudless sky overhead, and the bright faces around, made her almost dance with gladness.

She stood for a long while viewing some chromos in a window,—two or three of children, which were very piquant and amusing, and appealed to her love of fun. Obeying her impulse she entered, and stole timidly around. Two gentlemen were talking, and one of the faces pleased her exceedingly. A large, fair, fresh-complexioned man, with curly brown hair, and a patriarchal beard, snowy white, though he did not appear old.

A young fellow came to her presently, and asked if there was any thing he could show her.

"I should like to see the gentleman—when he is—disengaged."

That speech would have done credit to Florence.

The youth carried the message, and the proprietor glanced around. Not the one with the beautiful beard, and Charlie felt rather disappointed.

They talked a while longer, then he came forward.

"You wished to see me?"

Charlie turned scarlet to the tips of her fingers, and stammered something in an absurdly incoherent fashion.

"Oh! you did not interrupt me—particularly," and he smiled kindly. "What can I do for you?"

"Will you tell me—who made the first design—for—those pictures in the window,—the children, I mean?"

"Different artists. Two, I think, are by ladies."

"And how did they get to do it? I mean, after they made the sketch, who painted it?"

"Those are from the original paintings. The artist had the thought, and embodied it in a sketch."

"But suppose no one wanted to buy it?"

"That *has* happened;" and he smiled again. "Why? Have you been trying your hand at pictures?"

"Yes," answered Charlie in great doubt and perplexity. "Only mine are done in pencil. If you would look at them."

Charlie's eyes were so beseeching, that he could not resist.

She opened her small portfolio,—Hal's handiwork. The gentleman glanced over two or three.

"Did you do these yourself?"

"Yes;" and Charlie wondered that she should be asked the question so frequently.

"Who taught you?"

"My brother, a little; but I think it comes natural," said Charlie in her earnestness, knowing no reason why she should not tell the truth.

"Darol, here is a genius for you!" he exclaimed, going back to his friend.

Charlie watched them with throbbing heart and bated breath. She was growing very sensitive.

"That child!" "Come here, little girl, will you?" said Mr. Darol, beckoning her towards them.

"Who put the faces in these?"

"I did;" and the downcast lids trembled perceptibly.

"How long have you been studying?"

"Oh! I could always do that," answered Charlie. "I used to in school. And some of them are just what did happen."

"This,—Mr. Kettleman's troubles?" and he scrutinized her earnestly.

"There was a man working in the mill whose name was Kettleman, and he always carried a dinner-kettle. But I thought up the adventures myself."

Charlie uttered this very modestly, and yet in a quiet, straightforward manner, that bore the impress of sincerity.

The first picture was Mr. Kettleman purchasing his kettle. A scene in a tin-shop; the seller a round, jolly fellow, about the shape of a beer-cask; and Mr. Kettleman tall and thin, with a long nose, long fingers, and long legs. He was saying, "Will it hold enough?" The faces *were* capital.

In the second Mrs. Kettleman was putting up her husband's dinner. There were piles and piles of goodies; and his cadaverous face was bent over the mass, the lips slightly parted, the nose longer than ever, and asking solemnly, "Can you get it all in, Becky?"

The third showed a group of laughing men round a small table, which was spread with different articles. One fellow held the pail up-side-down, saying, "The last crumb." The head of Mr. Kettleman was just in sight, ascending the stairs.

Lastly the kettle tied to a dog's tail. Mr. Kettleman in the distance, taller, thinner, and exceedingly woebegone, watching his beloved but unfortunate kettle as it thumped over the stones.

There were many irregularities and defects, but the faces were remarkable for expression. Mr. Darol laughed heartily.

"How old are you?" asked Mr. Wentworth, glancing curiously at the slender slip of a girl.

"Fifteen."

"You don't look that."

"You have a wonderful gift," said Mr. Darol thoughtfully.

"Oh, that is real!" exclaimed Charlie eagerly, as they turned to another. "My brother was in a store once, and sold some pepper for allspice. The woman put it in her pie."

"So I should judge from her husband's face;" and they both laughed again, and praised Charlie to her heart's content.

By degrees Mr. Darol drew Charlie's history from her. She did not conceal her poverty nor her ambition; and her love for her one talent spoke eloquently in every line of her face.

"My child, you have a remarkable genius for designing. The school at Cooper Institute will be just the place for you. Wentworth, I think I shall take her over to Miss Charteris. What is your name, little one?"

"Charlie Kenneth."

"Charlie?" in amaze.

"It was Charlotte, but I've always been called Charlie."

"Just the name for you! Miss Charlie, you have a world of energy and spirit. I know you will succeed. And now it would give me great pleasure to take you to the studio of an artist friend."

The tears came into Charlie's eyes: she couldn't help it, though she tried to smile.

"Oh!" with a tremulous sob, "it's just like a dream. And you are so good! I'd go with one meal a day if I could only draw pictures!"

And Charlie was lovely again, with her face full of smiles, tears, and blushes. Earnest, piquant, and irregular, she was like a picture herself.

It seemed to Charlie that in five minutes they reached Miss Charteris's studio; and she stood in awe and trembling, scarcely daring to breathe. For up to this date she had hardly been able to believe that any woman in the world besides Rosa Bonheur had actually painted pictures.

"I have brought you a new study, Miss Charteris. A romance and a small young woman."

"Well, Paul Darol! I don't believe there is your equal in the world for picking up the lame and the halt and the blind, and the waifs and strays. What now?" and Miss Charteris laughed with such a musical ripple that Charlie turned and answered her with a smile.

"First look at these, and then let me tell you a story."

"Very fair and vigorous sketches;" and Miss Charteris glanced curiously at Charlie.

Then Mr. Darol began with the story, telling his part first, and calling in Charlie to add sundry helps to the other.

"And so, you see, I ventured to try your good temper once more, and bring her to you."

"What shall I do,—paint her? She might sit for a gypsy girl now, but in ten years she will be a handsome woman. What an odd, trustful child! This promises better than some of your discoveries."

"Well, help me to get her into the School of Design, and make a successful genius of her. She is too plucky for any one to refuse her a helping hand."

Miss Charteris began to question Charlie. She had a vein of drollery in her own nature; and in half an hour Charlie was laughing and talking as if she had known her all her lifetime. What pleased Mr. Darol most was her honesty and unflinching truth. She told of their poverty and struggles, of the love and the fun they had shared together; but there was a little tremor in her voice as she said, "We had one sister who was adopted by a rich lady."

The matter was soon settled, being in the right hands. Charlie was registered as a pupil at the school; and Miss Charteris taught her to re-touch photographs, and found her an opportunity to do a little work. It was something of a hardship to go on boarding with Mrs. Wilcox; but they were so fond of her, and so proud of what they could not understand!

So you do not wonder, I fancy, that Charlie's letter should be such a jubilate. Ah, if she could only earn a little money to take back with her!

She saw Miss Charteris and Mr. Darol quite often. He was like a father, but sweeter and dearer than any one's father she had ever known. When she went home, she meant to coax Hal to return with her, just for the pleasure of meeting such splendid people; "for he is the best of all of us," she used to say to Miss Charteris.

Ah, Charlie, if you dreamed of what was happening in the Old Shoe!

CHAPTER XVII.

LOST AT SEA.

The autumn was unusually warm and pleasant, without any frost to injure the flowers until the middle of October. Hal enlarged his green-house arrangements, and had a fine stock of tuberoses. He had learned a good deal by his experiments of the past year.

He had been careful not to overwork; since he was improving, and took every thing moderately. But at last it was all finished,—the cold frames arranged for spring, the plants housed, the place tidy and in order.

The loss of the school had been a severe disappointment to Hal. He was casting about now for some employment whereby he might earn a little. If Mr. Sherman would only give him a few days' work, now and then, they could get along nicely; for Granny was a most economical manager, and, besides, there was eighty dollars in the bank, and a very small family,—only three of them.

Hal came home one day, and found Granny sitting over a handful of fire, bundled in a great shawl. Her eyes had a frightened look, and there was a blue line about her mouth.

"Why. Granny dear, what is the matter?" he asked in alarm, stooping over to kiss the cold wrinkled cheek.

"I d-d-don't know," the teeth chattering in the attempt to speak. "I b-b-lieve I've got a chill!"

"Oh, so you have, poor dear child!" and Hal was as motherly as the old gray hen outside. "You must go to bed at once. Perhaps you had better bathe your feet, and have a bowl of hot tea."

"And my head aches so! I'm not used to having headache, Hal."

She said this piteously, as if she fancied Hal, who could do every thing in her opinion, might exorcise the pain.

"I'm very sorry, dear," stroking the wrinkled face as if she had been a baby. "Now I'll put some water on to heat."

"O Hal, I'm so cold! 'Pears to me I never shall be warm again."

"Yes, when I get you snug in the bed, and make you some nice tea. What shall it be,—pennyroyal?"

"And a little feverfew."

Hal kissed the cold, trembling lips, and went about his preparations. The water was soon hot; and he put a little mustard in the pail with it, carrying it to the bedside in the other room, and leading poor Granny thither.

The place was steaming presently with the fragrance of pennyroyal. Hal poured it off into a cool bowl, and gave Granny a good drink, then tucked her in the bed, and spread the shawl over her; but still she cried in her pitiful voice,—

"I'm so cold, Hal!"

After the rigor of the chill began to abate, a raging fever set in, and Granny's mind wandered a little. Then Hal was rather alarmed. Granny had never been down sick a day in her life, although she was not so very robust.

"Dot, darling, you must run for Dr. Meade," Hal said, as the child came home from school. "Granny is very ill, I am afraid."

Dr. Meade was away, and did not come until eight in the evening.

"I fear it is going to be a run of fever, Hal," he began gravely. "At her time of life too! But we'll do the best we can. There is considerable fever about."

Hal drew a long breath of pain.

"You will be the best nurse in the world, Hal;" and the doctor smiled, placing his hand on the boy's shoulder re-assuringly.

Hal winked away some tears. They lay quite too close to the surface for a man's nature.

"I'll leave her some drops, and be in again in the morning. Don't worry, my dear boy."

Granny could hardly bear to have Hal out of sight, and wanted to keep hold of his hand all the time. Dot prepared the supper, but they could taste nothing beyond a cup of tea.

"Dot," he said, "you must go up stairs and sleep in my bed to-night. I shall stay here to watch Granny."

"But it will be so—lonesome!" with her baby entreaty.

"It is best, my darling."

So Dot kissed him many times, lingering until after the clock struck ten, when Hal said,—

"My birdie's eyes will be heavy to-morrow."

Granny was worse the next day. Indeed, for the ensuing fortnight her life seemed vibrating in the balance. Everybody was very kind, but she could bear no one besides Hal. Just a little delirious occasionally, and going back to the time when they were all babies, and her own dear Joe lay dying.

"I've done my best for 'em, Joe," she would murmur. "I've never minded heat nor cold, nor hard work. They've been a great blessing,—they always were good children."

For Granny forgot all Charlie's badness, Joe's mischief, and Dot's crossness. Transfigured by her devotion, they were without a fault. Ah, how one tender love makes beautiful the world! Whatever others might think, God had a crown of gold up in heaven, waiting for the poor tired brow; and the one angel would have flown through starry skies for her, taking her to rest on his bosom, but the other pleaded,—

"A little longer, for the children's sake."

At last the fever was conquered. Granny was weak as a baby, and had grown fearfully thin; but it was a comfort to have her in her right mind. Still Hal remarked that the doctor's face had an anxious look, and that he watched him with a kind of pitying air. So much so, that one day he said,—

"You think she *will* get well, doctor?"

"There is nothing to prevent it if we can only keep up her appetite."

"I always feed her," returned Hal with a smile, "whether she is willing to eat or not."

"You are a born nurse, as good as a woman. Give her a little of the port wine every day."

Then the doctor turned to the window, and seemed to glance over towards the woods.

"Quite winterish, isn't it? When have you heard from Joe?"

"Not in a long time. Letters do not come so regularly as they used. I think we have not had one since August. But he writes whenever he can, dear Joe. The last time we received three."

"Yes," in a kind of absent way.

When Dr. Meade started to go, he kept his hand for several minutes on the door-latch, giving some unimportant directions.

"God bless you, Hal!" he said in a strained, husky tone, "and give you grace to bear all the trials of this life. Heaven knows, there are enough of them!"

What did the doctor mean? Hal wondered eagerly.

That evening Mr. and Mrs. Terry dropped in for a friendly call.

"When did you hear from Joe last?" asked Mr. Terry.

"In August."

"Wasn't expecting him home, I suppose?"

"Not until next summer. Has any one heard?" and there was a quiver in Hal's voice.

"I don't know of any one who has had a letter;" and Mr. Terry appeared to be measuring his words. "Joe was a nice bright lad, just as full of fun as an egg is full of meat. Cousin Burton took a wonderful fancy to him; though I suppose he'd have gone off to sea, any way. If it had not been Burton, it would have been some one else."

"Yes. Joe always had his heart set upon it."

"Father and Joe used to get along so nicely. We never had a boy we liked better. He was a brave, honest fellow."

It seemed almost as if Mrs. Terry wiped a tear from her eye. But Granny wanted to be raised in the bed, and some way Hal couldn't think until after they were gone.

He was thankful to see the doctor come in the next morning.

"Oh!" he exclaimed in a low tone, "you were talking of Joe yesterday: has anybody heard from him, or about him?"

The hand that clasped the doctor's arm trembled violently.

"Hal, be calm," entreated the doctor.

"I cannot! Oh, you *do* know,—and it's bad news!"

"My dear boy—O Hal!" and he was folded in the doctor's arms.

"Tell me, tell me!" in a yearning, impatient tone, that seemed to crowd its way over sobs.

"God knows it could not have hurt me more if it had been one of my own! But he was a hero—to the last. There isn't a braver young soul up in heaven, I'll answer for that. Here—it's in the paper. I've carried it about with me three days, old coward that I've been, and not dared to tell you. But it's all over the village. Hush,—for Granny's sake. She must not know."

Hal dropped on the lounge that he and Granny had manufactured with so much pride. He was stunned,—dead to every thing but pain, and that was torturing. The doctor placed the paper in his hands, and went into the other room to his patient.

Yes, there it was! The words blurred before his eyes; and still he read, by some kind of intuition. "The Argemone" had met with a terrific storm in the Indian Ocean; and, though she had battled bravely, winds and waves had proved too strong. All one night the men had labored heroically, but in vain; and when she began to go down, just at dawn, the life-boats were filled, too few, alas! even if there were safety in them. Nothing could exceed the bravery and coolness of the young second mate. The captain lay sick below; the first mate and the engineer were panic-stricken; but this strong, earnest voice had inspired every one through the fearful night. When it was found that some must be left behind, he decided to stay, and assisted the others with a courage and presence of mind that was beyond all praise. The smile that illuminated his face when he refused to step into the already overladen boat was like the smile of an angel. They who saw it in the light of the gray dawn would never forget. One boat drifted in to Sumatra, the other was picked up by a passing vessel. But the few who remained must have perished in any case, and among them no name so deserving of honor as that of Joseph Kenneth.

Hal read it again and again. Joseph Kenneth! Was that dear, laughing Joe, with his merry eyes, and the sauciest trick of winking in the corner of one; little Joe who had stood on his head, played circus, and, with the aid of a few old shawls, been lion, tiger, elephant, and camel; dear Joe, who had cuddled up in bed cold winter nights and almost smothered him,—Hal; who had made ghosts out of the bolster, and frightened Kit half to death! Why did he think of these foolish things now? Oh, this brave Joseph Kenneth never could be their little Joe! God surely would not give Granny this pain and anguish to bear at the last!

A hand was laid on Hal's shoulder.

"Oh! it can't be true"—

"There's just one chance out of a thousand. Hal, it seems to me the saddest thing I ever heard, and yet so grand. You see what the passengers said of him. Ah, I think he did not need to knock long at St. Peter's gate!"

The doctor wiped his eyes.

"But—never to have him—come back"—

"He has drifted into a better port, my dear boy: that must be our comfort. We shall all cross the river by and by; and it is never so hard for the one who goes, as for those who stay and bear the pain and loneliness. And some time it will be sweet to remember that he gave his brave young life for others."

Hal's eyes were tearless, and there was a hard, strained look in his face.

"Don't tell Granny now. She couldn't bear it."

"No;" and Hal's voice was full of pathetic grief.

"And oh, Hal, be comforted a little! I know there is an overwhelming anguish in it; but for the sake of those still left"—

"Yes." Hal's ashen lips quivered.

The doctor brushed away the soft hair tumbled about his forehead, and held the cold hand in his.

"God has some balm for every ache, my boy."

Hal sat there until Granny called for something, every moment growing more incredulous. But a heavy weight hung about his heart, even though he refused to believe. It seemed as if there could not be despairing certainty before to-morrow.

When Kit came home on Saturday night, and just threw his arms around Hal's neck, sobbing as if his heart had broken, it gave a strange reality to the grief and sorrow.

"I heard it on Monday,—the loss of 'The Argemone.' How proud Joe was of her! And my heart's been aching for you every day. The cruel thing of it all is, never to have him come home again."

Dot had to be taken into confidence then; but she was a discreet little thing, and quite to be trusted. She did not suffer so deeply, for Joe was only a pleasant dream to her; and she tried to comfort Hal with her sweet, winsome ways.

Granny *did* improve slowly. She began to sit up in the rocking-chair, walk to the window and look out, and occasionally smile, in her faint, wan fashion. They would never hear the merry chirruping laugh again, Hal thought.

But all the details of life had to be gone through with, as usual. There was the poultry to be prepared for market; for this source of their income could not be overlooked. In fact, Hal and Dot were not quite as economical managers as Granny; and then every thing was very high. They required more luxuries in sickness, and Hal would not stint. But, when this was gone, there would be the money for the flowers, and their little hoard in the bank still remained unbroken.

It was not any fear of want that troubled Hal. The old dreams and ambitions seemed to be slipping away. Sometimes even the idea of attaining to a green-house failed to charm; though he still loved his flowers passionately, and they comforted him as nothing else could have done.

One day Granny thought of Joe.

"Have we had a letter since my illness?" she asked.

"No," answered Hal faintly.

"Not since—let me see,—it was August."

Hal made no reply.

"Why—it's strange! He never did such a thing before! Hasn't any one heard?"

"I believe not." Hal turned his head, and went on with some writing.

"Seems to me you take it pretty easy," said Granny, a little vexed. "Joe never was the one to forget his home folks. Hal, something's happened: mark my words!"

Poor Hal brushed away a tear.

Then Granny gave Dot a mysterious confidence, and asked her to inquire of Mr. Terry.

"He always wrote to them, and they must know."

Dot said, in return, that they had not received a letter.

Granny then began to worry in desperate earnest, and besieged every visitor with questions and surmises. Hal was in a sore strait. Of course she must know sometime.

She made herself so nearly sick, that Dr. Meade saw the danger and harm, and felt that she had better know the truth.

"Will you tell her?" faltered Hal.

He undertook the sorrowful office. Tenderly, kindly, and yet it was a cruel wound.

"Oh, it cannot be!" she cried. "God wouldn't take him from me now that I'm old and sick and helpless! Let me see the paper."

They complied with her request, but the doctor had to read it. Her old eyes could not see a word.

"Oh, oh! Drowned in the sea! And I never wanted him to go! My poor darling! who was always so bright, so happy, and who loved his poor old Granny so well! Let me go back to bed now: I don't want to live. They're all up in heaven,—*my* Joe, and little Joe, and poor Dora. There is no use of staying here."

Hal soothed her with fondest love and caresses; but nothing could change the longing in her heart, the weary look in the eyes that seemed to be discerning the shore beyond, and the sad voice with its one refrain, "Poor, dear Joe!"

After that she failed rapidly. Hal scarcely left her. She used to ask him to read all the old letters over again, from the first boyish pride that so exulted in the trip to Albany. And she would recall some act of tenderness, or a gay prank at which they all had laughed.

One evening Hal felt unusually weary. There had been a warm rain for two days, with most un-December-like weather. A fire felt absolutely uncomfortable. He generally slept down on the lounge now, to be near if Granny wanted any thing. Before retiring he paid his flower-room a visit. Every thing was doing splendidly. So far business had not been very brisk; but that morning he had received an order for the next week,—Christmastide, —for all the flowers he could cut.

"Dear sweet children," he said, talking softly to himself. "If I could only have put some in *his* coffin, and on his grave! but to think of him lying in the sea, with the endless music over his head, and the shells tangled in his hair. O Joe! it doesn't seem a bit true, and I never can make it so."

Yet he knew in his heart that it was; and he tried to remember that Joe was up in heaven, past all pain and care, ready to welcome them as they came, one by one,—Granny first. It would be easier to give her up, because she was going to be with darling Joe.

He left the door against the hall open, it was so warm; then he took a last look at Granny, and dropped on his couch. It was a long while before he fell asleep, and then he slumbered soundly. Once he awoke with a shiver, and reached out for the blanket he had thrown off earlier in the night.

The light in the window roused him at length. How oddly it looked, and oh, how cold! Why, the panes were frosted with a thousand fairy devices! And then Hal sprang up, hurried into his clothes, and ran to the flower-room. The windows were white with frost, and the thick papers rolled to the top. Worst of all, the fire had gone out!

For a moment Hal stood in blank despair. His beautiful buds that were to be out in a few days, his tender, delicate plants! How had it happened? There must have been more ashes in the bottom of the stove than he thought; and the fire, being weak, had not kindled at all. He tore it out with eager hands. Not a spark remained. The stove was as cold as a stone.

But there was no time to waste in grief. Hal kindled his fire, and then began to drench his plants. Something might be saved.

Presently Dot's little feet pattered up the stairs.

"How we all slept!" she said. "And oh, dear! its as cold as Greenland, after the beautiful summer weather. But Hal, dear, what is the matter?"

"My fire went out."

"Will it hurt the plants?"

"Some of them;" and his voice had a great tremble in it.

"Oh, it is too bad, Hal! doesn't every thing seem to happen to us?" and tears sprang to the fond eyes.

Hal gave a long, pained sigh.

"Can't you save any of them?"

"Yes: some, I think. It might have been worse."

Dot kissed him tenderly,—it was all she could do. Then she ran down, and began to prepare breakfast.

The sun was rising; and Hal dropped the papers to keep it dark for the present, and allowed his fire to come on gradually. At first he began to take hope, for the flowers held up their heads crisply.

Alas! by noon they showed signs of drooping; and before night the buds of the tuberoses began to be slightly discolored. Poor Hal could have cried out of pure sorrow. He loved them all so dearly, and it almost seemed to him as if they suffered as well.

But the next day the ruin was plainly established. He went about with his scissors, clipping here and there. The heliotrope displayed a mass of blackened clusters; but it could be trimmed for new blossoming. Many of the more forward, choice rosebuds were ruined but the plants were not deeply injured. The bouvardias were quite spoiled; but the mignonette and alyssum were unharmed.

Hal cut a few the day before Christmas, and sent them over to Mr. Thomas. It was such a sore loss and disappointment, that it hung around him like a heavy burden. They had been counting on the money with so much pleasure.

"Never mind," exclaimed Dot cheerfully. "We will not have any extra Christmas. Granny will not be able to sit up, and there'll be no one home but Kit."

Hal brushed away a tear. To tell the truth, he felt miserably lonesome, and sick at heart. Every day the sense of loss grew upon him. He had given up hope for Granny; though she was no worse, and perhaps had improved a little in appetite. But then she did not care to get well. And the faces lost out of the home group made such a sad break.

They had received two more hopeful little notes from Charlie; but, if she was happy and prosperous, would she not be weaned away, like the one other. Joe, in his deep sea-grave, had always been tender and true.

"Christmas isn't much to us now," Hal answered, recalling the old gayety. "Yet it is too bad to put such black shadows in your life, my darling."

"The sun has never been so bright for me, you know," Dot said, in her sweet, soft voice, in which there was not a touch of complaint. "It seems as if the path had grown shady before I came to it, so I don't miss the gayety. And, while I can have you and Granny, I'll be quite satisfied."

"You are a comfort and a treasure. I'm so glad to have *you*, Dot, though you were a wee baby and always sick. Now and then a neighbor used to say, —'What a blessing it would be if that child should die!' But Granny never thought so."

Dot nestled closer.

The morning had been cloudy, and about ten o'clock it commenced snowing. They did their housework, and prepared their simple dinner.

"I had resolved to go to town to-day, and buy some Christmas," said Hal. "I believe we never were quite so blue before."

"I don't suppose Kit will be able to get home this evening," Dot said slowly.

"No."

"Then we'll keep it by ourselves, Hal. It will not be so very bad."

"But to have no little gifts,—and Granny sick in bed"—

"It will not be a merry Christmas for us, dear; but there may be something pleasant in it."

Hal sighed sorrowfully. Oh, for the sweet, lost childhood!

CHAPTER XVIII.

A SONG IN THE NIGHT.

It snowed steadily all day; and evening closed around them in the midst of this soft, noiseless storm. The roads were beginning to be blocked up, the houses were hooded in ermine, and no one passed by the windows. Not a soul had been in that day. So, after the lamp was lighted, they drew closer together. Hal read a while from a book of poems that Mrs. Howard had lent him.

"It is nearly bed-time," he said at length.

"I don't feel a bit sleepy."

"Hal," began Granny, stretching out her thin hand, "don't leave me. I feel so strange."

"Worse, my own dear?"

"Not in pain, but sort of restful, as if I'd come to something—no, I'm not afraid, Hal. I've been praying all along that I might die, and maybe it's coming. I'm a poor old body, not worth much,—and Joe's *there*, you know."

She gave her head a feeble nod. Hal swallowed over a great sob.

"When will it be Christmas?"

"To-morrow."

"Maybe I'll be up among the angels,—a poor, ignorant, foolish old body like me! It's wonderful to think of! But Joe'll be there, to take his dear Granny by the hand, and keep her from stumbling, and making mistakes, and doing all the things that would shame or vex any one. And Christ loved us all, you know. He died for us. I think I've understood it better since Joe stood there on the ship, refusing to get into the boat lest he might swamp it. He died for some one: not in *that* fashion, for he didn't have any sins to bear, and wasn't reviled and wounded; but still he gave his sweet life,—his dear life that was so much to me."

Dot crept up to the bed.

"After I'm gone you and Dot'll love each other. It will be sad for a little while, but God will remember you, and bring you comfort. I've cried to him a' many times, when it's been dark all round; and, when all other friends fail, you'll find him true and strong. I've done the best I could. It's been poor enough; but then I never had learnin' and all that to help me. I took you when you were all little chaps, motherless and fatherless, and I've tried to keep you together. But they've strayed off, Hal. There's only you and Dot to give Granny a last kiss."

Dot was sobbing on Granny's pillow.

"Don't, deary, don't," in her quivering, entreating voice. "We must all die some time. God knows when it's best. And I ain't of any use now, my work's all done. I'd like to see 'em all again, Hal,—dear little things; only I never can believe they are all men and women. And, if Flossy comes back, give her my love. She was so pretty, with her long golden curls! I don't wonder the grand lady liked her. And Charlie,—Charlie was such a good girl all last summer, working like a woman! Yes—if I could only see 'em once more!"

Hal wiped away his fast falling tears. It seemed too hard that Granny's unselfish life should not be crowned at the last. To die here, almost alone!

"You remember the old Christmas, Hal? The last time we were all together! Ah, how sweet it was! And the presents, and the old shoe full!"

Granny's voice sunk to a tremble of delight.

"It was so happy, so merry! All of 'em laughing and talking, and their bright pretty faces full of fun. But—maybe—I'll see 'em all in heaven. Don't cry, Dot."

Hal drew her to his breast, and soothed her with tender kisses. Then he sat down in the old rocker, and took her on his knee.

"There never was such a Christmas, never! I was so glad to have you all, so proud of you! And I've done my best"—

"Yes, Granny, God, who watches over all things, will bear witness to that. You were mother and father to us. And how you have toiled and worried and made sacrifices, how you have loved us, will all be written in the Great Book. I'm glad you are going to have a reward there."

"I shall see Joe."

Then she was quiet for a long while.

"I can't remember any thing about the Christmas," said Dot with much perplexity.

"Tell her, Hal. I'll listen; and it will seem all fresh again," pleaded Granny in a faint, far-off voice.

"You were such a weeny little thing, and couldn't talk plain; but then you had always been sick."

"And cross," Kit says.

"You did use to cry—sometimes; and then at others you were like a little lamb. All children cry occasionally."

Dot felt, somehow, as if she had not outgrown the trick yet; but the tears fell close to Hal's heart.

"But about the Christmas?"

"Oh, yes!"

Then Hal began. The preparations beforehand, the secrecy and plotting, the stockings stuffed to overflowing, and the wildest of merriment the next morning. It appeared to Dot that she could see it like a picture.

"And O Hal, that we should be so lonely now! Hasn't God let us slip out of his mind for a little while?"

"I think not, my darling."

"But how *can* you always believe? Why did God let Joe die, when we wanted him so much; and Flossy go away? And all the other things,—the sweet pretty flowers that were frozen?"

"My dear child, we cannot answer the questions. Trials always appear very hard to those who have them to bear; but maybe God gives us one to save us from some other that would be a great deal harder. And with it there is grace to endure."

"As when you were hurt. I wonder that you could be so patient, Hal!" and the little arms crept up around his neck.

"It was part my nature, you know. I used to be sorry at school, that I wasn't like the other boys; for, somehow, I never *was*: but, when God knew what I would have to bear, he made me patient, and almost girlish, loving to stay in the house, and all that. If I'd been like Joe, I should have fretted sorely when I found I should never be able to go to sea. He was so full of life and energy, you know, so ambitious, that it would almost have killed him. It was best to have it happen to me."

Dot sighed, her small brain being greatly puzzled.

"But I don't see why every one cannot be happy and prosperous. Isn't there enough to go round to all?"

"God knows best. And, when it troubles me sorely, I think of the little Christ-child, who was born eighteen hundred years ago, all goodness and sweetness and meekness, and of the trials he had to bear for our sakes. All the lowly life, the reviling, the unbelief, the persecution, the being homeless, and sometimes almost friendless, and at the last the shameful death. We shall never have all that, my darling; and so we ought to bear our lesser sorrows patiently."

Dot made no answer.

"My darling," said Hal, glancing at the clock, "ought you not to go to bed? It is almost midnight."

"And you?" reaching up to kiss the dear face.

"I am going to stay here by Granny."

Dot looked into his face with great awe.

"Hal, I've never seen any one die; but I want to stay too. There's only just you and I; and she'll want us to kiss her for the last time, when the angels come."

Hal pressed the little face in his trembling hands, but could not deny the wistful eyes.

Then he rose, and looked at Granny. She had fallen into a peaceful slumber. It did not seem as if she could die just then; and yet, at this hour of rejoicing, some souls were slipping out of the world.

He came back to his seat, and to his little sister. Dot's head was pillowed on his knee, and presently she began to drowse. Poor little bairn!

So he kept his vigil by himself, thinking over the old days, when they were all here. Oh, if Granny could have seen them once more! If the brave and lovely men and women could come back to the old home-nest, all outgrown,—and he smiled sadly to himself,—just to clasp each other's hands, and glance into each other's eyes, to speak some word of comfort and blessing, to smooth the path of the dear heart yonder, who had given herself for them without stint or grudging, a holier sacrifice than even a mother's love.

His mind was sorely troubled when he thought of Florence. Since childhood she had "lain in the roses and lilies of life." They had borne the burden and sorrow, the trials, the deprivations, days of toil, nights of anxious care about the future. And it seemed as if none of them had been especially prospered. She had gone to luxury at a bound. Where was she to-night? Did any remembrance of them ever cross her soul, amid her wealth and pleasure?

Poor Joe again! It was the sad refrain to which his life would be forever set, like a strain of minor music. He loved Joe so dearly! There was such a soreness, such an aching and longing in his heart, that it sometimes seemed as if he could stretch out his arms, and search among the tangled seaweed until he found Joe, and lift him out of his cold bed. One bright dream broken off in the middle.

There had been so much to take up his attention this winter, that he had hardly felt anxious for Charlie. Her cheerful little notes were like stray sunbeams, and she *had* promised to come back. Ah, if it could only be in time to say good-by to Granny!

Now and then he shut his eyes, and breathed a tender prayer,—that God would keep them all; that, no matter how far they strayed from each other, they might never stray from him.

The lamp burned dimly in the room beyond. Granny still slept peacefully, and Dot's baby hand was fast clasped in his. All was still to awesomeness. Even the storm without must have ceased.

"Hal," called the dear voice.

Gently as he laid Dot down, the movement woke her.

"Give me a little drink, Hal, please," Granny asked.

He brought her some wine.

"I wonder if there is any thing that I could eat?"

"I left some chicken-broth on the stove to keep warm, and there is a little jelly."

"I've had such a nice sleep, Hal! I feel so rested! It was almost like being in heaven, for Joe seemed to have his arms around my neck. Is it morning?"

"Almost."

"Oh!" exclaimed Dot, "it is clear and beautiful, with hosts of stars! I wonder if any shepherd watches them and thinks"—

"'In Bethlehem of Judea,'" said Granny in a chanting tone. "'Unto you is born a Saviour, which is Christ the Lord.'"

"How strange it seems! Christmas morning!"

Hal brought the chicken and the jelly. Granny ate remarkably for her. Then he placed his fingers on her pulse. It certainly *was* stronger.

"I do think she is better," he said to Dot, who had followed him to the kitchen.

"O Hal! maybe she won't die. I never saw anybody"—

"She was nervous last night, thinking so much of Joe," rejoined Hal softly in the pause that Dot did not finish.

"I'm so glad to have her better!"

"Children," Granny said when they came back, "it is Christmas morning, and you ought to sing. Everybody keeps Christmas."

Dot glanced up in tearful surprise. What was she thinking of,—angels in heaven?

"They sang on the plains of Judea, you know."

An awesome chill crept over Hal. Was this the change that sometimes preceded the last step over the narrow river? Had Granny received that solemn call?

"Sing," she said again. "Some of the bright Christmas hymns."

Hal's heart was throbbing up to his throat. He did not know whether he could trust his voice.

"What shall it be, Dot?"

She thought a moment. "'Wonderful Night,'" she answered. "But, oh! I feel more like crying. I can't help it."

The two voices rose tremblingly in the beautiful carol.

"Wonderful night,

Wonderful night!

Angels and shining immortals,

Thronging the heavenly portals,

Fling out their banner of light.

Wonderful, wonderful night!"

They sang until they forgot sorrow and toil and poverty, and the great fear that overshadowed them. The soft voice of the child Dot growing stronger, and the pain in Hal's slipping away, changing into faith and trust. For, as he sung, he grew wonderfully calm, even hopeful.

"It's like heaven, children! I've been thinking it all over, and God *does* know best. If they were all here, it would be harder for me to go."

The two kissed each other amid fast falling tears. When they glanced up again a faint streak of dawn stole in at the window.

"How strange!" exclaimed Dot. "We have not been to bed at all, only I had a nap on your knee." Then very softly,—

"Merry Christmas, Hal."

"Merry Christmas to you, my little darling."

Then Hal looked at the fires, and hurried them up a trifle. How lovely it was without! Over the whole earth lay a mantle of whitest ermine. Tree and shrub were robed in fleecy garments,—arrayed for this Christmas morning. As the sun began to quiver in the east they sparkled with a thousand gems.

It seemed like the beginning of a new life. Why, he could not tell, but he never forgot the feeling of solemn sweetness that stole over him as he stood by the window in the flower-room, looking over to the infinite, fancying that earth and heaven met this morning; the fine gold of the one blending with the snowy whiteness of the other. So pure was the soul of the little child born eighteen hundred years ago.

Within, it was all fragrance and beauty. The plains of the Orient could not have been more odorous in that early dawn. Unconsciously he hummed over two or three lines,—

> "Midnight scarcely passed and over,
>
> Drawing to this holy morn;
>
> Very early, very early—
>
> Christ was born."

They went about their simple homely duties, as if some unbidden guest had entered, whose presence filled the space out of which a dear face had vanished.

"Granny *is* better, I am sure," Dot said, preparing some breakfast for her.

"I am so thankful!"

"Listen to the church-bell! How faintly it comes ploughing through the snow; but oh, how sweet! Hal, I can't help feeling happy. I wonder if it is wrong, when we were so sad last night?"

Something floated through Hal's brain,—"Sorrow may endure for a night, but joy cometh in the morning." He brushed a tear away from his eye; but it was tenderness rather than sorrow.

While Dot was cooking her dainty breakfast, Hal took a turn at shovelling snow, clearing the old doorstep, and part of the path. It made his cheeks rosy, and the fresh crisp air took the tired look out of his eyes.

"Granny has been asking for you," Dot said, as he came in.

He warmed his hands, and entered the room. Dot lingered by the window, glancing up and down the unbroken road. Not a sound anywhere. It absolutely seemed to her as if a little bird ought to come out of the snowy trees, and sing.

Something attracted her attention,—a man striding along, muffled up to the ears, looking this way and that, as if considering how best to extricate himself from the last plunge, and make another. No, it was not Dr. Meade,— no one for them thus early in the morning.

Still she looked, and smiled a little. The strong, manful tread was good to behold. When he reached the house, he paused, appeared to be considering, then wheeled about.

She laughed this time. He placed his hand on the gate-post, and leaped over. It was such a boyish, agile spring! In the path he stamped off the snow, came straight to the door, and knocked.

Dot started, and opened it. A tall, laughing fellow, with a bronze brown beard and swarthy cheeks, lighted with a healthful glow of crimson. What was there so oddly familiar in the laughing eyes?

For an instant he did not speak. Dot began to color with embarrassment, and half turned to summon Hal.

"Oh, it's Dot, little Dot! And you have forgotten me!"

The rich, ringing voice electrified Hal. He made a rush in a blind, dazed way; for the room swam round, and it seemed almost as if he were dying.

"Oh, it isn't Joe! dear old Joe!"

And then Hal felt the strong arms around him. The glowing cheek was against his, and there were tears and kisses, for Hal was crying like a baby. I've done my best with him, I want you to observe; but I'm afraid he will be a "girl"-boy to the end. But nothing ever was so sweet as that clasp; and Joe's love on this side of the shining river seemed the next best thing to the infinite love beyond.

"Oh, I can't believe it!" he sobbed. "Did God raise you from the sea, Joe? for we heard"—

"Yes," with a great tremble in the tone. "It's just like being raised from the dead. And oh, Hal, God only knows how glad I am to come back to you all!"

Hal hid his face in the curly beard, and tried to stop the tears that *would* flow in spite of his courageous efforts.

There was a call from the other room,—a wild, tender cry,—and the next instant Joe was hugging Granny to his throbbing, thankful heart. You could hear nothing but the soft sobs that sounded like summer rain, blown about by the south wind. Ah, how sweet, how satisfying! What was poverty and care and trouble and loss, so long as they had Joe back again?

"Oh!" cried Granny, "I'm willing to die now. I've seen him, my darling!"

"Why, Granny, that would be blackest ingratitude. Here I've lived through all my narrow escapes, and they have been enough to kill any ten men, and, by way of welcome, you talk of dying. Why, I'll run back, and jump into the sea!"

"She has been very sick," said Hal.

"But she means to get well now. Dear old Granny! We couldn't keep house without you."

They knew well enough then that it was Joe, and not a Christmas ghost; for no one ever did have such a rich merry voice, such a ringing laugh, and oh, the dear bright eyes, shining like an April sky!

Granny looked him all over. How he had changed! A great strong, splendid fellow, whose smiling face put new hope into one.

"I almost feel as if I could get well," she said weakly.

"Of course you will; for, Granny, I have the silk gown, and we'll have just the jolliest time there has ever been in this little shanty. But where are all the rest?"

"Kit is at work in Salem, and he meant to come home last night; but I suppose the storm prevented."

"It was terrible! I've travelled night and day to reach home by Christmas. And last night, when the trains had to go at a snail's pace, or were snowed in, I couldn't stand it, so I took a sleigh; but we lost the road, and twenty other things; and then the horse gave out: it was such fearful, wearing work. And, when I came in sight of Terry's old store, I wouldn't stop, but trudged on afoot; for I wanted you to know, first of all, that I was safe and alive."

"It's just like a dream; and oh, Joe, the merriest Christmas there ever can be!"

"Where's that midget of a Charlie?"

"Ran away! It's very funny;" and Hal smiled, with tears in his eyes.

"But you know where she is?"

"I think she is in New York,—I'm pretty sure; and she has promised to come home."

"Well, that beats my time! Ran away! She threatened to do it, you know. And here I've forgotten all about little Dot! You don't deserve to be kissed nor made much of, you small woman, when you never gave me a word of welcome, but, instead, a cold, unfriendly stare. You don't remember Joe, who broke his delicate constitution carrying you round on his back to keep you from crying."

With that he caught her up, and perched her on the edge of Granny's bed. She was very shy, and turned a brilliant scarlet. This great strange fellow their dear, sweet Joe? She could not believe it!

"And you really were not drowned," said Granny, still anxious.

"Not exactly," with a droll twinkle of the eye.

"We heard"—

"Yes, the brave little 'Argemone' went down, and she was a beauty. But such a frightful storm! You can form no idea of it. Some day I'll tell you all. Our time is too precious for the long story now."

"And you wouldn't get in the boat," said Granny, her pale washed-out eyes alight with pride.

"There were three young fellows of us besides the sick captain, and we had no wives nor babies; so it seemed right that we should give the others the first chance. It was a miracle that they were saved. I never thought they would be. We lashed ourselves to some timbers, and trusted the winds and waves. What those days and nights were I can never tell you! I know now what that brave old soldier and sailor, St. Paul, meant when he said, 'A day and a night have I been in the deep.'"

Hal gave the sun-browned hand a tender squeeze.

"An Arabian trading vessel picked us up at last. We thought Jack was dead, but after a long while he revived. We were all perfectly exhausted. I could send no word, and then I resolved to come home just as soon as I could. I fancied you would hear of the loss. Did that make Granny ill?"

"No, she was sick before."

"But I'll get well now," she rejoined humbly. "I didn't want to, you know. Heaven seemed so much better."

Joe bent over and kissed her, wondering if he ever could repay the tender love.

"Have you ever heard from"—

There was no need of a name.

"She was married more than a year ago. I wrote that to you. There have been no tidings since."

"Are you going to have any breakfast?" asked Dot. "My muffins will be spoiled."

"Yes, indeed! I'm hungry as a bear. Granny, shall I carry you out?"

She laughed in her old cracked, tremulous fashion, good to hear. To Hal it seemed the beginning of a new life.

"I guess I'll lie still and think a bit, for I can't make it true. It's just as if we watched for him last night, Hal, and to-day is a day of great joy."

Dot's coffee and muffins were delightful. Then she broiled over a little of the chicken that had been left from the day before, and they had quite a sumptuous breakfast.

"How odd it seems to have Dot any thing but a baby!" laughed Joe. "It's quite ridiculous for her to set up housekeeping. Small young woman, you can't impose upon me."

"But she is royal at it;" and Hal gave her a fond smile.

"Now tell me all that has happened: I'm crazy to know. I believe I've not heard a word in six or eight months," declared Joe.

So Hal went back to the summer,—losing the school, Charlie's running away, Granny's illness, Kit's going to Salem, the mishap of the flowers, even the vigil of last night, when they believed Granny dying.

"But it *will* be a merry Christmas," Joe said with a great tremble in his voice. "And you can never guess how glad I am to be safe and alive, to comfort you all. Dear, dear Granny!—the best and bravest heart in the wide world, and the most loving."

CHAPTER XIX.

IN THE OLD HOME-NEST AGAIN.

They sat over their breakfast, and talked a long while. And then, after another glimpse at Granny, they went up to see the flowers, which had begun to recover rapidly from their misfortune.

"Why, Hal, it's a perfect little green-house, and oh, how fragrant! There are some tuberoses coming out. What an awful shame about that cold night! So you have wrecks on the land as well as on the sea?"

"I don't mind now. Your return makes up for all the misfortunes. We will have enough for some bouquets to-day;" and Hal's face was one grateful smile.

"And what will we have for dinner?" asked Dot. "It ought to be a feast. I wonder if Kit will get home in time? Oh, I'll tell you! we will not have our dinner until about three."

"Sensible to the last, Dot. Why, it is almost ten now; and our breakfasts have just been swallowed."

"We will have some chickens," exclaimed Hal.

"And a cranberry pie."

"Who is to make it,—you, or Hal?" laughed Joe. "He used to be my very dear Mrs. Betty. I don't know how we should ever have lived without him. Hal, I must confess that there's some rare good fortune in store for me. I had to stop a while in New York; and to think I should stumble over one of the very men who was last to leave 'The Argemone.' And he tells such a marvellous story! I suppose every thing looked different out there in the storm and darkness and night, with death staring us in the face; for, after all, I only did my duty, and our poor captain lying sick too! I don't mean ever to go very far away while—while Granny lives; but there's nothing like the sea for me!"

"Oh!" exclaimed Hal, with a soft little sigh.

"Well, the upshot of it was, that they, the owners, and this Mr. Parker, made me take a little gift,—five hundred dollars. I know where I can get enough more to build a real green-house. You see, the fall off the hay-wagon did for you; and you'll never be a great hulking fellow like me, fit to take the rough and tumble of life."

Hal clasped the arm that was thrown protectingly around him.

"No, you'll never be very strong; and you shall have the green-house. That will set you up for old age even."

"Dear, noble Joe!"

"Not half as noble as you. I often used to think of you, Hal, out there, miles and miles away, amid all manner of strange sights; and it was my one comfort that you'd always stand by Granny. What comrades you have been! And after this, you see, I shall be able to do my share."

Hal winked away some tears.

"Here's where we used to sleep. Oh! did you dream then that I'd be so tall I should have to go round, bowing my head to every doorway, just as if I believed in Chinese idols? And here's the old garret, where we dreamed our dreams. Hal, my darling, I'm glad to see every old board and crack and crevice in this blessed place!"

They went down presently. Joe stole off to Granny again, while Hal and Dot went about their household affairs. Hal soon had a couple of chickens for roasting. Dot made some savory dressing, stirred up her fire, baked her pie first, and then put the chickens in the oven. Hal shovelled away the snow, and took out two beautiful heads of celery, crisp and creamy.

Dr. Meade dropped in. You may imagine his rejoicing. They made him promise over and over again, that he would not tell a single soul in Madison. They wanted this dear Christmas Day to themselves.

"He's a hero to be proud of, Granny," exclaimed the doctor delightedly. "Such a great stalwart fellow, with a beard like a Turk, and a voice like an organ! Why, he overtops us all! Dot, if I were in your place, I should give his pockets a wide berth; for he could stow away such a weeny thing before your disconsolate friends would miss you."

Dot laughed, as if she wasn't much afraid.

"The excitement has not hurt Granny?" queried Hal.

"No, indeed! It's better than quarts of my tonics, and gallons of port wine. She only wanted a good strong motive to give the blood a rush through her veins."

"I was quite afraid last night."

"She'll weather it through, and come out in the spring like a lark. O Hal, my dear boy, God is wonderful! 'And so He bringeth them to the haven where they would be.'"

"Yes. I've been thinking of it all the morning."

"Merry Christmas, everybody. Not a word will I say."

Joe was still watching by the window, when another sleigh stopped, and a brisk little figure sprang out, running up the walk. He opened the door.

"Hillo!" he cried. "Here comes Kit, scalp-lock, fiddle, and all."

"Oh!" in the utmost wonder and amazement, glancing around as if suddenly bereft of his senses. "Oh, it isn't Joe, raised out of the sea! It can't be!"

"Pity the poor fishes," said Joe comically. "Think of the banquet to which they might have asked all their relations."

And then Kit was in his arms, crying and laughing; and, if Joe's head had not been securely fastened, it never could have stood the pressure.

"Oh, dear darling old Joe! How were you saved? What *did* Granny say?"

And then the little goose had to go and cry over Granny.

"You have really achieved a fiddle," exclaimed Joe at length. "Kit, my dear, you are on the high road to fame."

"Not very *high*," returned Kit. "But it's splendid to have. Hal gave it to me, and I can play quite well."

"We shall have to give a party some day,—a golden wedding for Granny."

"Or a golden Christmas. O Joe! I can't believe it a bit. I was awfully disappointed last night when it stormed, and they said I shouldn't come home. I thought how lonely Dot and Hal would be this morning."

The two smiled at each other, remembering the Christmas hymns in the gray dawn.

Dot's dinner began to diffuse its aroma around the room. What with boiling and baking, she had her hands full.

"Let us put both tables together," she said to Hal "It will give us so much more room. And it's to be a regular feast."

"Over the prodigal son," rejoined Joe. "Kit, here, who spends his substance in fiddles and riotous living."

"No: it is Dot who does the latter."

Dot laughed. "You will not complain, when I ask you to share the riotous living," she said.

The tables were set out, and Dot hunted up the best cloth. White enough it was too. Then the plates: how many were there? For somehow her wits seemed to have gone wool-gathering, and she had a misgiving lest some of them might disappear.

"Oh!"

Kit gave a great cry, dashed open the door, and flew down the walk, his scalp-lock flying, until he went head first into a snowbank.

"Kit's demented, and there's a girl at the bottom of it," said Joe. "O Kit! you've gone the way of mankind early."

"It's Charlie!" almost screamed Dot, following as if she had been shot out of a seventy-four pounder.

"Charlie! Oh, what a blessed, blessed Christmas!"

They dragged Charlie in,—not by the hair of her head, for that was hardly long enough. Charlie, in a pretty brown dress and cloak, a squirrel collar and muff, a jaunty hat with green velvet bands and a green feather. She was quite tall, and not so thin; and a winter of good care had completed the bleaching process commenced at the mill. She was many shades fairer, with a soft bloom on her cheek, while her mouth no longer threatened to make the top of her head an island.

"O Hal! and where's Granny? And"—

She paused before Joe.

"Why, Charlie, you're grown so handsome that you really don't know your poor relations."

"It's Joe! What a great giant! Oh! when did he come?"

"And we thought him drowned," said Dot, half crying. "We heard it ever so long ago! It was so splendid to have him come back!"

"Shut the door," exclaimed Hal.

"Why, I thought it was dreadful cold," said Kit, glancing round at the wide open door.

"Cold isn't any word for it! If we had a cast-iron dog we should have to tie him to the stove-leg to keep his hair from freezing off. It's lucky I wear a wig."

"You're the same old Joe," said Charlie, laughing.

"But where have you been, Charlie?"

"In New York. I've such lots and lots to tell you. But oh, I must see Granny!"

So Granny had to be hugged and kissed, and everybody went to look. They all talked and laughed and cried in the same breath; and nobody knew what was said, only they were all there together again, and Granny was alive.

"I intended to come home yesterday, but it stormed so fearfully; and to-day there were so many detentions, that I began almost to despair. But I had some Christmas for darling Granny, and I couldn't wait. See here,"—and Charlie began to search her pockets energetically. "Fifty dollars, Granny; and I earned it all my own self, besides ever so much more. And I'm going to be a —a"—

"Genius," said Kit. "Hooray for Charlie!"

"It's all about the pictures. Mr. Darol sold some designs for me, and I wanted Granny to have the money; but I never dreamed that she had been sick. And did you miss me much? I never told Mr. Darol about it until yesterday. I suppose it wasn't right. And oh! Granny, I'm sorry if I've given you the least mite of pain; but all the time I've been as happy as Joe's big sunflower."

"We shall set Granny crazy," said thoughtful Hal.

"Oh, my dinner!" and Dot flew to the stove-oven like the "moon-eyed herald of dismay."

There was no damage done. The chickens were browned to a turn. She took them out on a dish, and made her gravy, and then Hal came to help with the vegetables. Potatoes, onions, carrots stewed with milk dressing, cranberry sauce, celery,—altogether a fit repast for anybody's Christmas dinner.

"If Granny could only come?"

"I've been thinking that we might take her up a little while at dessert. She asked to sit up before Charlie came. What a day of excitement!"

"O Hal! it's all lovely. And I can't help thinking how good God was not to let her die in the night, when we were to have such a happy day. He saw it, with the angels keeping Christmas around him; didn't he, Hal?" said little Dot.

"Yes, my darling."

"And I'm so full of joy! I can't help crying every other minute! And to think of that magnificent Charlie earning fifty dollars!"

Hal went to summon the "children," and explain to Granny, that if she would be very quiet, and take a good rest, she might get up when the dessert was brought on. The old woebegone look had vanished from her face, and the faded eyes held in their depths a tender brightness.

She assented rather unwillingly to the proposal, for she could hardly bear them out of her sight an instant. Hal closed the door between, but she begged him to open it again.

"I'd like to hear you talk. I'll lie still, and never say a word."

A happy group they were, gathered round the table. Dot was perched up at the head, and Hal took the opposite end, to do the carving. They had time, then, to look round and see how pretty Charlie was growing. The contact with refinement, and, in a certain sense, society, had improved her very much. If any thing, she had grown still farther out of the Wilcox sphere.

Then she had to tell her story.

"You really don't mean Mary Jane Wilcox?" interrupted Joe. "Why, we used to go to school together!"

"I never thought of them," said Hal, "when I was considering where I could write. Then Granny was taken sick, and the bad news about Joe,—and somehow I had a fancy that you were safe."

"Mrs. Wilcox has been like a mother. She *is* good, and I do like her; but, somehow, she is not our kind, after all. But oh, if you could only see Mr. Darol! I am going to stay a whole week, and he is coming out here. I told them all about you, Hal."

Hal colored a little.

"I'm glad I went, and made a beginning. There is ever so much hard work before me; but it is what I like. I am actually studying wood engraving. And Miss Charteris found me some work to do in my leisure time. She is as lovely as she can be, and a real artist. Think of her getting five hundred dollars for a picture!"

"And if you should ever do that!" said Kit admiringly.

"No: I haven't that kind of genius. But they all do say that my talent for designing is remarkable; and I shall be able to earn a good deal of money, even if I do not get as much at one time. I'm so glad, and so thankful!"

They all looked at brave Charlie; and, somehow, it didn't seem as if she were the little harum-scarum, who never had a whole dress for six consecutive hours, who ran around bare-headed and bare-footed, and was the tint of a copper-colored Indian. Why, she was almost as elegant as Flossy, but with a nobler grace. There was nothing weak about her. You felt that she would make a good fight to the end, and never go astray in paths of meanness, deceit, or petty pride.

Then they had to tell what had happened to them. She had all the rejoicing over Joe, without any of the pain and anguish. For, now that he was here, she could not imagine the bitter tears which had been the portion of the household.

How gay they were! There was no china on the table, no silver forks, no cut-glass goblets; but the dinner was none the less enjoyable. There never were such roasted chickens, nor such cranberry sauce, nor such celery! And certainly never such glad and loving hearts. The sorrows and successes drew them the more closely together.

What if Granny had let them stray off years ago, to forget and grow cold! Ah! she had her reward now. Every year after this it would pour in a golden harvest.

"We will have our dessert in style," said Hal.

"Kit, please help take off the dishes, for I know Dot must be tired."

"I will too," responded Charlie promptly.

They gathered up the fragments, and carried them in the pantry, took away the dishes, brushed off the cloth, and then came the crowning glories. First, two beautiful bouquets, with a setting of crisp, fragrant geranium leaves; then a dish of apples, rosy-cheeked and tempting.

"It is fortunate that I made a good large pie," said Dot with much complacency.

Hal bundled Granny in a shawl; but, before he could help her out of bed, Joe's strong arms had borne her to the kitchen. Hal brought the rocking-chair, and they made her comfortable with pillows.

They all, I think, saw a strange beauty in her on this Christmas Day. The little silvery curls,—they always *would* curl; the pale, wrinkled face; the faded eyes, with their youth and glory a thing of the past; the feeble, cracked voice; the trembling hands,—all beautiful in their sight. For the hands had toiled, the voice had comforted, the lips had kissed away pains and griefs. Every furrow in the face was sacred. What watching and anxiety and unfaltering labor they bespoke!

Dot poured her a cup of tea: then she proceeded to cut the pie.

"Dot, you are a royal cook!" exclaimed Joe. "We have discovered your special genius."

198

It was very delightful. Granny had a little slice, and added her praises to the rest so lavishly bestowed.

"There never was but one such Christmas. If I were a boy, I should pronounce it 'red-hot,'" laughed Joe. "I'm almost sorry to outgrow the boyish tricks and slang."

"And you can't cool it," appended Kit, with a melancholy shake of the head.

"If there was one face more," began Granny slowly.

Yes, just one was needed to complete the group.

The sun stole softly out of the window. The happy day was drawing to a close. Would life, too, draw to a close without her?

"Hark!" exclaimed Dot.

For the merry jingle of sleigh-bells ceased suddenly. Was it some unwelcome guest to break in upon the sanctity of their twilight hour?

A knock at the door. Charlie, being the nearest, opened it. A lady dressed in deep mourning, and a tall, fine-looking gentleman. She certainly had never seen either of them before.

The veil was raised. Oh, that face, with all its fairness and beauty; the golden hair, the lustrous eyes! They all knew then.

"O Granny, Granny!" and Florence was kneeling at her grandmother's feet, kissing the wasted hands, her sad, pathetic voice broken with sobs. "I had to come: I couldn't stay away. I've been selfish and ungrateful, and God has punished me sorely. And, when I turned to him in my sorrow, he brought before me all my neglect, my pride, my cruelty. O Granny! can it be forgiven?"

"There's nothing to forgive, child."

She kissed the sweet, wet face. At that moment she forgot every thing save that this darling had come back.

"Yes, there is so much, so much! You don't know. For, after I was married, I might have come. Edmund was tender and noble. This is my husband, Mr. Darol."

She rose as she uttered this, and made a gesture with her outstretched hand. Mr. Darol bowed.

"This is my dear grandmother Edmund; and these are my brothers and sisters. It is so long since I have seen any of you, that you seem strangers to me."

There was a peculiar silence in the room.

"Oh!" with a low, imploring cry,—"have you no welcome for me? Have I forfeited *all* regard, all remembrance?"

Hal came round to her side; but she was so stately and beautiful, that he felt almost awed.

"It is Hal, I know. Oh! take me back in your midst: for only yesterday I buried my little baby; and I know now the sense of loss that I entailed upon you."

They all crowded round her then. Not one had forgotten darling Flossy. Kisses and fond clasps. They were so glad to take her into their circle.

"This is Joe," she said, "and Kit, and Dot. O Charlie! to see you all once more! and to have you all alive! For I have been haunted with a terrible fear lest some of you might have fallen out of the old home-chain. Not a break, thank God!"

Then she brought them to her husband. Oh, how wild she had been when she fancied that she *might* be ashamed of them!—this group of brave, loving faces, full of the essential elements of nobility.

Ah, Florence, if you had known all their deeds of simple heroism!

Charlie helped her take off her wrappings. She had not changed greatly, except to grow older and more womanly.

"Granny has been ill!" she exclaimed in quick alarm.

"Yes, nearly all winter. But she is better now. O Flossy, I am so glad you came to-day!" and Hal's soft eyes swam in tears.

"It was Christmas. I could not help thinking of the dear old Christmas when we were all together. O Hal! if you could know all my shame and sorrow!"

"Joe," said Granny feebly, "will you take me back to bed? I'm tired again. I'm a poor old body at the best. Then you can come and sit round me."

"Shall I send the driver away?" asked Mr. Darol of Florence.

"Yes: I can't leave them to-night. You will not mind?"—

She glanced around as she uttered this, as if apologizing for the poor accommodations.

"No, I shall not mind," in a grave tone.

Granny was carried to bed again. Hal shook up the pillow, and straightened the spreads. Joe laid her in tenderly, saying, as he kissed her,—

"You have us all home again in the old shoe!"

The room was neat and orderly; poor, to be sure, but with a cheerful air. Hal brought in the flowers, and Kit some chairs, and they made quite a party.

"But think of the dishes!" whispered housewifely Dot. "And not a clean one for morning, we've used so many. But, oh! wasn't it elegant? And Florence is a real lady!"

"We had better slip out, and look after our household gods," Hal murmured in return.

Before they were fairly in the business, Charlie joined them.

"Let me help too," she said. "I don't hate to wash dishes quite as much as I used; and I am so happy to-night that I could do almost any thing!"

They were a practical exemplification of the old adage. Many hands did make light work. In a little while they had their house in order.

"But what a family!" exclaimed Dot. "Where are we to put them all?"

"I've been thinking. Florence and her husband can have my room, and we will make a bed for Kit and Joe in the flower-room. They won't mind it, I guess."

"Dot can sleep with Granny, and I can curl up in any corner for to-night," said Charlie.

"Hal never had a wink of sleep last night. We talked and sang Christmas hymns, and Granny thought that she would not live."

Charlie gave a sad sigh.

"You are angels, both of you," she answered. "And when Mr. Darol comes,—oh! isn't it funny that Florence's husband should have the same name? I wonder"—

Charlie was off into a brown study.

"Oh!" she exclaimed, "isn't it odd? Florence's name is Darol, and there is my Mr. Darol. Why, I do believe they look something alike,—Flossie's husband, I mean."

To which rather incoherent statement no one was able to reply.

"Perhaps we had better put my room in order," suggested Hal, returning to the prose of housekeeping.

Dot found some clean sheets and pillow-cases. Charlie followed them, and assisted a little. The bed was freshly made, a clean napkin spread over the worn washstand, towels as white as snow, and every thing neat, if not elegant.

"Though, of course, it will look very common to Flossy," said Dot with a sigh. "I feel almost afraid of her, she is so grand."

"But she isn't a bit better than we are," returned Charlie stoutly. "I think Hal is really the noblest of the lot, and the most unfortunate. But I told Mr. Darol all about the green-house, Hal!"

Hal colored. Charlie was a warm and courageous champion.

Then they went down stairs. Florence still sat at the head of Granny's bed, and had been crying. Hal remembered his hard thoughts of Flossy the night before with a pang of regret; for, though they had been poor and burdened with cares, death had not come nigh *them*, but had taken Florence's first-born in the midst of her wealth and ease.

Charlie went round to them. "Florence," she began a little timidly, "do you live in New York?"

"Yes."

"I've been there since the last of August."

"You?" returned Florence in surprise. "What are you doing?"

"Studying at the School of Design."

"Why, Charlie! how could you get there?"

"It was very strange. I almost wonder now if it really did happen to me. You see, I worked in the mill, and saved up some money; and then I went to New York. You remember Mrs. Wilcox, don't you? I've been boarding there. And, while I was trying to find out what I must do, I met a Mr. Paul Darol, who is a perfect prince"—

"O Florence! we have heard all this story," interrupted Mr. Darol. "It is the little girl for whom Uncle Paul sold the designs. She wanted some money to take home, you know. He never mentioned the name."

"Then he is your uncle," said Charlie, quite overwhelmed at her success.

"Yes; and you are a brave girl, a genius too. Florence, I'm proud enough of this little sister. Why didn't Uncle Paul think,—but you don't look a bit alike."

And this was Charlie! Here were the brothers and sisters of whom she had felt secretly ashamed! Joe, the dear, noble fellow; Hal, tender and devoted;

heroic Charlie; ambitious Kit; and fond little Dot. Oh! instead, *she* was the one for whom they needed to blush,—her own selfish, unworthy soul, that had stood aloof the past year, when she might have come to their assistance. How it humbled her! She even shrank away from her husband's eyes.

"I think Granny is growing weary," Hal said presently, glancing at the pallid cheek. "She has had a great deal of excitement to-day; and now, if you will come up stairs and look at my flowers, we can let her have a little rest."

They all agreed to the proposal.

So Hal gave her a composing draught; and, though Joe was fain to stay, Granny sent him away with the others. They had all been so good, that she, surely, must not be selfish; and, truth to tell, a little quiet would not come amiss.

For, happy dream! she *had* lived to see them all come back. What more could she ask? That she might recover her health, and feast on their smiles and joyousness; and she prayed humbly to God that it might be so, in his great mercy.

CHAPTER XX.

WHEREIN THE OLD SHOE BECOMES CROWDED.

They trooped up the narrow stairs. Why, the old loom-room looked like a palace! Hal had made some very pretty brackets out of pine, and stained them; and they were ranged round the wall, upholding a pot of flowers or trailing vines, and two or three little plaster casts. Here were some bookshelves, the table surmounted by a very passable writing-desk, Hal's construction also. But the flowers were a marvel.

"Hal's dream was a green-house," exclaimed Florence. "But I don't see how you found time for it all"—

"It has been profit as well as pleasure," said Hal with a little pride. "Last winter I sold a quantity of flowers, and, in the spring, bedding-plants and garden vegetables."

"Oh!" returned Florence, choking back the sobs, "do you remember one summer day, long, long ago, when we all told over what we would like to have happen to us? And it has all come about."

"Even to my fiddle," said Kit.

"And my running away," appended Charlie with great satisfaction.

Hal brought in some chairs.

"We're going to sit in the corner on the floor," said Charlie; and the three younger ones ranged themselves in a small group.

Florence and her husband walked round to view the flowers, guided by Joe.

"You appear to have wonderful success," remarked Mr. Darol. "These tuberoses are very fine."

"They were frosted about ten days ago, and have hardly recovered. That is, I lost most of my blossoms."

"Oh, what a pity!"

"And all our Christmas money," said Dot softly.

"No matter," returned Charlie. "You can have all of mine. I meant every penny of it for Granny."

"And now I want to hear what you have been doing all these years. I know it was my own act that shut me out of your joys and sorrows; but if you will take me back"—and the voice was choked with tears.

Hal pressed the soft hand.

"You will find Edmund a brother to you all," she went on. "It is my shame, that after my marriage, knowing that I could come any time, I hesitated to take the step."

"It is a poor old house," exclaimed Hal tremulously.

"But holds more love and heroism than many grander mansions," Mr. Darol said in his deep, manly tone. "Florence is right: I should like to be a brother to you all. I honored Charlie before I fancied that I should ever have a dearer claim."

"And I've been a sort of black sheep," returned Charlie frankly. "Hal and Joe are the heroes in this family."

"It is so wonderful to have Joe safe!"

"And to think how sad we were last night," Dot began. "We did not expect any one to help us keep Christmas but Kit."

"O Dot! tell me all about it," said Charlie eagerly. "I do like to hear it so. And how Joe came home."

Dot was a little shy at first; but presently she commenced at Hal's losing the school, Granny's sickness, Joe's shipwreck, the trouble and sorrow that followed in succession, the misfortune of the flowers, and then she came to the night when Granny wanted to die and go to heaven. Only last night; but oh, how far off it appeared! She told it very simply, but with such unconscious pathos that they were all crying softly Florence leaned her head on her husband's shoulder, hiding her face.

"And I never knew a word of it!" exclaimed Charlie with the quiver of tears in her voice. "I didn't want to tell you about my going, for fear you'd worry over me, or, if I should be disappointed, you would feel it all the more keenly. But I never thought any thing sad could happen to you."

"I should like to hear the first part of Charlie's adventures," said Mr. Darol. "How did she come to know that she had a genius?"

"She used to be punished enough in school for drawing comical faces," answered Joe. "Little did Mr. Fielder think that you would make an artist!"

"But I planned then to run away and live in the woods. I believe I once took you off, Kit."

"Yes; and we were threatened with the jail, weren't we, because we made a fire. But how you did talk, Charlie! You were always splendid on the fighting side."

"I was made to go right straight ahead," said Charlie. "And, if I had been afraid, I should never have done any thing."

"And we want to hear how you did it," pursued Mr. Darol.

So Charlie related her trials and perplexities, her fruitless journeys, and her vain endeavors, until she met Mr. Paul Darol, who seemed to understand just what she wanted.

"I don't see how you had the courage," Florence remarked. "And if I'd only known you were there, Charlie!"

Charlie shrugged her shoulders. Now that the fight had been made, and terminated successfully, she was rather glad to have gone into it single-handed: not from any vanity, but a kind of sturdy independence that had always characterized Charlie Kenneth.

And then they rambled farther back, to the time of Hal's sad accident. Perhaps the most truly noble thing about them was their fearlessness and honesty. They were not ashamed of the poverty and struggle: there was no petty deceit or small shams to cover the truth.

Ah, what heroic lives they had all been, in a simple way! For it is not only in great matters that men and women must fight: it is the truth and endurance and perseverance which they bring into every-day events that moulds character. Not a poor, false, or useless soul among them, unless it was hers, Florence thought.

Hal stole down a time or two to see Granny, who had fallen into a peaceful sleep. And presently the old clock struck ten. Dot and Kit were nodding.

"I am going to put you in our old room," Hal said to Florence. "It is the best I can do."

"No: let me sit up and watch with Granny."

"That is not at all necessary. Last night she was nervous. I fancy she was haunted by a dim impression of impending change, and thought it must mean death. Instead, it was the dearest of joys."

"O Hal! I don't feel worthy to come among you. Not simply because I chose to go away, to have luxury and ease and idleness, while you were in want and sorrow; for in those old days I thought only of myself. But, a few months after I was married, Mrs. Osgood died, and I was quite free to choose.

Don't shrink away from me Hal, though the cowardice has in it so much of vile ingratitude. I had not the courage to be true to my secret longings. She had filled my weak soul with her beliefs; and I persuaded myself that my debt to her was greater than that to my own kindred."

"O Florence, hush! let it all go, since you *have* come back," pleaded unselfish Hal.

"And then my precious baby came. Hardly four months ago. He had your tender eyes, Hal; and they used to reproach me daily. But I made a hundred excuses and delays. And then God took him, to let me feel what a wrench the soul endures when its cherished ones are removed. All these years I have been like one dead to you, without the sweet comfort of those who know their treasures are safe in heaven. When we came back from *his* grave yesterday, I told Edmund my deeper shame and anguish, my disloyalty to those who had the first claim. And if any of you had been dead, if I could never have won Granny's forgiveness, ah, how heavy my burden would have proved!"

"But we all consented to your going," Hal said, longing to comfort her.

"Because you knew how weak and foolish I was, with my sinfully ambitious longings. And oh, if my husband had been less noble!"

"You shall not so blame yourself on this blessed Christmas night. Is there not to be peace on earth, and tenderness and good will for all? And it seems as if you never could have come back at a more precious moment."

Hal, foolish boy, cried a little in her arms. It was so sweet to have her here.

After a while the children were all disposed of. Hal apologized to Joe for the rather close and fragrant quarters.

"Don't worry, old comrade. When you've slept on a whale's backbone, or a couple of inches of tarred rope, you take any thing cheerfully, from a hammock to a bed of eider down."

Kit cuddled in his arms. Dear old Joe was the best and bravest of heroes to him.

Hal threw himself on the lounge, covered with shawls and overcoats, for the bedclothes were insufficient to go around. He laughed softly to himself. Such a houseful as this the "Old Shoe" had never known before. What was poverty and trouble now? A kind of ghostly phantom, that vanished when one came near it. Why, he had never felt so rich in all his life!

Granny was none the worse the next morning for her excitement. Dot bathed her face, combed out the tiny silver curls, and put on a fresh wrapper.

Charlie helped get breakfast, though she was not as deft-handed as Dot. The two tables were set again; and, when they brought Granny out, she was more than proud of her family.

That seemed to be a gala-day for all Madison. When the news was once started, it spread like wild-fire. Joe Kenneth wasn't drowned after all, but had come back safe, a great, tall, handsome fellow. Florence had returned with her fine-looking husband; and wild, queer Charlie had actually been transformed into the family beauty.

"There never was a finer set of children in Madison," said Mr. Terry, clearing his voice of a little huskiness. "And to think they're Joe Kenneth's poor orphans! I tell you what! Granny Kenneth has been one woman out of a thousand. Didn't everybody say she had better let the youngsters go to the poor-house. And now they're a credit to the town. Think of Joe being praised in the papers as he was! That went to my heart,—his giving up a chance for life to some one else. He's a brave fellow, and handsome as a picture. There isn't a girl but would jump at the chance of marrying him. He will be a captain before he is five years older, mark my words."

Dr. Meade was brimful of joy also. He kissed Charlie, and laughed at her for running away, and was much astonished to find how fortunate she had been But Joe was everybody's idol.

"I think some of you ought to be spared," exclaimed the good doctor. "I don't see where you were all stowed last night. I have two or three rooms at your service; and, indeed, am quite willing to take you all in. But, anyhow, Kit and Joe might come for lodgings."

"We put them in the flower-room," said Charlie.

"Which accounts for their blooming appearance, I suppose;" and the doctor pinched Charlie's ear.

Between themselves, they had endless talks. It seemed as if all the stories would never get told. And, strangely enough, they came to pity poor Flossy, who, among them all, had the only lasting sorrow.

Charlie took to Mr. Darol at once; and before the day ended they were all fast friends.

"I think yours is a most remarkable family," he said to Florence. "There is not one of the children but what you might be proud of anywhere."

"I am so glad you can love them!" and the grateful tears were in her eyes.

"And, when we return home, it seems as if we ought to take Charlie. There she will have just the position she needs."

"O Edmund! I don't deserve that you should be so good to me. I was longing to ask it. But I have been so weak and foolish!"

"My darling, that is past. I will say now, that my only misgiving about you has been the apparent forgetfulness of old family ties. But I knew you were young when you left your home, and that Mrs. Osgood insisted upon this course; besides, I never could tell how worthy they were of fond remembrance."

"And did not dream that I could be so basely ungrateful!" she answered in deepest shame. "I abhor myself: I have forfeited your respect."

"Hush, dear! Let it all be buried in our child's grave. Perhaps his death was the one needful lesson. And now that we have found them all, we must try to make amends."

Florence sobbed her deep regret, nestling closely to his heart.

"Your brother Hal interests me so much! It seems that he will always feel the result of his accident in some degree, on account of a strained tendon. He has such a passionate love for flowers, and the utmost skill in their care and culture. But he ought to have a wider field for operations."

"Oh!" she said, "if we could help him. Charlie has worked her way so energetically, that she only needs counsel and guidance. Kit and Dot are still so young!"

"I don't wonder Uncle Paul was attracted. There is something very bright and winsome about Charlie. I had to laugh at her naïve confession of being a black sheep."

"She used to be so boyish and boisterous! not half as gentle as dear Hal."

"But it seems to be toned down to a very becoming piquancy;" and he smiled.

"How very odd that she should have met your uncle!" Florence said musingly. "How surprised he will be!"

Dr. Meade came over again that evening, and insisted upon the boys accepting his hospitality; so Joe and Kit were packed into the sleigh, and treated sumptuously.

Granny continued to improve, and could sit up for quite a while. She enjoyed having them all around her so much! It was like the old time, when the gay voices made the house glad.

And so the days passed, busy, and absolutely merry.

Charlie and Florence helped cook, and Joe insisted upon showing how he could wash dishes. On Sunday they all went to church except Dot,—Granny would have it so.

On Monday Mr. Darol came. Charlie had given him very explicit directions, but she was hardly expecting him so soon. Sitting by the window she saw him coming down the street in a thoughtful manner, as if he were noting the landmarks.

"O Mr. Darol!" and she sprang to the door, nearly overturning Dot.

"Yes: you see I have been as good as my word. How bright you look! So there was nothing amiss at home?"

"Indeed there was! but, in spite of it, we have all been so happy! For everybody came home at Christmas, even Joe, whom they thought drowned. This is my little sister Dot. And oh, this is my brother Hal!"

Mr. Darol clasped the hand of one, and gave the other a friendly pat on the soft golden hair.

"I dare say Charlie has told you all about me: if she has not she is a naughty girl. Why"—

For in the adjoining room sat Florence, close to Granny's chair. No wonder he was amazed.

"That's Florence, and you've seen her before. And Mr. Edmund Darol is here," went on Charlie in a graciously explanatory manner.

"They are my brothers and sisters," said Florence with a scarlet flush.

He looked at her in deep perplexity.

"Mrs. Osgood adopted Florence," Charlie interposed again. "It was all her fault; for she would not allow the relation to be kept up, and"—

"This is your grandmother?" he interrupted almost sharply, feeling unconsciously bitter against Florence.

"This is dear Granny."

He took the wrinkled hand, not much larger than a child's, for all it had labored so long and faithfully.

"Mrs. Kenneth," he said, "I am proud to make your acquaintance. One such child as Charlie would be glory enough."

Charlie fairly danced with delight to see Granny so honored in her old days. And as for the poor woman, she was prouder than a queen.

"You've been so good to *her!*" she murmured tremulously, nodding her head at Charlie.

"She is a brave girl, even if she did run away. I have used my best efforts to make her sorry for it."

"But oh! Mr. Darol, the work was all undone as soon as I came home. For when I found them sick, and full of trouble, it seemed so good to be able to take care of myself, that I think running away the most fortunate step of my whole life."

"I am afraid that we shall never bring you to a proper state of penitence;" and he laughed.

"You were so good to her!" said Granny again, as if she had nothing but gratitude in her soul.

"It was a great pleasure to me. But I never dreamed that I had made the acquaintance of one of your family before."

"He will never like me so well again," thought Florence; "but that is part of my punishment. I have been full of pride and cowardice."

Mr. Darol made himself at home in a very few moments, for he was interested beyond measure.

"It *is* a poor place," ruminated Charlie, glancing round; "but we cannot help it, I'm sure. All of us have done our best."

Then she dismissed the subject with her usual happy faculty, and became wonderfully entertaining; so much so, indeed, that, when Mr. Darol glanced at his watch, he said,—

"In about half an hour my train goes down to the city. I have not said half that I wanted to. I have not seen your brother Joe, nor the hot-house; and what am I to do?"

"Stay," replied Charlie; and then she colored vividly. "Our house is so small that it will not hold any more; but Dr. Meade has already taken in Kit and Joe, and he is just splendid!"

Mr. Darol laughed.

"Are there any hotel accommodations?"

"Oh, yes! at the station."

"Then I think I will remain; for my visit isn't half finished, and I am not satisfied to end it here."

Charlie was delighted.

After that they went up to the flower-room. It seemed to improve every day, and was quite a nest of sweets.

"So Miss Charlie hasn't all the family genius," said Mr. Darol. "It is not every one who can make flowers grow under difficulties."

"They were nipped a little about the middle of the month. One night my fire went out."

"And it blighted the flowers he meant to cut in a few days," explained Charlie, "so that at first there did not seem a prospect of a very merry Christmas."

And Charlie slipped her hand within Mr. Darol's, continuing, in a whisper, "I can never tell you how glad I was to have the money. It was like the good fortune in a fairy story."

He looked at the beaming, blushing face with its dewy eyes. Ah! he little guessed, the day he first inspected Charlie Kenneth's drawings, that all this pleasure was to arise from a deed of almost Quixotic kindness.

Yet he wondered more than ever how she had dared to undertake such a quest. Strangely courageous, earnest, and simple-hearted, with the faith of a child, and the underlying strength of a woman,—it seemed as if there might be a brilliant and successful future before her.

And this delicate brother with a shadow in his eyes like the drifts floating over an April sky,—he, too, needed a friend to give him a helping hand. Who could do it better than he, whose dearest ones were sleeping in quiet, far-off graves?

CHAPTER XXI.

HOW THE DREAMS CAME TRUE.

Charlie insisted upon Mr. Darol remaining to supper; and he was nothing loth.

"Dear me!" exclaimed Dot, "we shall have to echo the crow's suggestive query,—

> 'The old one said unto his mate,
>
> "What shall we do for food to *ate?*"'"

"Make some biscuit or a Johnny-cake," said Charlie, fertile in expedients. "Dot, I've just discovered the bent of your budding mind."

"What?" asked the child, tying on a large apron.

"Keeping a hotel. Why, it's been elegant for almost a week!—a perfect crowd, and not a silver fork or a goblet, or a bit of china; rag-carpet on the floor, and a bed in the best room. Nothing but happiness inside and out! Even the ravens haven't cried. You see, it isn't money, but a contented mind, a kitchen apron, a saucepan, and a genius for cooking."

"But you must have something to cook," was Dot's sage comment.

"True, my dear. Words of priceless wisdom fall from your young lips,— diamonds and pearls actually! Now, if you will tell me what to put in a cake"—

"A pinch of this, and a pinch of that," laughed Dot. "I am afraid to trust your unskilful hands; so you may wait upon me. Open the draught, and stir the fire: then you may bring me the soda and the sour milk, and beat the eggs —oh, there in the basket!"

"Dot, my small darling, spare me! I am in a hopeless confusion. Your brain must be full of shelves and boxes where every article is labelled. One thing at a time."

"The fire first, then."

Dot sifted her flour, and went to work. Charlie sang a droll little song for her, and then set the table. Their supper was a decided success. Edmund came in, and was delighted to see his uncle. There was hero Joe, gay as a sky-full of larks. It didn't seem as if any of them had ever known trouble or sorrow. Even Granny gave her old chirruping laugh.

The next day they had some serious talks. Hal and Mr. Darol slipped into a pleasant confidence.

"I've been thinking over your affairs with a good deal of interest," he said. "It seems to me that you need a larger field for profitable operations. I should not think Madison quite the place for a brilliant success. You need to be in the vicinity of a large city. And, since three of the others will be in New York principally, it certainly would be better for you. Would your grandmother object to moving?"

"I don't know," Hal answered thoughtfully.

"Floriculture is becoming an excellent business. Since you have such a decided taste for it, you can hardly fail. I should recommend Brooklyn, Jersey City, or Harlem. Besides the flowers, there is a great demand for bedding-plants. You haven't any other fancy?" and he studied Hal's face intently.

Hal's lip quivered a moment. "It was my first dream, and I guess the best thing that I can do. I could not endure hard study, or any thing like that. Yes, I have decided it."

"I wish you would make me a visit very soon, and we could look around, and consider what step would be best. You must forgive me for taking a fatherly interest in you all. I love young people so much!"

Hal's eyes sparkled with delight. He did not wonder that Charlie had told her story so fearlessly to him.

"You are most kind. I don't know how to thank you."

"You can do that when you are successful;" and he laughed cordially.

They had all taken Flossy's husband into favor, and their regard was fully returned by him. Indeed, they appeared to him a most marvellous little flock. As for Florence, the awe and strangeness with which she had first impressed them was fast wearing off. As her better soul came to light, she seemed to grow nearer to them, as if the years of absence were being bridged over. Fastidious she would always be in some respects, but never weakly foolish again. She had come to understand a few of the nobler truths of life, learned through suffering,—that there was a higher enjoyment than that of the senses, or the mere outward uses of beauty.

They all appreciated the manner in which she made herself at home. They gave her the best they had, to be sure; and she never pained them by any thoughtless allusion to her luxuries. She had not lost her old art with the needle, and Dot's dresses were renovated in such a manner that she hardly knew them.

Granny would never allow her to regret her going with Mrs. Osgood.

"It was all right," she would say cheerfully. "The good Lord knew what was best. I don't mind any of it now,—the losses and crosses, the sorrows and sicknesses, and all the hard work. Your poor father would be glad if he could see you, and I've kept my promise to him. So don't cry, dearie. If you hadn't gone away, I shouldn't 'a' known how sweet it was to have you come back."

Florence and Mr. Darol made their preparations to return. They decided to take Charlie back with them, and install her in her new home; though Charlie did not exactly like the prospect of having her visit abridged.

"I meant to stay all this week," she said decisively. "I cannot have another vacation until next summer."

"But you will go back with me to my sad house, and help me to forget my baby's dead face," Florence returned beseechingly. "O Charlie! I do mean to be a true and fond sister to you if you will let me."

So Charlie consented; though she would much rather have staid, and had a "good time" with Dot and Hal.

"If Florence was not here, I should like to perch myself on a chair-back, and whistle 'Hail Columbia' to all the world. Dear old shoe! What sights of fun we have had in it! I am rather sorry that I'll soon be a woman. Oh, dear! You always *do* have some trouble, don't you?"

"Charlie, Charlie!" and Dot shook her small forefinger.

Joe was going too. "But I shall be back in a few days," he said to Granny.

"O Joe! if you wouldn't go to sea any more,—and when you've been a'most drowned"—

"O Granny! best mother in the world, do not feel troubled about me. We are a family of geniuses, and I am the duckling that can't stay brooded under mother-wings. It's my one love, and I should be a miserable fish if you kept me on dry land. I have been offered a nice position to go to Charleston; and as I am not rich, and have not the gout, I can't afford to retire on a crust. But you'll see me every little while; and you'll be proud enough of me when I get to be a captain."

Granny felt that she could not be any prouder of him if he was a king.

There was a great thinning-out again. Kit bemoaned the lonesomeness of the place; but Dot's housewifely soul was comforted with the hope of a good clearing-up time.

In two days Joe returned.

"Florence is as elegant as a queen," he reported; "not the grandest or richest, but every thing in lovely style. Charlie went wild over the pictures. And there are great mirrors, and marble statues, and carpets as soft as spring-hillsides. You never imagined, Granny, that one of us would attain to such magnificence, did you?"

Granny listened in wide-eyed wonder, and bobbed her little curls.

"And Darol's a splendid fellow! Flossy always did have the luck!"

That night Hal and Joe slept in the old room, which Joe declared seemed good.

"We had a long talk about you, Hal. Mr. Paul Darol is wonderfully interested in you. He is just as good and generous as he can be, and has two beautiful rooms at a hotel. You know, in the old dream, it was Flossy who was to meet with a benevolent old gentleman: instead, it has been Charlie, the queer little midget. What a youngster she has been!"

"She is as good as gold."

"Mr. Darol thinks her the eighth wonder of the world. But he wants you to have the green-house; and I said I intended to help you to it. When he found that we did not mean to take any thing as a gift, he offered to loan the whole amount, to be paid as you were prospered."

"How very, very generous!" said Hal with a long breath.

"It *was* most kind; but you cannot do much here. I believe I like the Brooklyn project best."

"I wonder if Granny would consent to leave Madison?"

"I think she will. You see, I can spend a good deal of time with you then."

Joe was to start again the middle of January. Granny fretted at first; but dear, merry Joe finally persuaded her that it was the best thing in the world.

Hal could not help shedding a few quiet tears, but then they had a glowing letter from Charlie. She and Florence had actually been to call on Mrs. Wilcox in their own carriage. They had taken her and Mary Jane a pretty gift; and Mrs. Wilcox was, to use her own expression, "clear beat." And Charlie declared that she was living like a princess. She could come home, and spend almost any Sunday with them.

While Hal was considering how best to inform Granny of the new project, circumstances opened the way. In the march of improvement at Madison, an old lane was to be widened, and straightened into a respectable street; and one end of it would run through the old Kenneth cottage.

Poor old Shoe! Its days were numbered. But there were no more rollicking children to tumble in and out of windows, or transform the dusty garret into a bedlamic palace. And yet Granny could not be consoled, or even persuaded.

"I never could take root anywhere else, Hal, dear," she said, shaking her head sadly.

"But the old house has been patched and patched; it leaks everywhere; and a good, strong gust of wind might blow it over. We should not want to be in the ruins, I'm sure. Then, Granny, think of being so near all the children!"

Granny was very grave for several days; but one evening she said with a tremor in her voice,—

"Hal dear, I am a poor old body, and I shall never be worth any thing again. I don't know as it makes much difference, after all, if you will only promise to bring me back, and lay me alongside of my dear Joe."

Hal promised with a tender kiss.

Dr. Meade used to bundle Granny up in shawls, and take her out in his old-fashioned gig; and, by the time Joe came back, he declared she was a good deal better than new, and the dearest grandmother in the world. I think she was, myself, even if she was little and old and wrinkled, and had a cracked voice.

They formed a great conspiracy against her, and took her to New York. She never could see how they did it; and Joe insisted that it was "sleight-of-hand," he having learned magic in China. It was very odd and laughable to see her going round Florence's pretty home, leaning on Dot's shoulder, and listening, like a child, to the descriptions of the pictures and bronzes, and confusing the names of different things. But Dot declared that it was right next door to heaven; and, for sweet content, it might have been. Charlie almost went wild.

It seemed, indeed, as if Florence could never do enough to make amends for her past neglect. Edmund Darol treated Granny with the utmost respect and tenderness. He never tired of hearing of their youthful frolics and fun; but Charlie's running away seemed the drollest of all.

Mr. Paul Darol, or Uncle Paul as he had insisted upon being to all the children, took Hal under his especial protection. They visited green-houses, talked with florists, read books, and began to consider themselves quite wise. Then they looked around for some suitable places. At Jersey City they found the nucleus of a hot-house, and a very fair prospect; but, on the outskirts of Brooklyn, they found a pretty cottage and some vacant lots, that appeared quite as desirable.

"Indeed, the neighborhood is much better," said Mr. Darol. "Green-houses could soon be put up, and by fall you might be started in business. I think the sooner the better."

Hal's brown eyes opened wide in astonishment.

"Yes," continued Mr. Darol, with an amused expression, "Joe and I have quite settled matters. He allows me *carte blanche* for every thing; and, being arbitrary, I like to have my own way. When you decide upon a location, I will take care that it shall be placed within your power."

"You are so good! but I couldn't, I wouldn't dare"—And somehow Hal could not keep the tears out of his eyes.

"I think this Brooklyn place the most desirable. It is on a horse-car route, and near enough to Greenwood to attract purchasers thither. I'll buy the place, and turn it over to you with a twenty-years' mortgage, if you like. You see, I am not giving you any thing but a chance to do for yourself."

Hal and Joe talked it over that evening.

"How good everybody is to us!" said Hal. "There was Mrs. Howard, when I was so ill, and the Kinseys, while they were in Madison, and Dr. Meade, and"—

"Mrs. Van Wyck, who snubbed Flossy, and prophesied that I should come to the gallows. Hal, dear old chap, we have had ups and downs, and been poor as church-mice; but it is all coming around just right. And I'd take the place: I know you will succeed."

"But eight thousand dollars; and the green-houses, and the plants afterward"—

"Why, I'd be responsible for the place myself. The property would be worth a fortune in twenty years or so. And, with Mr. Darol to hold it, there wouldn't be the slightest risk."

"But if I should not live"—

"Nonsense! I'll come in and administer. I'll be thinking about your epitaph. Mine is already stored away for use:—

'From which it is believed,

The unfortunate bereaved

Went to sea, and was promiscuously drownded.'"

"Now, isn't that pathetic?"

"O Joe! you are too bad!"

"It's a sign of long life, my dear. I have had to be worse than usual, to balance your account."

Everybody said Hal must have the place. Mr. Darol actually purchased it, and took Dot over to see the cottage. It was not very large, but sufficiently roomy for them, and had only been tenanted for a year; a pretty parlor and sitting-room, with a nice large kitchen, and abundance of closets. The chambers up stairs were very pleasant, and commanded a beautiful view.

"Will it do for you, O morsel of womankind?" asked Mr. Darol. "I propose to buy you a dog, and call you Mother Hubbard."

Dot laughed, and blushed, and expressed her satisfaction.

Then Hal declared they must return to Madison, and he would consider what could be done.

"You can count on me for three hundred a year," said Joe with his good-by.

They wanted Granny to remain with Florence, but she would not: so they returned together.

Oh, poor little cottage! The chimney over the "best room" had blown down in a March gale, and the roof leaked worse than ever. The street was surveyed, and staked out; and, oddest of all, Mr. Howard had received a call to Brooklyn.

"I suppose we must go," said Granny. "Dot needs a pretty home, and this isn't"—

"The palaces have spoiled us," said Dot. "Think of having hot and cold water in your kitchen without a bit of fuss; and a bath-room, and the work so easy that it is just like playing at housekeeping. Why, Granny, you and I would have the nicest time in the world!"

Mrs. Meade had cared for the flowers while Hal was away, though they missed his loving hand. But he decided that it would be best to sell them all out, and dispose of the place as soon as he could. The township offered him three hundred dollars for the ground they needed; and presently Hal found a purchaser for the remainder, at twelve hundred dollars. By the time of Joe's next return Hal was ready to take a fresh start.

One thousand was paid down; and Joe promised three hundred of the interest every year, and as much more as he could do. Mr. Darol was to superintend the erection of the green-house,—two long rows, joined by a little square at the end, a kind of work-room, which could be opened or closed at pleasure. They were built on the back part of the two lots, and the space in front was to remain a summer-garden. The street had a lovely southern exposure, while a great elm-tree shaded the house.

They all came back to the Old Shoe for a farewell visit. It was June, and they had supper out of doors; for, somehow, half the neighborhood had invited itself. Everybody was sorry to lose Hal and Granny; and everybody thought it wonderful that the Kenneths had prospered, and had such luck.

Then Florence took Granny and Dot to a pretty seaside resort, where Charlie was to join them. Kit and Hal were to pack up whatever household treasures were worth saving, and afterward domesticate themselves with their brother-in-law.

Good-by, Old Shoe! Tumble down at your will. There is no more laughing or crying or scolding or planning for you to hear,—no tender children's voices singing Sunday-evening hymns in the dusk, no little folded hands saying reverent prayers. O old house, brown and rusty and dilapidated! there has been much joy under your roof; many prayers answered, many sorrows, and some bitter tears, that God's hand wiped away. Every crumbling board has some tender memories. And, as Hal and Kit sit on the old stone step for the last time, their hands are clasped tightly, their eyes are full of tears, and neither can trust his voice to speak.

Good-by! The birds said it, the wandering winds said it, the waving grasses, and the rustling trees. You have had your day, old house, and the night has come for you.

———————————

CHAPTER XXII.

CHRISTMASTIDE.

Hal watched the hot-houses with strange delight. They seemed to him on a most magnificent scale. The boiler was put in, the pipes laid, the force-pump and coal-bins arranged; then the stands of steps, rising higher, the wide ledge by the window for small plants and slips, lattices for vines, hooks for hanging-baskets, and every thing in complete order.

When Charlie rejoined Granny, Florence came back for a brief stay. She and Edmund went over to the cottage, and measured and consulted; and the result was, that one morning it looked wonderfully as if some one was moving in. Hal ran to inform them of their mistake.

The carpet-men said they had their orders, and wouldn't budge an inch. Down went carpets and oil-cloths. Such a hammering, and knocking-about, and unrolling! Kit stood it as long as he could: then he went out of doors, perched himself on a pile of stone, and played on his beloved fiddle.

The next day there was another raid. This time it was furniture. Florence and Edmund soon made their appearance.

"Oh!" exclaimed Hal.

"It is to be our gift," began Edmund. "Florence wished it so much! She feels that she took her pleasure when you were all toiling and suffering, and is better satisfied to make some amends. Besides, we have an interest in Dot and grandmother."

"And I am only going to put in the principal things," explained Florence. "There are so many that you will prefer to select yourselves."

The parlor and library, or sitting-room, were carpeted alike. The furniture was in green, with here and there a bright article to relieve it; a pretty book-case and writing-table, a *console* for Dot's small traps, easy-chairs in abundance, and every thing as pretty as it could be. The dining-room and kitchen were plain, but home-like, with an old-fashioned Boston rocker for Granny. But the three sleeping-rooms up stairs were perfect little gems,— Hal's in black-walnut, Granny's in quaint chestnut, and Dot's in pale green with a pretty green and white carpet to match.

"Why, I shall want them to come home right away!" exclaimed Hal. "O

Flossy!"

"Dear, brave Hal! God has been good to us all. Only love me a little in return."

The last of August, Hal's household returned. He and Kit had provided for them a gorgeous supper, with the best china, and a bouquet at each plate. Granny could hardly believe her eyes or her senses. Dot and Charlie ran wild, and made themselves exclamation points in every doorway.

"Oh! Oh! Oh!"

"And the surprise!"

"And so beautiful!"

"That I should ever live to see it!" said Granny.

They explored every nook and corner and closet.

"I like it so much," said old-fashioned little Dot, "because it isn't too grand. For, after all, we are not rich. And it was so thoughtful of Florence to choose what was simply pretty instead of magnificent!"

"Look at the goblets," said Charlie with a solemn shake of the head. "Dot, if any nice old gentleman comes along, be sure to give him a drink out of them, and put this K round where he can see it."

"The whole eighteen, I suppose, one after another," returned Dot drolly.

"I shall paint you some pictures," Charlie began presently; "and, Dot, when I get to earning money in good earnest, I'll buy a piano. I used to think I did not care much about it, and I never *could* learn; but sometimes, when Florence sits and plays like an angel, I can't help crying softly to myself, though you wouldn't believe I was such a goose. And, if you learn to play, it will be a great comfort to Hal."

"Yes," said Dot, crying out of pure sympathy.

They commenced housekeeping at once. Charlie was to remain with them until the term commenced.

"Isn't it a delight to have such splendid things to work with?" exclaimed Dot. "Why, Granny, don't you believe we have been spirited away to some enchanted castle?"

Granny laughed, and surely thought they had.

Hal, meanwhile, was stocking his green-houses. Loads of sand and loam had to be brought; piles of compost and rubble standing convenient; and the two boys worked like Trojans. And then the journeys to florists, that seemed to Hal like traversing realms of poesy and fragrance. Great geraniums that one could cut into slips, roses, heliotrope, heaths, violets, carnations, fuchsias; indeed, an endless mass of them. Hal's heart was in his throat half the time with a suffocating sense of beauty.

It was such a pleasure to arrange them! He used to handle them as if they were the tenderest of babies. Watering and ventilation on so large a scale was quite new to him; and he went at his business with a little fear and trembling, and devoted every spare moment to study.

Mr. Darol had paid the bills as they had been presented. One day Hal asked to see them. The request was evaded for a while; but one evening, when he was dining with Mr. Darol, he insisted upon it.

"Very well," returned Mr. Darol smilingly. "Here they are: look them over and be satisfied. Very moderate, I think."

The hot-house had cost thirteen hundred dollars; soil, and various incidentals, one hundred more; flowers, three hundred.

"Seventeen hundred dollars," said Hal in a grave and rather tremulous tone. "And seven thousand on the house."

"The mortgage is to remain any number of years, you know. Joe has arranged to pay part of the interest. And the conditions of these"—gathering them up, and turning toward Hal, who was leaning against the mantle, rather stupefied at such overwhelming indebtedness.

"Well?" he said with a gasp that made his voice quiver.

"This," and Mr. Darol laughed genially. Hal saw a blaze in the grate, and stood speechless.

"It is my gift to you. Not a very large business capital, to be sure; but you can add to it from time to time."

"O Mr. Darol!"

"My dear Hal, if you knew the pleasure it has been to me! I don't know why I have taken such a fancy to you all, unless it is for the sake of the children I might have had; but that is an old dream, and the woman who might have been their mother is in her grave. You deserve all this, and more."

The tears stood in Hal's eyes, and he could not trust his voice. How dark every thing had looked only a little year ago! *Could* he ever be thankful enough? And that it should all come through such a ridiculous thing as Charlie's running away!

"I am confident that you will prosper. And I expect you all to like me

223

hugely, in return. When I take Dot and Charlie to operas, I shall look to you to provide the flowers."

"A very small return," said Hal.

But he went home as if he had been a tuft of thistle-down on a summer-breeze. Ferry-boat and horse-car were absolutely glorified. And when he reached the little cottage with lights in every window, and the dear ones awaiting him, he could only clasp his arms around them, and kiss them. But they knew the next morning what had flushed his face, and made his eyes so lustrous.

"Ah, I told you he was a prince!" declared Charlie in triumph.

And then Hal's work commenced in earnest. Every morning he spent in his green-house, and began experiments of propagating, that were so interesting to him. Kit assisted, and Dot ran in every hour or two, to see how they prospered.

Kit had come across a German musician, hardly a square off, who was giving him lessons, and who used to wax very enthusiastic over him. There had been quite a discussion as to what should be done with him.

"Why, he must go to school," declared brother Edmund. "He's a mere child yet; but he has a wonderful talent for music, it must be admitted."

"He might become an organist," said Florence. "That gives a man a position." Somehow she did not take cordially to the violin.

Kit consented to go to school.

"But to give up my dear, darling old fiddle! It's mean, when the rest of you have had just what you wanted,—been adopted, and gone to sea, and had green-houses, and all that!" said Kit, half-crying, and jumbling his sentences all together.

"You shall keep the fiddle," said Granny. "I like it."

Florence also proposed that Granny should have a servant. At this Granny was dismayed.

"A servant! Why, do you suppose I am going to set up for a queen, because Hal has his beautiful hot-house,—an old woman like me?"

"But Dot ought to go to school, and then it would be too much for you."

"I am going to study at home," returned Dot with much spirit. "I haven't any genius: so I shall keep house, and help Hal with his flowers. And the work isn't any thing. A woman comes in to do the washing and ironing."

"And Hal is handy as a girl. No: I'd rather stay as we are," Granny said, with more determination than she had shown in her whole life.

Florence had to leave them "as they were." The simple, homely duties of every-day life were not distasteful to them. If Granny could not have been useful, the charm would have gone out of life for her.

Joe was delighted with every thing, and told Granny that if he wasn't so tall he should surely stand on his head, out of pure joy. He was to make his head-quarters with them when he was at home.

Miss Charteris had been added to their circle of friends, and enjoyed the quaint household exceedingly. Hal was an especial favorite with her, and she took a warm interest in his flowers.

In October, Hal began to have a little business. Baskets and stands were sent in to be arranged for winter; and now and then some one strayed in, and bought a pot of something in bloom. He began to feel quite like a business-man. His five hundred dollars had served to defray incidental expenses, and put in coal and provisions for the winter, leaving a little margin. If he could get his sales up to regular expenses, he thought he should be content for the present.

He took a trip to Madison one day. The cottage was nothing but a heap of crumbling boards. Had they ever lived there, and been so happy?

"It'll never be the same place again," said Granny, listening to the summer's improvements. "I am glad we came away. I couldn't have seen the old house torn down. Maybe it's the flowers here, and the children, that makes it seem like home to me; but most of all I think it must be you, dear Hal. And so I'm satisfied, as the good Lord knows."

Her caps were a trifle more pretentious, and her gowns more in modern style; but she was Granny still, and not one of them would have had her changed. When she sat in her rocking-chair, with her hands crossed in her lap, Hal thought her the prettiest thing in the house.

"Hooray!" exclaimed Kit, rushing home one evening out of breath, and covered with snow. "What *do* you think? Granny, you could never guess!"

"I never was good at guessing," returned Granny meekly.

"Something wonderful! Oh, a new fiddle!" said Dot.

"No: and Hal won't try. Well"—with a long breath—"I'm going—to play —at a concert!"

"Oh!" the three exclaimed in a breath.

"And it's the oddest thing," began Kit, full of excitement. "You see, there's to be a concert given in New York, to help raise funds to give the newsboys, and other homeless children, a great Christmas dinner. Mr. Kriessman has it in hand; and, because it's for boys, he wants me to play—all alone."

"O Kit! you can't," said Hal. "When you faced the audience, it would seem so strange, and you would lose your courage."

"No I wouldn't, either! I'd say to myself, 'Here's a dinner for a hungry boy,' and then I wouldn't mind the people. Mr. Kriessman is sure I can do it; and I've been practising all the evening. A real concert! Think of it. Oh, if Joe can only be here!"

Dot put her arms round his neck, and kissed him. Hal winked his eyes hard, remembering the old dreams in the garret.

He went to see Mr. Kriessman the next day.

"The boy is a genius, I tell you, Mr. Kenneth," said the enthusiastic professor. "He will be a great man,—you see, you see! He has the soul, the eyes, the touch. He fail!" and an expression of lofty scorn crossed the fair, full face.

"But he has had so little practice"—

"It will all be right. You see, you see! Just leave him to me. And he is so little!"

Hal smiled. Kit did not bid fair to become the family giant, it was true.

Not a moment did the child lose. Dot declared that he could hardly eat. Charlie was in high delight when she heard of it; for Mr. Darol was going to take her and Miss Charteris. Hal hardly knew whether he dared venture, or not.

But Joe did come just in the nick of time, and insisted that everybody should go, ordering a carriage, and bundling Dot and Granny into it; poor Granny being so confused that she could hardly make beginning or end of it. And, when they were seated in the great hall that was as light as day, she glanced helplessly around to Joe.

"Never you mind, Granny! I'm not a bit afraid," he whispered. "He will fiddle with the best of them."

'The wonderful boy violinist,' it said on the programme. "If he should not be so wonderful," thought Hal quietly, with a great fear in his soul. He could not tell what should make him so nervous.

Mr. Darol came and spoke to them. "Isn't it odd?" he said with a laugh. "Why, I never dreamed of it until Charlie told me! I wouldn't have missed it for any thing."

The concert began. There was an orchestral overture, then a fine quartet, a cornet solo, and so they went on. Hal followed the programme down. Then he drew a long breath, and looked neither to the right nor the left. That little chap perched up on the stage, Kit? making his bow, and adjusting his violin, and—hark!

It was not the story of the child lost in the storm, but something equally pathetic. Mr. Kriessman had made a fortunate selection. Curiosity died out in the faces of the audience, and eagerness took its place. Ah, what soft, delicious strains! Was it the violin, or the soul of the player? Not a faltering note, not a sign of fear; and Hal laughed softly to himself. On and on, now like the voice of a bird, then the rustle of leaves, the tinkle of waters, fainter, fainter, a mere echo,—a bow, and he was gone.

There was a rapturous round of applause. It nearly subsided once, then began so vehemently that it brought Kit out again. But this time he was the gayest little fiddler that ever played at an Irish fair. People nodded and smiled to each other, and felt as if they must dance a jig in another moment.

Joe bent over to Granny.

"Isn't that gay?" he asked. "Kit has beaten the lot of us. Granny, if you are not proud of him, I'll take you straight home, and keep you on bread and water for a month."

Proud of him! Why, Granny sat there crying her old eyes out from pure joy. Her darling little Kit!

"Dot," exclaimed Mr. Darol as they were going out, "we shall hear of you as an actress next. I never knew of such wonderful people in my life."

"Oh, it was magnificent!" said Charlie. "And the applause!"

"That I should have lived to see the day!"

"Why, Granny, it would have been very unkind of you if you had not," declared Joe solemnly.

How they all reached home, they never exactly knew. They laughed and cried, and it was almost morning before they thought of going to bed.

But the notices next day were as good as a feast. There could be no doubt now. Hal understood that from henceforth Kit and his fiddle would be inseparable. It was "born in him," as Joe said. As for Kit, he hardly knew whether he were in the body, or out of the body.

Hal and Dot set about making up accounts the day before Christmas. The three-months' proceeds had been two hundred and sixty dollars; pretty fair for a beginning, and a whole green-house full of flowers coming into bloom. He was on the high road to prosperity. So he fastened his glasses, put on his coal, and arranged his heat cut-offs for the night, and came into the house. There were Dot and Kit and Charlie, and the supper waiting.

"And there is the six-months' interest," said Hal. "Next year we can let up a little on dear, generous Joe. And to-night is Christmas Eve."

Joe rushed in.

"What do you think, Granny? I've just come from Flossy's. They have a beautiful little boy named Hal Kenneth,—a real Christmas gift, and no mistake. Here's to your namesake, Hal; though, try his best, he can never be half as good as you."

I do believe poor, foolish Hal had his eyes full of tears, thinking of Flossy's great joy. But Charlie and Kit cheered in a tremendous fashion.

After the supper was cleared away, they sat in a little circle, and talked. There always was so much to say, and Joe liked nothing half so well as to hear of every event that had transpired in his absence. They all kept such a warm interest in each other!

Somehow they strayed back to the last Christmas, and the "songs in the night."

"Sing again," besought Granny.

Dot's birdlike voice was first to raise its clear notes. One hymn was dearer than all the rest. The music quivered a little when they came to this verse, as if tears and heart-throbs were not far off:—

"Wonderful night!
Sweet be thy rest to the weary!
Making the dull heart and dreary
Laugh with a dream of delight.
   Wonderful, wonderful night!"

And then a tender silence fell over them. They clasped each other's hands softly, and the breaths had a strangled sound. Granny alive, Joe raised from the dead, Kit some day to be a famous musician!

Joe crept up to Granny, and kissed her wrinkled face. Somehow it seemed as if the furrows began to fill out.

"Oh," he said huskily, "there's nothing in the world so wonderful, nor so sweet, nor so precious as 'The Old Woman who lived in a Shoe!' When I think of her love, her patient toil, her many cares, and the untiring devotion with which she has labored for us all, I feel that we can never, never repay her. O Granny!"

"I've been glad to have you all, God knows. There wasn't one too many."

Not one of the loving arms that encircled her could have been spared. There she sat enthroned, a prouder woman to-night, poor old Granny Kenneth, than many a duchess in a blaze of diamonds. Fair Florence; laughing Joe, with his great, warm heart; sweet, tender Hal; racketing Charlie; Kit, with his scalp-lock waving in the breeze; and dear little Dot,—jewels enough for any woman, surely!

Ah, children! love her with the best there is in your fresh young souls. Make the paths smooth for her weary feet, remembering the years she has trudged on the thorny highway of life for your sakes. When the eyes grow dim, bring the brightest in your lives to glorify her way. Cling to her, kiss warmth into the pale lips; for when she has gone to heaven it will seem all too little at the best. True, she will reap her reward there; but it is sweet to have a foretaste of it in your smiles, as well. Dear Granny, who has made toil heroic, and old age lovely, and out of whose simple, every-day existence have blossomed the roses that still render this old world bright and glorious,—Love, Labor, Faith!

Lightning Source UK Ltd.
Milton Keynes UK
UKHW041041100820
367987UK00004B/814